# BIERGARTEN OF THE DAMNED

SEANA KELLY

This is a work of fiction. Names, characters, places, and incidents are either products of the writer's imagination or are used fictitiously and are not to be construed as real. Any resemblance to actual events, locales, organizations, or persons, living or dead, is entirely coincidental.

Biergarten of the Damned



Ebook ISBN: 9781641972185

KDP POD ISBN: 9798355348656

IS POD ISBN: 9781641972406



NYLA Publishing

121 W. 27th St., Suite 1201, NY 10001, New York.

http://www.nyliterary.com

*For C.R. Grissom*
*who never fails to shore up my*
*self-doubt and champion my stories.*
*Best. Critique Partner. Ever.*

## 1

# A Bloody Awful Wakeup Call

Dragons were prowling the Shire again. I couldn't see them but knew they were close by. No, I wasn't supposed to snoop, but come on! The crew was working on our folly, and I was having a hard time not peeking every chance I got.

They'd added a long hallway from our bedroom, deeper into the cliff, creating an entrance to our magical new underground home. Clive and I had fallen in love with the dragon folly in Wales and wanted something similar but all our own here in San Francisco.

It was the middle of the night and time for bed. While Clive walked Fergus for one last potty stop before sleep, I was lurking by the sheets of thick plastic hanging at the end of the hall, blocking our entrance to their workspace.

Sliding one sheet of plastic a few inches to the side, I listened intently for the sounds of nearby workers. Yes, their hearing was better than mine—which was excellent, I might add. No, I wasn't supposed to be reminding them they were working for a werewolf and a vampire instead of their usual clients, other dragons. I knew all of that, but a book had come to life right behind this plastic!

Eye to the open slit, I tried to commit a visual slice of the Shire to memory. It was perfect! Beautiful. Exactly how my mother had described it to me before I was able to read the Tolkien books myself. She would have loved it. Just seeing this little slice of Hobbiton made me feel like she was standing right beside me.

A pond! There was a serene pond right near the entrance. A silvery fish broke the surface, leaving bubbles in its wake as it swam under a lily pad. These dragon builders were insanely good and really freaking magical. I knew that wasn't a real fish, but there was nothing about its behavior or appearance that gave it away. Clive would get to walk in what looked and felt like sunlight. I knew, from the folly in Wales, that the limitless blue sky above was really a magicked cavern ceiling, but all my senses were telling me I was above ground in Middle Earth.

I pulled out my phone, opened the camera, and pushed my hand through the plastic. Holding my phone as high as I could reach, twisting it this way and that, I took pictures of our new home. It felt like things were finally settling down, that Clive and I would soon be living our happily ever after.

When I heard puppy claws on the barroom floor, I hurried down the hall and returned to our bedroom ahead of my fellas. Fergus bounded in as I innocently sat on the end of the bed in my pajamas.

Clive followed, untucking his dress shirt from his black trousers. He paused when he moved to his cuff, studying me. "What are you up to?"

"Moi? Nothing."

He gave me a look that said he didn't believe me, as he draped his shirt and pants on the chair. Moving from the nocturne to this little apartment was particularly difficult for Clive. No valet. No housekeepers. No studio-sized closet for his massive wardrobe of dark suits and snowy white dress shirts. Poor bub.

"I was just thinking about our new home, and I can't wait." I slid my phone out from under my leg so we could look at the pictures.

"Soon, darling." He flipped the comforter back and slid into bed.

"Aren't you even a little curious?" I crawled up the bed and slid in beside him.

"Of course I am, but I'd rather wait to see it when it's complete. Come here, now. It's late." He held out his arm for me to snuggle in.

I plugged in my phone, turned off the lamp, and slid into his arms. Crazy crap may have happened on the regular, but if I had Clive at the end of the day, all was good. Resting my head on his shoulder, I wrapped an around his waist and dropped off.

In the early days of our relationship, I'd wondered if waking up next to a dead-ish body on the daily would prove to be off-putting. Gentle Reader, it was not. Yes, my vampire husband was out—the sun being up—but he was still Clive. The feel of him, the smell of him, brought me comfort and contentment. Head on his shoulder, arm wrapped around him, I was exactly where I wanted to be.

It didn't feel as though I'd slept long, though. Why was I awake? I listened intently. Was Fergus, my Irish Wolfhound pup, shaking his collar? Nope. Soft puppy snores were my white noise. Clive groaned and flinched in his sleep. Yes, most considered vampires dead during the day, but I believed it was more akin to a period of stasis. He could be awoken, if necessary. He wouldn't survive direct sunlight, but being extremely old and powerful had its perks. So, while Clive thought it silly to refer to his daylight death as sleep, I knew he was wrong. If he could wake—ever—he wasn't dead.

What had me concerned at the moment, though, was that my guy never moved around or made noises when he slept. As an aside, I totally won the lottery on the bedmate-who-doesn't-snore thing. When he flinched again, Fergus hopped onto the bed and growled. Running my hand down Clive's chest, I tried to soothe whatever was upsetting him. I felt something wet. Confused, I peered at my hand in the dark.

The smell of blood had me bolting up and fumbling with the lamp on the nightstand. Flinging back the stained sheets, I discovered red smeared across Clive's abdominals but couldn't find a wound. Fergus sniffed at the stains and whined quietly

"Wha—"

A slash tore across his perfect, chiseled face. He grimaced in pain but still didn't wake, even as blood bloomed from his forehead across his nose and down his cheek. My hand flew to my mouth. Fergus hopped over Clive and leaned into me, shaking. What was happening?

As I watched, his skin healed, the cut knitting together. I pushed up to get a washcloth and he jolted again, a jagged slash appearing on his thigh. It was as though an invisible blade was carving him up.

Clutching his shoulder, I dove deep into his mind. I'm a werewolf, yes, but also a wicche—a necromancer, to be specific. I might not have been able to do basic spells, but I could communicate with the dead. As well as the mostly dead. *Clive!* No response. We'd done this before. He'd been sluggish but able to reply, his thoughts and memories laid open for me. Not this time, though. It was as though he was cut off from his own mind.

A chill ran down my spine when I realized I was hearing breathing. It was like dry dead leaves stirred by the wind. Clive didn't breathe anymore. Something was in here with me, something that wasn't my husband.

*This one's mine.* The voice was a deep, gravely threat.

*You're wrong,* I responded. Visualizing my magic as a thread coiled in my chest, I drew it out, wrapped it around my hands, and shoved with all my strength. *He's mine!* Like dark sludge, the entity slipped through my fingers. I didn't know what he was other than beyond my control.

A snide, humorless chuckle echoed all around me. *I have prior claim. You best run along now before I take an interest in you. And your little dog too.*

The thing lashed out again and I felt Clive recoil. He was in pain. I had to protect him. Whatever this was, it didn't feel fae. Gloriana's ring would hold no sway, but it was a weapon, and I needed to use every one I had. Uncoiling my magic again, I wrapped it around Clive, holding tight to the tether. Thumbing the ring, I reached up for the wicche glass around my neck and called on my werewolf ancestors, the whole Quinn line back to the first werewolf, and then let loose a shattering howl, mentally digging my claws into the dark corners of Clive's mind, staking my claim on my mate.

I felt the intruder crouching. Watching.

Clive shook, seizing, while Fergus barked, but I hadn't feel the other entity leave. He was silent, waiting for me to pull out of Clive's mind so he could resume his torture. Whatever this thing was, it felt strangely familiar. Not a vampire; at least, I didn't think so. Not the fae. I couldn't feel wicches. Maybe an immortal, like Stheno or Meg? I hadn't known them to do anything like this before, but that didn't mean they couldn't. Pulling Fergus into my lap, I comforted my poor pup. Clive had said his maker, Garyn, was gifted with exceptional mental powers, but this felt distinctly male.

I glanced over at the beautiful carved wooden box on my dresser holding the magical chess set. I'd found it in an art gallery in Canterbury. The delicate pieces were carved to represent Gloriana, the queen of the fae, and her people on one side, with Finvarra, king of the fae, and his people on the other side. Finvarra's side of the board was trying to kill me—long story—while Gloriana's side fell somewhere between neutral and helpful. Maybe this was one of Finvarra's people attacking Clive. I had no idea the full extent of what the fae could do.

The thing was, though, this entity made my stomach twist, like that demon Sitri who had invaded my mind and taken away my will so easily a few months ago. Clive had killed him for what he'd done to me, but perhaps this was another one. If that was the case, we were screwed. I had no power over demons. Maybe Dave...but Dave was missing more work than he was making. Something was up with him. Owen had said a demon had come into the bar to see Dave, to harass him, while Clive and I were in Europe.

Were they connected? Dave was having issues with a demon and something evil and outside my control was attacking Clive. My guy would be at this thing's mercy every daylight hour.

*Clive? Please, can you hear me?*

*Hmm…hello, love.*

I dropped my head to his shoulder and let out a breath. Either the thing had left or had pulled back enough for me to find Clive. The terrifying part was that I didn't think anything I'd done had had any effect on the entity squatting inside him. Which meant there was nothing I could do to keep it from returning to continue the torture.

Clive pulled me in tight. *Stay.*

*Yes. I will.* Even though I had no power to stop it, I couldn't leave Clive alone, vulnerable to attack. So I lay there beside him, lamp on, wide awake, alert to any movement. We hadn't had nearly enough time together. Our whole very long lives, that's what we'd promised each other when we married.

Hours later, when I felt Owen push on the ward, I grabbed my phone, sending him a quick text. A minute later, I felt him pushing against the ward at our apartment door.

"Come in."

He hurried through the overstuffed living room and poked his head in our bedroom. "Are you okay?"

While I explained what had been going on, he sat on the edge of the bed, staring at the bloodstains. "I don't see any scars."

"No. Vamps can heal that kind of thing. If they couldn't, they'd all be covered in a million scars. But the time it took him to heal himself got slower and slower. The thing was draining him."

I sat up, resting my hand on Clive's chest, my sea green silk pjs covering me from neck to ankle. "Look at him."

"Believe me, I am," Owen said.

Pulling up the sheet that had dropped low across Clive's waist —I was watching for slashes—I said, "No. Look at his face. He has shadows under his eyes. He never does."

The grin dropped as Owen moved forward. "You're right. I've

never seen him look anything but model perfect." He rested a hand on my knee. "What can I do?"

"No idea. I don't know what *I* can do." I took Clive's hand and held it.

"If you really think it might be a demon, maybe you need a priest or something." Owen gave Clive a wary look, as though waiting for a demon to pop out of his mouth.

I couldn't really blame him. The idea that a demon was crouching nearby was wigging me out too. "Oh yeah, priests are going to line up to help a vampire with his exorcism needs."

There was another push on the ward. "Fyr's here."

Owen got up and moved to the door. "We'll get set up. If you need to stay here today, we're covered."

"How is Fyr doing, you know, when I'm not around?" The poor guy was dealing with past trauma, horrible betrayal, moving to a new country. It was a lot.

"He's good. He knows the job. That's not an issue, although he is still learning about the bookstore. It's more his dealing with customers. He's fine with the wicches. The fae, though, are another story. With the Wicche Glass Tavern closed, more of them are showing up here all the time. He glares at them, like he's waiting for an attack. I've spoken with our regulars to explain the hostility. It doesn't help that Alice isn't here to keep him calm."

"I told him he could bring J'Alice with him. Two wolfhounds are better than one."

"It's Alice. She's scared of the magical stairway. The first time Fyr brought her, she whined and wouldn't move. When he picked her up, she yelped, trying to get away. So he had to run her back home. It can be weird to get used to. She stays with Coco at the jewelry store when Fyr's at work. I told you he took George's old apartment above Drake's Treasures, right?"

I nodded.

"Anyway, the customers here understand and they're trying not to flinch when his eyes go red and smoke streams from his nostrils." Owen shrugged. "The fact that he's a Thor-looking god with a sexy accent has helped some to see past the anger issues."

"Some like yourself?" I asked, eyebrows raised.

"Eh. I have my own gorgeous dragon." He grinned. "No offense, but the vibe in the bar is very different when he's working it instead of you."

I gave him my squinty eye. "Meaning?"

"Let's just say a lot more of our customers are paying close attention to barrels being moved or cases being carried. I mean, those muscles are distracting."

"I have muscles!" I stopped myself from flexing an arm, but just barely.

"Sure you do, honey. Anyway, I better get out there before Fyr has to deal with Grim. Come on, Fergus." He patted his leg. "Let's go potty, buddy."

P'fft. What did Owen know? I was werewolf strong. I slid my arms under Clive and lifted him easily to prove my point. Blood streaked the sheets beneath him. Instead of putting him down, I carried him to the shower. It wasn't easy, but I got rid of the bloody smears all over his body.

After drying and dressing him in comfy sleepwear—which I wouldn't have been able to do if I didn't have muscles—I sat him in a chair and stripped the sheets off the bed. The blood had soaked through. Even though I wasn't that kind of wicche, I used the scouring spell Owen's mom Lydia had taught me. It worked a little. The stains were lighter.

When I texted Owen asking for help, he did a proper job of cleaning the mattress. After I remade the bed, I slid Clive back in. The shadows under his eyes had lifted a bit. He was healing from the attack. Slowly.

Feeling decidedly useless, I pulled up photos on my phone and shared them with him. I mean, not really, but sort of. I knew he was out, but it felt good to look at honeymoon photos and talk with him about them. If nothing else, I supposed, I was comforting myself.

I tapped on a selfie I'd taken of us on the balcony of the George V in Paris. The Eiffel Tower glowed in the night sky behind us.

"I never want you to tell me how much that hotel cost. My guilt over the price tag will color my memories of a perfect honeymoon...Look, the glass pyramid of the Louvre all lit up. We need to go back some day. We could spend a week wandering through...Oh!" I smacked his shoulder. "I really want to go to the British Museum too. Someday...Look at you, so handsome. I think the Mona Lisa is checking you out...I loved that café. It was something out of a Van Gogh...I know you hate the catacombs, but I kind of want to go exploring. There's an immortal tucked away in there. I felt him. I want to know who it is...I really wished you'd been with me while I wandered around Canterbury. We walked the same roads, you and I, but a thousand years apart. It's nuts...Look..."

I whiled away the afternoon talking about anything and everything, my head on his shoulder, my arm wrapped around him. I couldn't protect him, couldn't keep him safe, and that terrified me.

My fingers brushed back and forth over his abdomen. "I don't think I could survive losing you. You changed that. You changed me. I was fine on my own. I'd been doing it for seven years, twenty-four, really. Hey, wait. I'm twenty-five. Huh, that one got past me this year. It had been just Mom and me and later just me. But that was okay. I'd trained my whole life for isolation. I was good at it. I had my Slaughtered Lamb and I had my books. I was fine.

"Then you had to saunter into my life, mixing everything up. I was okay on my own, but you made me see a different life. More, you made me want it. How did you do that? You're a tricksy one, I'll give you that. Dangling love and happiness just out of reach, making me stumble toward it. And you were there, arms out, ready to catch me if I fell, ready to hold my hand when I was brave enough, when the want outweighed the fear.

"I thought I'd spend my life alone, and that was okay. I was comfortable. Alone meant I didn't have to face the damage that had been done, the trauma and the fear. I could keep it shoved down and hidden, curling in on it at night when it was quiet and dark.

"And if sometimes I desperately longed for that hand to hold, well, the desperation faded eventually. I had work and I had books and I was safe. That was what was most important, the safety and the silence. I didn't want to remember, so I avoided looking in mirrors, kept myself covered. And then you come along, offering warmth and touch and safety, and you started peeling away the layers. Slowly, gently, revealing myself to me, showing me I'm worthy of love, that I'm strong enough to face it.

"I can't go back now. You've changed me for good. So, you see, you have to be okay. I wouldn't survive it."

He rolled me over, staring down at me, taking in my tears, and kissed me softly. "I'm not going anywhere, love, and I don't saunter."

Laughter bubbled up, and I wrapped my arms around him.

He dropped a kiss on my nose. "And what do you mean you're twenty-five now? When was your birthday? Why didn't you tell me?"

I shrugged awkwardly. "December thirteenth, and I don't know. We were busy battling Abigail and Leticia. I was getting blown up and burned. We had a lot on our plates."

# 2

# FoCing Club Now Accepting Members

"I believe gifts are in order," Clive said, settling between my legs.

"Oh no you don't." I poked his shoulder. "You've already bought me too much. Look at this joint." I gestured to the boxes and racks of clothes. He'd filled almost two closets worth of clothing, accessories, shoes, and jewelry for me. When we moved out of the nocturne, two huge suites worth of stuff had to be squished into my little apartment behind The Slaughtered Lamb's bar. "It's like an episode of High-Class Hoarders in here."

He ran his lips down the column of my neck. "How about a party? We could have it here or I could rent the ballroom at the Palace Hotel," he suggested while nibbling on my ear.

"No parties, thank you." I tilted my head up, giving him better access. "And we just had a wedding reception here. We're all partied up."

He slid down my body, unbuttoning and kissing, driving me crazy. "I'll think of something."

"Clive, wait. I need to talk to you." I shook his shoulder.

"All in due time. I'm otherwise occupied at present," he murmured as he slid my pajama bottoms off, taking my panties with them. He pushed my legs apart with his wide shoulders and I stopped thinking or speaking coherently for quite some time.

Later, stretched out on top of him, I told him about the slashes and the dark foul thing that had been squatting in his mind. I felt his shock, so I knew he felt my terror. I explained what I'd done to try to get rid of it, but that I knew none of it had worked.

Lifting his head, he kissed my brow. "We'll figure it out."

"Clive—"

"I'll make some calls. We'll come up with a plan." He rubbed his hands up and down my back, trying to soothe me.

Tilting my head, I rested my chin on his chest so I could watch his expression. "I know you've lived a long time, but have you ever gone up against demons before?"

He gave a barely perceptible shrug. "Most consider us demons, so…"

"No. Don't make light of this. I held you while your skin split open again and again. I couldn't stop it."

He stared up at the ceiling, lost in thought, hugging me tightly against him. "I imagine this is something like what you felt when your aunt was trapping you in visions. Knowing someone else is at the helm in your mind, your body; it's rather off-putting, isn't it?"

I smacked his shoulder. "I'd say it's more than off-putting."

"Yes, but you're American." He gave me another kiss. "We have all night. We'll come up with a plan."

"Hey, vampires don't actually have a problem with holy water, right? I mean, you held on to that cross in New Orleans. We could get a tub of water blessed and then have you sleep underwater. That'd work."

Clive tore his eyes from the ceiling to give me a pitying look. "I hesitate to say there are no bad suggestions when brainstorming, but perhaps we'll put a pin in that one and then forget it."

He grinned and shook his head at the insult he recognized in my expression. "Darling, will you have us kidnap a priest and bring him down into the Slaughtered Lamb to bless bathwater? I could be wrong, but I would bet that abducting clergy would do more to strengthen the demon's case against me than weaken it."

"What did you do to piss off a demon?"

"That is the question, isn't it?" Patting my bottom, he said, "Come on. Let's get cleaned up and take over for your poor over-worked employees. I'd imagine they'd like to leave now."

Sighing, I rolled out of bed. "I'll shower first, since I actually know what I'm doing out there."

By the time I got the water running, Clive was right behind me. Well, I supposed water conservation *was* important, although probably not the way we took showers. I had to move clothing racks in order to get to my bureau to pull out undies, jeans, socks, and a sweater. Clive had given me a rainbow assortment of running shoes, but I'd taken to wearing the same gray pair every day. Digging around for fashionable stuff was way too much work. After a few months of living the high life in the nocturne, I'd reverted to living out of three drawers.

I walked through the kitchen. Empty again. What was going on with Dave? He didn't even bother to call in anymore. I needed him, not just to talk about Clive's problems, but to be here. He was part of The Slaughtered Lamb, right from the beginning. Why wouldn't my grumpy, foul-mouthed, half-demon cook tell me what was going on?

The bar was crowded. Fyr, the hot, Thor-looking dragon we'd found in England, was behind the bar, building a pint of Guinness, and Owen, wicche extraordinaire and my right-hand man, was hurrying back from the bookstore to clear empties off tables.

"Sorry, guys. I'm here." I took Owen's tray from him and finished collecting the empties, taking them back to the kitchen to fill the washer.

Owen followed me in. "How's Clive?"

"I'm fine," Clive said, walking through the warded doorway from our apartment to the bar's kitchen. He was wearing a perfectly worn-in pair of jeans with a light blue button-down shirt, open at the collar, the sleeves rolled up.

I grinned, taking it all in.

He glanced down at himself. "You said this was appropriate for working in a bar. Is it the shoes? Are these not intended for men?"

I hadn't even scanned down far enough to see the shoes. He was wearing dark gray running shoes, similar to my own.

"Fyr wears heavy work boots," he continued, "and Owen's choice of footwear seems clothing dependent. You always wear running shoes, so I thought this was a safe bet. Was that incorrect?" How was it a thousand-year-old vampire was so adorably unsure of himself?

Grabbing his hand, I swung it and squeezed before dropping a kiss on his cheek. "You look perfect."

He nodded, seeming pleased. "Excellent. What shall I do first?"

Owen gestured toward the bar. "I was just going to—well, Stheno's here."

When he stopped talking, I interpreted. "We need a case of red wine from the storeroom. Can you get the crate that has a big S on the side? It's a special vintage I buy just for her."

Brushing his hands together, Clive went through the side door in the kitchen into the storeroom.

I smacked Owen's elbow. "You have to tell him what to do. You're the manager."

He waved a hand dramatically toward the storeroom door and then dropped it when Clive walked past us into the bar, carrying a huge crate of wine bottles. "It's freaking Clive," he whisper shouted. "I can't tell an ancient, all-powerful Master vampire to go clean the toilets!"

"Technically, you can, but I get it. How about if we handle the toilets? Clive and Fyr can handle any heavy lifting. You know, he still doesn't know how to work the espresso machine. You can teach him that."

Owen was already shaking his head. "That's all you, sister. That thing is a temperamental pain. I'm not pissing off a vampire. You can put your jugular on the line to teach him how to make coffee." Crossing his arms, he said, "I'm fine doing everything else, but I won't be *his* manager. That's gotta be on you. The patrons are still scared shitless of him.

"I mean," he sighed, "I get you guys want this to work but cleaning tables and pouring beers will eventually make him one of the guys, like it did Audrey. Some people were still scared of her, but most got over it. The thing with Clive, though, is you don't want people to get over their fear of him. He's got to be seen as the scary-as-hell vamp in town in order to keep other nocturnes from attacking us. Yes, Russell is Master now, but everyone knows Clive is still here. He's a layer of protection for us all. If his legend is reduced to bartender, it puts us all in danger."

Clive swung back through the door, expression pensive as he leaned against the nearby counter. "He's right. I've been battling with just this since I made my decision. You summed up the issue well."

"So you don't want to work here?" Oh, no. Clive gave up the nocturne for a life together and he was already regretting it. "We could move into the nocturne's pool house, if you want to be back in the thick of vampire central."

Grinning, he shook his head. "That chapter has ended. We're building our new life here."

Owen backed up to the door, checking his watch. "I'll get out of your hair. George is picking me up in fifteen."

Nodding, I said, "Of course. I'm sorry. I'll be right out."

Owen swung through the door and Clive took my hand, leading me back into our soundproofed apartment. Pulling me down next to him on the small couch, we sat a minute, each lost in our own thoughts.

"He's right. This isn't me. I'm more than happy to help whenever you need it, but the thought of someone tapping me on the shoulder to ask for a refill..." He shook his head. "No."

"What *do* you want to do?"

Running his thumb over the back of my hand, he said, "I'm not really sure. I don't recall ever being quite so adrift in my life. I've always had a purpose."

"Are you sorry you gave up the Master of the City gig? You didn't have to do that for m—"

"Shh. I did it for me and hopefully us. Russell should have been heading up his own nocturne a century ago. I love this town and he's the right choice to look over and protect it. I've just been doing the job for so long—what? A little over two hundred years—that I'm feeling strangely adrift without all the irritating responsibilities."

Fergus trotted through the doorway. I put my hand out and he hopped up on the couch to snuggle between us. The little charmer had already won over my patrons. There was a clipboard on the bar, people signing up to take him for walks. He was spending time with lots of different supernatural beings and becoming a kind of therapy dog for the bar.

Scratching under Fergus' chin, Clive continued, "I've had a few vampires reach out to me, asking for information and advice."

Fergus rested one of his oversized paws on Clive's leg. He was an intuitive one, my wee warrior. I kissed the top of his head and he flopped over into my lap.

"Now that I'm not attached to a nocturne, controlling a city, they seem to feel more comfortable calling. I'm powerful but officially unaffiliated—though they all know I back Russell and San Francisco without question. It appears they would like to be considered a friend of mine."

"Friends of Clive. FoC." I snickered. "We should start a FoCing club."

Grinning, he shook his head.

"We could make FoCing t-shirts and keyrings. We'll make mad money on the merch."

"Go relieve Owen." He gave Fergus tummy scratches. "He has a date. I think I'll sit here, with my feet up." So saying, he rested his casually clad feet on the coffee table. "Fergus and I will have a quiet think."

"You're sure?"

He gave me a kiss. "Darling, I'm perfectly fine. In fact, I've never been happier. I'm just in that uncomfortable in-between place. I'll figure it out. I always do."

## 3

# FuckFuckFuckityFuck

I rushed back out to the bar, tapping Owen on the back and taking over building a Guinness. "Go have fun and say hi to George for me." I glanced around the bar, trying to figure out who was drinking all the Guinness. We hardly ever got asked for this stuff.

"It's for the guy sitting by the bookstore entrance." Owen grabbed his jacket and pulled it on. "We got a new book order and even though I could have taken care of it this afternoon when it was quiet, I left it for you."

"Thank you!"

"All right, I'm outta here." Owen jogged up the steps as Stheno, my gorgon friend, walked in from the bookstore.

She was looking fabulous in skintight black jeans, little wedge boots, and a fitted leather jacket with a matching eyepatch. Her long, wild, corkscrew curls bobbed in the nonexistent breeze. Even those who didn't know who she was could probably feel the power she exuded. Hopping up on a stool, she crossed her legs and casually looked around the crowded bar.

"Hey, kid. When you're done with that, pour me a glass of wine. Owen said he'd grab a bottle from the back." She drummed her fingers on the bar and gave an upnod to a wicche I was pretty sure she'd been hooking up with. "Got anything to eat?"

"I can check. Dave hasn't shown up for work the last couple of days, so possibly not." I finished the pint for the new guy, took it to him, and collected the cash. When I slid back behind the bar, I opened the crate and took out a bottle. I also had a slightly oversized wine glass just for Stheno. It fit an entire bottle of wine. "How have you been?"

Fyr, crouching behind the bar to fix a tap line, stood, causing heads to swing around. He gave the fae with the Guinness a dark look. Owen was, of course, correct. Most eyes followed Fyr as he reached up to grab a whiskey bottle off the wall. The fabric of his flannel work shirt strained at his broad, muscular shoulders and bagged at his narrow waist. Strands of his long blond hair had fallen from its band, so he pulled it out, snapped it around his thick wrist, and finger-combed his hair out of his face. There was a palpable hush in the room as he shoved it back, coiled it up, and then pulled the band from his wrist and secured his hair out of the way again.

"Sam." He nodded to me and then turned to Stheno, brows furrowed. Tilting his head, he focused his dragon green eyes on her. She was an unknown. I could almost see the gears turning as he tried to figure out what manner of supernatural she was.

"You've been holding out on me, kid," Stheno breathed. "Dragon?" she asked him.

Fyr nodded.

"I do love a fiery mouth."

Fyr blinked.

"On me," she elaborated. "I'm Stheno."

His eyes warmed when he grinned at her. "Fyr. Why the eyepatch?"

Tilting her head, she looked up at him through her lashes. "It's a gripping story I'd be more than happy to tell you. When do you get off?" The look she gave him made smoke trail from his nostrils.

Fyr turned to me. "She fae?"

"She is not. I'll let Stheno introduce herself properly, though. Suffice to say, I trust her implicitly. With my life, that is. With your virtue?" I shrugged.

"In that case"—he took the bar towel out of his waistband and walked around the bar—"my shift ended an hour ago."

Stheno took his arm as they walked up the stairs. "I've got a place not too far…"

As I hadn't yet opened the wine bottle, I just slid it back into the crate for her next visit. I'd run the place by myself before. I could do it again. It was crowded, but steady. I kept on top of orders and clearing tables. When Fergus trotted out, he came behind the bar, sniffed all the usual spots, and then leaned into me, a paw on my shoe. Once I'd slid a cup of tea to the wicche at the end of the bar, I crouched down to give him two-handed, full-body scratches. He wiggled in ecstasy and then flopped across my foot.

I picked up my wee furry friend. We'd only had him a short time, but he'd already put on more weight, and those legs of his were getting longer. I sat him on my hip, holding him close.

"You made sure he was okay before you left, right?" I whispered, scratching his chest.

He sniffed my ear and then bumped his nose against my jaw. I took that as a yes.

"I believe it is my turn to walk Fergus."

I turned to find the unsettlingly yellow gaze of Ule, our owl shifter, as he pointed to his name on the clipboard.

I grabbed Fergus' leash, clipped it on, and walked the pup to Ule. When Fergus rounded the corner of the bar, he stopped to stare at the Guinness-drinking fae, the hair between his shoulders standing. Growling, he lunged for the guy, but I had his leash in my hand.

I dropped down beside him again, wrapping my hand under him, palming his chest and tummy. "My dude, we don't maul the customers." I grimaced at the unknown fae. "Sorry. I'm Sam and this is my place. I don't think we've met yet."

The guy watched my dog, a strange look on his face before it relaxed into a smile. "Poldo. No problem. I have cats. Maybe he's smelling them."

Nodding, I rose and handed the leash to Ule. "It's probably that." More quietly, I looked straight into Ule's unblinking eyes and said, "Take care of my guy, okay. Don't let anything happen to him."

Ule bowed. "On my life."

I hadn't been expecting quite that serious of a vow, but I'd take it. "The poop bags are in that little roll dangling off the carabiner."

Walking Fergus up the steps, he said, "I've done this before."

It was good that Fergus was getting familiar with his new home and all my regulars. I worried every time he was taken away from me, though.

I cleared a few tables and took orders for a pint of mead and a pot of tea. I felt Poldo's eyes on me as I got to work. We got new customers all the time, but Fergus was a good judge of character and Finvarra, the fae king, hated my guts, so…

Clive appeared at my side a moment later. "Problem?" He scanned the room, nodding to Hepsiba, the old wicche sitting in the corner by the window, who'd been sitting in just that spot almost every day since I'd opened The Slaughtered Lamb.

Heavy steps pounded on the stairs. My heart gave a quick tug. Dave? His motorcycle boots, black jeans, black t-shirt, deep red face, and shark-black eyes appeared. On the long stairway from the mundane world into our home down here, he'd dropped the glamour he wore to keep the humans from screaming and running. Aboveground, he was a muscular Black man, who was bald and perpetually angry. In reality, he was a muscular half-demon with dark red skin, who was bald and perpetually angry.

"You're here." Maybe tonight he'd talk to me, because I needed answers.

"Good catch, Sam," he grumbled. Nodding to Clive, he walked past us and swung into the kitchen.

I began to follow my long-absent cook and then stopped

myself. I was the only one working out here. "Could you watch the joint for me for a minute so I can talk to Dave?"

Clive nodded, crossed his arms over his chest, and stared out the window wall at the night sky, still holding pink streaks, the last remnants of sunset. High tide wouldn't be for another few hours.

The Slaughtered Lamb was located where the Pacific Ocean becomes the San Francisco Bay. The water swirled and crashed against the aquarium-grade glass about three feet above the barroom floor. At high tide, my bookstore and bar were submerged six to eight feet below the surface.

While Clive watched the water, daring anyone to ask him for help, I headed to the kitchen. When I pushed through the door, I found Dave with his head in the refrigerator, a trash can by his side.

"Is there a reason you can't clear out rotting food?" he grumbled.

"I did. Some of it. If it was obvious." Something was going on. He wasn't his usual grumpy self. I felt heat coming off him, so I stood on the opposite side of the island. "What's wrong? Why haven't you been coming to work?"

A blue glow ran across his deeply red skin. It was like a match had been dropped into a pool of gas. "Just get out, Sam." The glow sputtered out and his shoulders seem to droop as he continued emptying the refrigerator.

"I need to talk to you." And I'd really prefer not to be scorched, if at all possible.

"Not now." He slammed the frig door and yanked up the sides of the garbage bag, knotting off the top.

"That's what you said the last time I tried to talk to you. And the time before." When he glared at me, I knew I had to keep going. "Please tell me what's going on. You hardly ever show up to work anymore and when you do, it's like this. You keep everyone at a distance with your rage."

"And yet here you stand. In my way." Disgust lined his face. What had I done?

"If you're not ready to tell me, to let me try to help"—he scoffed at that—"can I ask for *your* help?"

"What, Sam?" He dropped the garbage bag. "What more do you fucking want from me? How much more *help* do I owe you?" While he fumed, flames ran down his fingers.

Clive was suddenly standing in front of me, facing Dave. "You have better control than this. Sam's done nothing to incur your wrath. If you can't control your temper, you shouldn't be here."

"Exactly," he said, shoving out the kitchen door.

"Wait!" I ran after him. To his credit, Clive didn't try to stop me.

My customers shrank back in their chairs as Dave strode across the bar and up the stairs. I followed, knowing there was section of the stairway that was in between, not Slaughtered Lamb, not Land's End lookout, where maybe we could talk.

I grabbed his hand and then yelped, pulling it back. It was bloody and blackened, the pain horrendous. I'd basically grabbed an open flame.

"What the fuck, Sam?"

"Please talk to me? You're breaking my heart here." Funneling pain into the wicche glass, I sat on a step and tugged at his smoking jeans with my other hand. "Please."

"I've got nothing to say." But he came down three steps and sat.

"Okay," I said, resting my hand palm up against my leg. "But you're my family and you're obviously in some kind of trouble. Please let me try to help."

He sat, silently staring ahead, his gaze carefully not on me or my wound.

"Is Maggie okay?" It was only thing I could think of that would have him this upset. Had Maggie dumped him or been hurt?

"Why?" he snarled.

"I called her, looking for you, trying to find out what was going on. She didn't answer or return the call." Maybe he'd accidentally hurt her, like he had me.

He stood abruptly. "This is none of your damn business. You get that, right? We're not family. Hell, we're not even friends. I just work here. And you know what? I don't do that anymore either. It was a shit job and I'm done."

"Dave, please, come on." When he turned and continued to stomp up the stairs, I followed. "You don't mean that."

"I'm not your daddy. I'm not your grumpy uncle. We're nothing to each other. Grow the fuck up."

Stealing myself, I didn't react, not now. "Fine. In that case, I have a question."

He turned, his face a mask of fury. "What?"

"Clive is being attacked in his sleep." I saw it. Momentary shock before the mask was back in place. "There was something dark and evil crouching in his mind and slashing his skin open while he slept. I couldn't get rid of it. It felt like—I'm not sure—but it felt like the demon Clive killed for me."

He shook his head, continuing up the stairs, nearing the human world. "You can't kill a demon. All Clive did was unmake him for a short time. And piss him off."

I stopped and swayed, pitching forward. Knee down, good hand gripping the stair lip above, the blood rushed from my head. A demon. An actual demon was torturing Clive while he slept. I tore up the stairs to ask for help, but when I emerged, Dave was already speeding out of the parking lot, laying rubber as he spun onto the main road.

# 4

# It Burns!

When I returned, Clive was waiting at the bottom of the stairs, his gaze traveling over me, looking for the hurt. He washed away what was left of the pain as he gently took my injured hand. When he glared up the stairs, I shook my head.

"My fault. I know better than to touch him when he's riled up." We didn't need another demon pissed off at Clive for defending me.

"Where's the first aid kit?"

Grim, the dwarf who had hopped onto the stool at the end of my bar the first night I'd opened and then resumed his seat every afternoon since, slid off said stool and walked around the back of the bar, grabbing the kit. He waved us over, opening it.

I'd been avoiding looking at my hand. The sight of it made me lightheaded. I let Clive and Grim work on me while I pretended that charred thing wasn't attached to me. This wasn't even the worst burn I'd endured. I'd be fine. I vaguely registered Clive calling Dr. Underfoot and then Owen's sister Lilah, who was a wicche healer.

Poldo, the new Guinness-drinking elf, was watching the proceedings a little too intently. All my patrons were glancing over, wearing similar expressions of concern. The new guy seemed more avid than sympathetic.

Ule returned with Fergus, who lifted his lip in a sneer at the new guy and then raced around the bar to me, rearing back on his hind legs, his front paws scratching at my jeans, trying to climb me. Ule left the leash by the clipboard for the next dog walker to use.

I crouched down, while Clive kept a firm grip on my hand, to pick up Fergus. Leaning across me, the pup sniffed wildly, trying to determine the problem.

When I said, "I'm okay, buddy," he gave me a soulful look, licked my chin, and then his head swung back to the new guy, who was no longer in his seat. Fergus squirmed, needing to get down.

"Darling, stay still," Clive murmured.

Careful not to pull my hand, I bent and placed Fergus back on the floor so he could investigate and patrol. After a thorough search of the bar and the kitchen, stopping to sniff at the doors of the restrooms, he paused at the stairs and lifted a paw to follow a scent trail. At least three other people and I said "No" at the same time. It warmed my heart that so many of us were looking out for him.

Sucking it up, I looked around Clive's shoulder at my hand. My stomach dropped and my throat constricted. It looked as though most of the skin was gone and what was left had been blackened. Clive moved to the side, blocking my view again.

"Lilah will be here shortly. I caught her in her car." He bent over my hand and I felt his tongue.

The pain spiked and I channeled what Clive wasn't able to relieve into the wicche glass around my neck. Light footsteps hurried down the stairs. Lilah emerged a moment later, wrapped in a long sweater, her dark hair pulled up and tucked into a knit hat.

She hurried over. Clive slid us toward her, but remained standing between me and my hand. Thunking my head against his back, I thanked the universe for giving me a man who understood

I needed to run after an angry demon and who loved me enough to block my sight of my own ouchy.

When Lilah finished, she moved to the side so I could see her. "How does it feel now?"

"No idea. Clive's still siphoning off the pain." I glanced around behind the bar. Yup, still just me bartending. "Can I get you something to drink?"

She gave me a sad smile. "I'm good. I was driving home after a dinner date."

"How was it—Oh, Clive, the tobacco tin with the salve Dr. Underfoot gave us last time is in the first aid kit." I turned back to Lilah. "The date, I mean."

"Meh. I liked the restaurant, though, so not a total loss." She watched Clive gently stroke the ointment over my burns. "I need to ask the doc if he can make some of that for me."

"You can have some." I tapped Clive's shoulder. "Split what we have with Lilah. I'm sure we have containers in the kitchen."

Clive held up the repurposed tobacco tin, showing me we only had a quarter left of what the doc had given us. "I think not," he ground out, "especially as one of your employees has a rather disturbing habit of burning you."

Oh. I was trying so hard to block the pain and the sight, I hadn't realized just how angry Clive was. "Hey." I nudged him with my shoulder. "I'm okay."

"You're not, no." Lifting my hand, he kissed the back of it. *I don't care what's going on in his life. He bloody well knows better than to lose control with someone so fragile.*

*I'm not fragile! I'm a badass werewolf.*

He turned, framing my face in his hands. *That, you are.* His gaze traveled over me and his expression softened before he leaned in to kiss me.

We broke apart when we heard more footsteps coming down. Owen, George, and George's twin Alec had arrived. Owen and George moved out of the way so Alec could get the full effect of The Slaughtered Lamb.

"Wow," Alec breathed. "I mean, they explained it, but wow."

Fergus raced between visitors, sniffing shoes, making assessments.

Hurrying around the bar, I pulled Alec into a one-armed hug. "Look at you!" My eyes filled with tears, which I wiped away quickly on a laugh. I couldn't help but remember how I'd seen him, a skeletal heap in the corner of his cell, an emaciated, escaped prisoner George had finally rescued after twenty years of wasting away in a dark dungeon. He'd put on some weight. Still thin, he no longer looked close to death.

"You're taller." I had to look up now.

Alec nodded, grinning.

George slung his arm around his brother's neck. "He's shot up four inches just since he's been here."

"And I've got the growing pains to go along with it. My legs are killing me. Actually..." He pointed to an empty chair before walking over to sit down. Rubbing the heels of his hands over his thigh muscles, Alec stared out, watching the water crash against the window before swirling down and out. His face was darker and healthier than it had been before. Fresh air, sun, and regular meals had him looking more like his gorgeous twin.

He glanced around and noticed Lilah. "Hi, again. I thought you had a date tonight."

She took the seat beside him. Owen and George moved another table over and sat down as well. "I was. The food was great, the guy not so much. I was driving home when I"—she glanced at my hand—"decided I could use a drink and a gorgeous view. I'd earned it."

George's gaze went unerringly to my hand before he patted his brother's shoulder. "Okay, are you ready to do some beer tasting?" When Fergus put a paw on George's thigh, the dragon picked him up and tucked him under a strong arm, his hand cradling Fergus' chest. Animals were drawn to George.

Alec laughed. "Bring it on. Oh, and Sam?" He reached out a hand for me.

I gave him my good one.

He squeezed it once and then used it to pull me closer. Once I was beside him, he leaned forward and very carefully took my injured hand in his. He studied the wound and then gave me a sad smile. "You don't have to protect me from the bad stuff. Okay?" When I nodded, he said, "Good. Now, what are you serving me?"

Unlike the dragons, who'd no doubt scented the wound, Owen hadn't noticed until Alec had examined my hand. There'd been a moment of horror in his expression before his gaze had shifted to his sister. Hand resting on George's thigh, Owen gave it a quick pat and then stood and went behind the bar.

"I'll give you a hand, Sam." He pulled six short glasses from under the bar. "I'll do this. Can you pour George a brown ale? Lilah and I prefer IPAs." He was giving me the easier job, filling glasses from the taps, as I only had one working hand at the moment.

"Okay," Owen said, carrying a tray holding the six half-filled glasses back to the table. "Here you go." He lined them in front of Alec, light to dark.

I loaded my three beers on a tray and went around the bar to pick it up, but Clive beat me to it, serving George, Owen, and Lilah before dropping the tray back on the bar. He waited for me to take the seat next to Lilah and then sat beside me, his arm protectively around me. It was late and most of my customers had already left, though a few stayed to watch the beer tasting.

"First up," Owen said, "is a lager. This will be the lightest, in terms of color and flavor."

Alec picked it up and sniffed. Turning to George, he said, "Do you remember the cousins, uh, Jordie and Wills?"

When George laughed, nodding, Alec filled in the rest of us. "This was in December one year, when we were at the keep in Wales. Jordie and Wills snuck into the kitchen in the middle of the night to steal beer. If we were seven or eight, they must have been ten or eleven." He took a small sip and let it sit on his tongue a moment. "Anyway, they stole a couple of the dark beers"—he motioned to George's glass—"and drank themselves sick. When we got up in the morning, we found them passed out in the great hall, lying on the floor by the now cold fireplace, a puddle of vomit next to Jordie." He shook his head, grinning.

"As I recall, they had a hard time sitting down at lunch," George added, taking a drink of his brown ale. Fergus sniffed the glass and then turned back to the excitement at the table, giving George's hand a little lick.

Grinning, Alec took another sip of the lager. "Good times. Meanwhile, this is okay. I didn't expect beer to be so bubbly."

"That's a lager thing. They're more carbonated than other beers," Owen explained. "The next one is a pilsner."

Alec took a sip and again let it settle on his tongue.

"I wish I had some food for you." Unfortunately, I no longer had a cook. Considering, I said, "I have nuts." I popped up to go get them, but Alec waved me down.

"These two took me to dinner so I wouldn't be trying this on an empty stomach." He held up the pilsner and sniffed before taking another sip. "This one's better than the last one, but I'd still chose a soda over this."

"Next is an India Pale Ale. It's what Lilah and I are drinking," Owen said. He kept glancing over at me, a question in his eyes.

I hid my hand under the table, palm up on my leg.

"Better. I can see why you guys like it, but I think this is like coffee." He took another sip.

"How is beer like coffee for you?" Clive asked.

Alec swallowed on a grin. "Sorry, no, I meant—sometimes, when I need out of Grandmother's house, I stroll down to their place." He gestured to George and Owen. "They gave me my own room on the lower level." His expression was haunted for a moment before he blinked and shook it off. "Twenty years of living underground." He shrugged. "Heights bother me."

Alec picked up the next glass and raised his eyebrows at Owen.

"That's an Irish Red."

"I like the color." He took a sniff and then a sip. After a

moment, he said, "Hm, that one actually has an interesting taste. I can't tell you what that taste is, but it's interesting."

Fergus squirmed to get down and George lowered his arm.

"We're taking Alec to lots of different restaurants so he can try different kinds of cuisine. Up until now, his choices were...limited," George said, resting a hand on his twin's back.

Alec scoffed, "That's one way of putting it."

# 5

# Making Friends, One Lemon Drop at a Time

"Some people say the Irish Red has a caramel maltiness, others more of a toffee or a buttered toast taste," Owen volunteered.

I waved as the wicches who'd been sitting in the corner left. When Fergus completed his security rounds, he hopped on his back legs, his front paws on my leg as he sniffed furiously at my injured hand. I picked him up with my good one and held him on my lap.

"That's it. It reminds me of toast." He turned to Clive. "Sorry," he said, picking up the thread. "After so many years—Sometimes I forget to talk out loud. I was saying that I split my time between my grandmother's house and George and Owen's. This morning, Owen was up early, making us breakfast. The food smelled great, but the coffee was disgusting. We had a discussion about when they started drinking it and why. What they like about it. We kind of came to the conclusion that if you don't start drinking it at a certain time in your life, you probably won't. I have a feeling beer may be like that for me."

George nodded. "I started drinking coffee in college and so did Owen. Staying up late to study for tests or finish writing research papers the night before they were due—"

"That was me," Owen broke in. "There's no way George was waiting until the last minute."

Alec laughed, the tension around his eyes disappearing. "Not this one," he said, patting his twin on the shoulder. "He was always the responsible one."

George shook his head, embarrassed yet hopeful, watching Alec laugh. "My point was that we each started drinking it out of necessity and then acquired a taste for it over the years."

"Same for me," Lilah said. "Though it was in high school. My friends liked going out for flavored iced coffees, so I started drinking them too. Although I much prefer boba tea."

Owen high-fived his sister across the table.

"What's boba?" Alec asked.

"Delicious!" Lilah laughed. "It's a milky tea, sometimes with a fruity flavor. It has tapioca pearls that sit on the bottom. You drink it with a wide straw so you can suck up the pearls with the tea. Have you had chai?"

He shook his head.

"I'm off tomorrow. Do you want to go get boba with me?" Lilah kept the invitation light. From Alec's reaction, it was clear the idea of going out, especially without a close relative, was causing fear to rear back and bite him in the face.

A few more people left, waving to me before they headed up the stairs.

Alec took another sip, a war waging inside him, before nodding. "Yeah. Thanks. I'd like to do that." He paused, looking down at the beer a moment. "Uh, if I start to act crazy—"

"Not crazy," George interrupted. "He has some very understandable anxiety. If things get too busy or noisy or the lights are too bright, it can trigger a panic attack. The best thing to do is just move him quickly away from the people and the noise and let him relax someplace dim and quiet."

I leaned forward to catch Alec's eye. He was clearly embarrassed by what he believed was a weakness. "Welcome to the club. I've had panic attacks for seven years."

Hesitant, he put down his beer, seemingly unsure if I was being honest or just trying to make him feel better.

I glanced around the bar. Everyone else had left. Clive rubbed my back. I was among friends and Alec needed to know he wasn't alone.

"When I was seventeen, I was abducted and held in a shack in the woods for a day and a half. I was tied down, blindfolded—"

"Trapped in the dark," he breathed, and I nodded.

"He was a werewolf. Sometimes he attacked as a man, using a knife to slice me up, raping me repeatedly. Sometimes he was the wolf, claws and teeth tearing at me." I pulled up my sleeve, showing him some of the countless scars covering most of my body.

"I had panic attacks all the time. It took almost, what?" I glanced at Clive. "Maybe six months before I left Helena's apartment—she was the wicche who took me in when I was dumped in San Francisco." I shook my head. "Long story.

"Anyway, it's a hard road back and we can only do what we can only do. Give yourself a break. Healing on the inside takes a lot longer than healing on the outside. Lots of people don't get that, and, honestly, good for them. What happened to us shouldn't happen to anyone. So if you're having a bad day and the hurt is too close to the surface, you may react and people may give you strange looks, but that's okay.

"It just means they, thankfully, haven't lived what we have. We need to shake those awkward moments off and give ourselves a really big break because we're out here trying. Right?" At his cautious nod, I continued, "It doesn't matter if anyone else understands that the simplest things can require herculean strength. We know it and we need to give ourselves credit for doing, or at least attempting, the extraordinarily difficult simple things.

"And just so you don't think I've put it all behind me now, The Slaughtered Lamb is still warded against werewolves. Seven years later and other supernaturals can come for a drink or a book, but no wolves. Maybe someday I'll take down that barrier, but I'm not ready yet and that's okay."

I shrugged. "If you are having one of those hard days, you can always call me. I'm close by and can run over."

He nodded again but didn't speak. George's eyes were glassy as he reached out to hold his brother's hand.

Alec gripped it hard, cleared his throat, and let go. "This one looks like what George is drinking."

"That's right," Owen said. "That's a brown ale."

Alec met my gaze and nodded, acknowledging my offer, before picking up the glass. "Okay, let's see if my brother's got any taste." He took a sip and held it a moment. Swallowing, he shook his head. "There are so many tastes in the world. It's crazy. This is a—what's it called?" He drew his finger back and forth along the line of glasses.

"Spectrum?" George guessed.

Alec paused, thinking. "Yeah, a spectrum of tastes, light to dark, weak to strong. Honestly, I don't know that I'd ever want to drink any of these again, but I prefer this end of the spectrum, the darker colors and stronger tastes. Even if they're not good, they're interesting."

I got up, dropping Fergus back to the floor, and went behind the bar, pulling bottles and a shaker. While Alec tried a stout, I mixed him a cocktail, being careful not to accidentally use my right hand.

"I feel like I should chew this one," Alec said. "I like this one the best of the six, but that's not saying much."

I shoved a glass of water to the edge of the bar. "Owen, give this to Alec so he can clean that taste out of his mouth." I rimmed another glass with a lemon, turned it over, and spun it in a shallow dish of tart sugar before righting the glass and pouring a perfect lemon drop into the glass.

"I'm not sure what you're brewing up back there, but I love lemon so I'm already looking forward to it."

I brought it around the bar and placed it in front of Alec before resuming my seat. "Try that one."

He studied the glass a moment. "Pretty." Picking it up by the stem, he frowned at the sparkling sugar on the rim. "How?"

"Drink from any side. That's part of the cocktail."

Nodding, he brought it to his lips, getting a taste of sugar on his tongue as he took a sip, and then closed his eyes, savoring. When he blinked them open, he grinned at me. "Now that's more like it."

"Right? I don't get the beer thing either." I knew he had a long road ahead of him, but he was already healing and it made my heart happy.

While Alec and George talked rugby, Owen leaned in and said, "I forgot to say earlier, my mom thinks she's heard the name Arwyn Corey."

I leaned in myself, wanting to know everything about the maker of the magical chess set. "Where? When?"

He shook his head. "She's not sure, but give her time. She always remembers."

"She does," Lilah agreed.

"She doesn't know much about European wicches, so she's pretty sure what she knows relates to a local wicche. Anyway, when she remembers, I'll pass it on." Owen took another sip and started chatting with his sister.

Local? I couldn't decide if that was amazingly cool or vaguely threatening. On a completely unrelated note, I'd had a thought.

*I've been thinking.*

*Sounds dangerous.*

*Since abducting a priest is out, I think we need to pay a call to our unfriendly neighborhood Fury who lives in a church.*

*Good thought, darling, but decommissioned churches go through some sort of ceremony, I believe, taking away the sanctity of the property.*

*True, but she scared off the priest a hundred years ago, before he could do the rite. She said her home is still holy ground and that it keeps away the dark and deadlies.*

*My brilliant wife.* He kissed me on the cheek and then stood, pulling his phone out of his pocket.

Alec checked his watch and downed the rest of his drink. "Okay. George starts work early. We should get going." He bent to the side, looking down at his foot, where Fergus was currently taking a nap.

"Sorry. He does that when he likes you and wants you to stay put. I can—"

"I got him." Alec picked up the floppy pup and cradled him. Fergus gave a great sleepy yawn, licked Alec's hand, and snuggled in.

"Why don't you take him tonight?" It popped out before I had a chance to think about it, but it felt right.

The lines of tension around Alec's eyes smoothed. "What?"

Motioning to the kitchen, where Clive was talking on the phone, I said, "We can't stay here tonight—dealing with a bad guy—so you'd be doing us a favor. I'd feel better if I knew he was safe with you." I grabbed his leash from the end of the bar. That did it. Fergus was suddenly wiggly and ready to go.

Laughing, Alec took the leash and snapped it onto Fergus' collar before putting him down. "Okay, sure." He glanced around the bar. "We should get food and toys, right?"

"Yes. Give me a minute to gather up a bag of stuff to take. He's mostly potty trained; you just need to take him out regularly. And he'll let you know. We take him out to go every few hours, but if we forget, he'll whine and pace in a circle-eight pattern."

I ran into the kitchen to grab a tote bag, scooped out the proper amount of kibble into individual baggies, and then threw in some potty bags and his favorite toys. Clive walked out of the apartment grinning, Fergus' dragon chew toy in his hand. He dropped it in my bag and I had to laugh.

Back in the bar, I handed the puppy bag to George. He lifted the gnawed-on rubber dragon by its torn wing.

Fergus gave a happy yowl, jumping and trying to get his dragon.

George's expression was one of long-suffering disappointment. "Really, Sam?"

Owen patted George's shoulder, reaching over and dropping the dragon back into the bag. "Don't worry. I'm almost positive Fergus is going to lose that toy in the ocean—it'll be a kind of burial at sea—and then we'll get him a replacement chew toy. A wolf. As he's a wolfhound, I'm sure he'll like that better."

Alec shook his head, grinning, and turned toward the stairs. "Come on, little man. Let's go home and play."

George mouthed *thank you* and then was right behind his brother. Owen and Lilah quickly said their goodbyes, following in their wake.

Mentally closing up the wards, I filled a tray with empties and carried them to the bar.

"Meg's out of town but said we could use her church."

My stomach finally began to unclench. We'd have a way to protect him during the day. "Great. Let's pack a bag and go." I'd leave the glasses to deal with in the morning.

"One caveat," he said.

I stopped beside him, waiting to hear what hoop Meg was planning to have us jump through.

"She says we're not allowed to use her bed, because—and I quote—eww."

Laughing, I pushed through the kitchen door and headed to our apartment. "Got it. No nookie in her bed. No problem. She's got a great couch. We can sleep there."

Our apartment was as neat and clean as it could be, given it was small and filled with way too much stuff. I found the luggage and then paused.

"Are we driving or running?"

Clive strolled in behind me. "Good question. Given the neighborhood, parking will be quite difficult and I'd rather not have my roadster towed during the day."

"Got it." I grabbed a backpack, as that would be easier to run with.

"Wait. Let me make a phone call." He walked back out to the kitchen.

Doing my best with one hand, I gathered pajamas, a change of clothes, and a toiletry bag.

When Clive walked back in, he handed me my overnight case. "The nocturne has paid for parking spots in the neighborhoods where it's necessary. As I can no longer just take one when I need it, I had to call Russell to ask if I could use it."

Dropping the clothes I'd been gathering on the bed, I walked to Clive and hugged him tightly with one arm. "I'm sorry."

He rubbed my back. "Adjustments. Little adjustments is all. Once the house is done, we won't been crammed in here. And now that I've remembered the issue, I'll rent spaces for us."

"You need a Norma," I said, referring to the nocturne's daytime human liaison who got stuff done. I missed her.

"Nonsense. It's just the two of us."

I leaned back to look at him, eyebrows raised.

"Yes, fine. It's been quite some time since I haven't had someone I could call and tell to take care of things for me. Adjustments, darling. We're setting up a new life. It takes time."

I pushed up and kissed him. "Right you are." He watched me struggle a moment, trying to fold the clothes I'd just dropped on the bed.

Wrapping his hands around my shoulders, he shunted me to the side, refolded them, and packed them in the overnight bag.

I gave him another kiss on the cheek.

Grinning, he zipped up the bag. "Anything else? Oh." He pulled the tin of Dr. Underfoot's burn salve out of his pocket. "I got this out of the kit for you. We'll put on another coat before you sleep. Come now," he said, kissing my forehead. "Let's go. You're dead on your feet."

Elbowing him in the side, I said, "Hey, you too."

Rolling his eyes, he helped me into my coat and then grabbed my bag.

"Wait. Don't you need something?"

Ushering me out, he said, "As you well know, I'll be dead to the world."

6

# Drunken Pixie Crooning

It was a lovely night for a drive. Cold, but clear. As it was well after midnight on a weekday, there were few other cars on the road.

Meg's home sat behind the Sts. Peter and Paul Cathedral in the North Beach district of San Francisco. It was small and old and probably should have been torn down, but Meg had bought it before anything could be done.

"You know," I said, "I don't think we need the nocturne's parking space. I remember seeing a dirt path that went around the back of her church. We won't have to try to find street parking. I think you can just pull up onto her property."

"Good memory," he said, changing direction and heading straight for Meg's. He drove down her street, looking for the break in the sidewalk that would indicate a driveway. The cars were parked bumper to bumper, but we finally found the break. A car was parked well into the driveway, but Clive was able to squeeze his sports car through.

"What if another car blocks us in completely?"

"I believe that would mean that we'll be picking up the car and carrying it to the street."

I laughed as he drove the path around the back of the church.

Meg kept it all locked up. I'm sure generations of locals assumed it would be torn down any day now, but she loved it and had updated the interior. It had a modern bathroom—hallelujah—and small kitchen area. When she'd let me spend the night—right after the New Orleans vamps attacked us—she had to fly me in, as all entrances were boarded up.

Clive might not have Meg's wings, but he can scale buildings like no one's business. After locking up his baby, he swung me around so I was clinging to his back. I had my right arm clenched across his throat, holding my hand carefully away from everything. In the left, I carried my overnight bag.

"Do the look-away spell, will you, darling?"

"You know I can't really do that kind of magic." It was a good thing Clive didn't need to breathe, as I hitched myself up with the arm around his neck before wrapping my legs around his waist. Heights and I were not friends, especially when I only had one good hand to hold on with.

"Even a weak spell is better than none."

As that was a good point, I did the spell as Owen had taught it to me. "Now or never."

He leapt straight up, landing easily on the edge of the roof near the bell tower. Meg had removed the bell because she kept hitting her head on it. Clive pulled a cord and the floor under where the bell should have hung swung up, revealing a way in. A rickety ladder led to a series of catwalks so high in the rafters, they were hard to see from the floor. The door was no doubt intended for bell ringers and roof repairmen, but it now served as Meg's entrance.

I'd had the misfortune of trying to use the ladder and catwalk the last time I was here. Never again. The whole high-wire apparatus felt like it was one industrious termite away from disintegrating on the spot. Clive, with more skill and flare than I have ever possessed, dropped through the hole while flipping the trapdoor closed, dropping fifty or sixty feet and landing lightly on the living room rug.

I released my chokehold on my hunny bunny and looked

around. It was dark, but I made out candles and matches on the sideboard. I tossed my overnight bag on the sheet-covered chair and started lighting candles.

While I fumbled with match strikes, Clive pulled sheets off the furniture. When I turned around, he was sitting on the couch, his feet up on the coffee table.

"It's surprisingly homey."

"Right? I love this place." I left one of the candles on the sideboard and put the other three on the coffee table. We had another problem. "This place should deal with the demon trouble, but it's not lightless. She has some original stained glass up there."

"Hmm." He stood and looked around. "That's a larger problem. You said you took a tunnel out. I could go down there."

"Hard pass." I shook my head vehemently. "There has to be an army of spiders down there, given the thick cobwebs. Nope nope nope." I looked around for something to jury-rig. "The pews are made of thick wood." I went over and picked up the end of one, checking its weight and condition.

"Good call." He picked up a long and ridiculously heavy pew, hefting it on his shoulder, and walked it to a side chapel with boarded-up windows. He put the first one down and then went back for another. "Grab that one, darling. We're going to tip them forward so their backs hit, creating a lightless diamond underneath."

"Pew fort!" I shouted, pumping my fists.

"As you like. Can you grab a candle? We'll see where the light gets in." Crouching, he stared down the tunnel we'd created.

I held a candle over the seam where the two wooden pews came together. He shook his head and picked up another pew, inverting it and dropping it like a cap on top of the diamond.

"What about the legs? That extra weight on one side might tip the whole structure over."

He gave me a quick kiss, a gleam in his eye. "I'm just getting started."

Deciding to be comfortable, I went back to the couch while he played with pews, creating an impregnable fort.

"Darling? I need you and your candle again." He slid under the mountain of pews. "And could you please push this last one into place."

The pew was on its back. I pushed it forward, blocking the hole he'd just slipped through, sealing him up. Grabbing the candle, I walked it all around the structure, moving the candle this way and that, trying to find any chinks in the armor before the sun rose.

"Are you seeing any light?"

"I am not."

It boggled my mind. For more nights than I could fathom, he'd engaged in these same activities, trying to ensure his survival during daylight hours. "I made the circuit twice. I think you're good."

"Excellent," he said, pushing back the pew I'd used to seal him in. "Well, barring an earthquake—"

"Hey, we don't tempt fate. Remember?" I did not need more things to worry about.

"Sorry, love." He took my hand and led me back to the couch. "I can put myself to bed when it's time." He picked up his topcoat from the chair where he'd dropped it earlier and then lay down on the couch.

I kicked off my running shoes and snuggled in, so we were spooning. Clive then flung his coat over us, mostly me, as vamps didn't feel the cold. He wrapped an arm around me, held me close, and the world was right again.

"Shall I tell you how construction is coming on the new house?"

"Yes, please." We'd—Clive had—purchased a house on Seal Rock Drive. It was the last on the road, closest to the ocean. It would give us a physical address, a home we could invite people to, and give Clive a garage he could drive one of his fleet of cars out of. The dragon contractors who were building our underground real home were connecting The Slaughtered Lamb to the Seal Rock house, including a huge underground parking lot.

The Seal Rock house had been turned into apartments decades ago. When it went on the market a few months ago, when we'd begun our relationship, Clive had purchased it. He'd said he hadn't had a plan for it then, hadn't known how things would play out between us. He just knew he was in love and considering alternatives to living in my tiny apartment. He'd also researched the huge waterfront mansions that Benvair and now George owned, but after the dragon contractors had agreed to make us our own folly, he'd known exactly what to do with the Seal Rock house.

"They've taken the interior down to the studs and have built it back up according to the blueprints I showed you."

I tapped his hand. "You know I only actually looked at the library, right? And it seemed way too small."

"I do, yes, and you realize that it's a scaled plan, correct? If I recall, the page you were studying was a thousandth actual size." He kissed the back of my neck.

"Oh, that's better then." I poked his arm and felt him laughing behind me. "I'm not a moron. I know how blueprints work. I was just hoping for a library floor, that's all."

"In our next home."

"I'm totally holding you to that."

"We have a crew working on the exterior as well. I dare say you may not recognize it. They're remaking it so we'll have the Tudor Revival style you like."

"Wouldn't it be easier to just tear it down and start again?"

"Yes and no. If we did that, it would be considered new construction and there'd be even more hoops to jump through, all of which take inordinate bureaucratic time. This is more complicated for the construction crew, but we're employing the same team who made The Slaughtered Lamb. They are highly skilled, magical craftsmen."

I was quiet for a while, visions of our new home, our new life, playing out in my mind's eye. I tapped the hand he had wrapped around me again. "You know you're going to freak out the neighbors. Someone who's paying attention is going to notice tons of different cars driving out of the same two-car garage."

"We were always going to be the strange ones on the block, darling. If the most scandalous charge they can lay at our feet is a secret auto chop shop, we'll be fine. Did you know," he said, adjusting his arm under my head, "that perhaps a hundred years ago, neighbors of the nocturne tried to get us railroaded out of town?"

I looked over my shoulder. "They knew you were vampires?"

"Lord, no. They believed us to be men who shared a love that dare not speak its name."

I laughed.

"It's true. They thought the nocturne was some kind of gay sex club."

"Maybe it was all the chandeliers."

Clive tickled me and I squirmed away.

"If only they knew how incredibly boring and stuffy you guys are."

After pulling me back into place, he said, "I'd love to take offense at that, but it's true. Our lives are long, dark periods of tedium broken up with savage violence. Blood and ennui."

"Good band name."

He chuckled. "And then a scarred little wolf moved into my territory and suddenly life wasn't so lifeless."

"Aww."

"Annoyance woke me from my stupor."

"Heeey." Rude.

"And what I discovered was a quiet bookworm who was slyly funny. I didn't need anyone to tell me our lone wolf's aura was a bright, shiny gold. The wicches needed it to feel comfortable coming to The Slaughtered Lamb to drink their teas and read their books. The first time I came into the bar to check on you, I knew. I'd intended to stay a moment, make sure the window wall wasn't leaking and that humans hadn't accidentally found their way in.

"What I hadn't expected was to find the little wolf—the one who jumped at shadows when I'd first met her—crouched down and shouting into a spittoon that he better get his stupid, drunk ass out if he knew what was good for him."

I slapped my good hand to my face, embarrassed all over again. "And you, Mister Impeccably Polished and Too Sexy For Real Life, cleared your throat and said—in your upper crusty British accent—'Has the spittoon offended you in some way?' "

"Yes, but I knew you were made of sterner stuff when you brazened it out. I'd expected a squeak and for you to run behind the bar. Instead, face blazing red with embarrassment, you popped up, shot your finger down at the spittoon and said, 'He won't get his stupid drunk pixie ass out of there and now we have to listen to slurred ABBA songs echoing around the bar.' You turned back, leaned over with your hands on your hips, and shouted, 'That's it, Terry! You're cut off!' And then, to my great and everlasting delight, I heard a high pitched moan of sadness before 'Dancing Queen' floated out of the copper spittoon."

## 7

# Meanwhile, Now I Have "Dancing Queen" Stuck in my Head

I grinned in the dark. "I miss Terry. I heard he went back to Faerie."

"It was then I knew there was more to you than the scared little wolf who'd come to me with a plan for her bookstore and bar. But what made me—a being who cannot see auras—know that you were as kind as you were adorable was when, as the song was winding down, we heard a metallic clang. You looked into the spittoon and then knelt down, hesitantly reaching in and ever so gently picking up the unconscious pixie.

"You ran him over to the sink and sprinkled cold water on him, all while asking the wicches if they could help. You were in a panic that the pixie you'd been berating had passed out and were trying to get him help."

"If he'd hit his head, he could have hurt himself."

"And no doubt did, as he was absolutely soaked. But that wasn't the shiny gold part of the story. When I asked you why you hadn't tipped the spittoon over and dumped him out before, you said that would have been rude. Terry might like to belt out songs when he was tipsy, but none of us were perfect and no one had the right to make another feel small and weak and unable to protect themselves. So you carefully carried him to the end of the bar and used two bar towels to make a little bed for him."

"The wicches assured me he didn't have a concussion or anything, so I figured he could just sleep it off where he'd be safe."

Clive kissed the side of my neck.

We were silent for a while, content to be together. "I don't think I can leave you today."

"We just checked. I'm safe on holy ground and will be out of the sun in Pew Mountain." He rubbed his hand over my hip. "I'll be fine, darling. I've been hiding from the sun for a millennium."

"Yeah, but anything could happen to you. What if neighborhood kids pick tomorrow to pull down boards and explore? I'm supposed to trust that nothing is going to happen to you? No. I don't like that. I can't leave you unprotected." I paused again, remembering. "And Dave quit, so we can't ask our demon questions."

"Ah, is that what you were discussing when he burned you?"

I shrugged one shoulder. "I kind of burned myself. He was ignoring me, walking away, and I grabbed his arm to stop him, which was stupid. It was after the burn, when I tried to get him to tell me what was wrong, that he quit."

"I see." He was pissed all over again. I could hear it in his voice.

"He won't be at work tomorrow to help. It'll be Owen and Fyr all day again."

"You're not asking them for a favor. These are your employees. You pay them to work. The bar opens at noon and the sun goes down at six. We'll be there shortly after sunset and then you'll be the one working all by herself for the next six to eight hours."

"Yeah, but it's my place. I'm supposed to be doing most of the work."

"And you usually are," he said, squeezing my hip. "Business has been good. People missed you and The Slaughtered Lamb. Fyr won't be enough. You should probably look into hiring more people, especially if your cook has, in fact, quit."

"He'll come back." He was just angry right now. He'd settle down and come back. I hoped.

"Go to sleep, darling. You were awake all last night, watching over me. You need rest."

As much as I wanted to argue the point—*You're not the boss of me!*—he was right. I was having a hard time holding on to my thoughts. Like quicksilver, as soon as I tried to grab one, it slid out of reach.

I woke soon after to the sound of Clive grunting and my injured hand itching. Brain sluggish, I tried to put the pieces together. What was going on? Remembering not to touch my hand, I shook it, trying to get rid of the maddening prickles.

I opened my eyes, checking to see if more skin was covering my fingertips and palm, if the healing spells and ointment were working. I had to blink and then blink again in the darkened building. Weak light filtered through the high stained glass windows. Shafts of colored sunlight broke up the darkness. Even with the dim light, though, I couldn't make sense of what I was seeing. I was holding my hand steady, but it was moving.

Clive made a sound and my heart raced in a panic. Sleep-deprived, my brain finally caught up, making sense of the unrelated details. Clive was under attack and thousands of tiny spiders were crawling all over my hand. Leaping up with a cry of shock, I tried to fling my hand across the room. Some spiders flew off into the darkness but most clung to my salve-covered wound. I felt the prickling itch across my cheek and over my scalp. I knew I had an injured hand, but logic had left the building. I swatted at my arms and legs, scratching my head, spinning away from the spiders swarming me.

A low, papery laugh broke through my panic. The spiders were still crawling down my neck and across my forehead, but my focus was on the man standing on what used to be the altar, beside Meg's bed.

"A little jumpy, aren't ya?" Sounding as though he gargled with gravel, he leered, and my heart dropped into my stomach. Possession. I hadn't even considered possession. "I found this one just for you. Do you like him?" The demon's words were mouthed by a homeless man with glazed eyes.

Skin crawling, I stood paralyzed as a spider scurried over my lower lip. I couldn't tear my eyes from the possessed man, who had moved into the side chapel and pulled at the legs of a pew, sending it crashing to the floor. He was toppling Pew Mountain, trying to turn my husband to dust.

"No!" When I leapt toward him, he turned back, teeth bared in a feral grin, his hand on another pew. Threat clear, I stopped.

"He's not the same one, obviously," the homeless man mouthed, "but he's remarkably similar to the one who flayed your mother, isn't he?" It was disorienting to have the man open his mouth and listen to the demon make comments essentially about himself.

I'd been wrong about the church. A demon didn't need to step foot on holy ground when he was able to possess someone who could. I was an idiot. I'd thought I was keeping Clive safe. A quiet grunt sounded from under the pews. The demon continued to slice Clive open while distracting me with spiders and a homeless puppet.

"Watch." He kicked the end pew, sending it a few feet away, opening Clive's daytime resting place. With a sneer, the demon-possessed man moved from the pews and stepped up on the altar again, holding his arms out and slowly spinning in a circle. "The clothes are almost identical. Crusty, urine-stained pants, too-large shoes with flapping soles, a worn, threadbare camo jacket. I thought it would be fun to reenact the moment you became an orphan. This time, it'll be the moment Clive becomes a widower."

He laughed, dry and papery, when Clive grunted again.

Spiders crawled across my chest and around my ear. It wouldn't be like last time. My mother had shoved me in a closet when she'd realized her sorcerer sister had finally hunted us down. My mother had spelled me so I couldn't move or speak. She'd tried to protect me. There'd been a gap in the door, though, so I'd seen my aunt and the dark, smoky demon she'd called. I'd watched the smoke dive into the homeless man who'd been sitting quietly in the corner. The man had risen unsteadily and pulled a long, sharp knife from his pocket. I'd been unable to move, to intervene in any way.

That wasn't the case now. My claws slid from my fingertips as I uncoiled my magic, felt it surge through me.

The demon's gaze dropped to my claws before the man's face split into a grin filled with blackened, broken teeth. "Excellent." He pulled a long, serrated blade from his jacket pocket and then lurched off the altar toward me.

We circled each other, my socked feet silent on the wooden floors. He telegraphed the move a split-second before he lunged and sliced the air. I'd already spun to the side out of the knife's path.

"Oh, good. At least you're making this entertaining for me." The menace and intelligence of the demon shone through the homeless man's eyes. "Now, I wasn't there, but I heard she didn't put up much of a fight." He tapped the blade against his own face, as though lost in thought and then used the tip to scratch his cheek, slicing through his own skin. The demon was fully in charge, the homeless man barely flinching.

"Probably trying to protect you, huh? If she kept everyone's focus on her, no one would think to go look for you in that closet."

*Shit.* Had he already known where I'd been or was he reading my mind now?

"How do you live with the knowledge that your mother endured unspeakable pain because of you?" He shook his head, disgusted. "Doesn't it ever bother you? All these people getting hurt, losing their lives, because they're trying to protect you? Think of all the people who'd be living now if you weren't."

He began to circle again, and I kept my distance. "Have you ever tallied it up? Your mom and dad, of course, but then your grandfather Alexander. He wouldn't have been killed by Marcus if your dad had still been around. Then there's Marcus. Your great-aunt Martha. Think how happy she and Galadriel would be right now if they'd never met you. Abigail. She'd been obsessed with ridding you from the family line and died for her trouble. You've spent so much time painting her as the villain, but really, Miss Shiny Gold, you've been at the center of countless deaths."

He gestured to the mountain of pews with the long knife. "And that guy. He's survived for a thousand years, but he meets you and the attacks begin. Right now, his skin is being split open and it's taking longer and longer to heal because he's getting weaker and weaker. If it weren't for you, he'd be sleeping safely in his nocturne, still Master of the City. He gave up the power and prestige he'd fought hundreds of years to earn because the other vampires were mean to you." His words had become whiny as he made an exaggerated sad face.

He stopped circling and cleaned his fingernails with the knife tip. When he looked up from his filthy hands, his gaze speared me in place. "And that's not even taking into account all the people you've killed. You're in infamous serial killer territory now. You know that, right?"

His arm shot out, quick as a snake, but he was slashing at air again. Instead of ducking out of the way, I flipped over the top of him, landing in a crouch and dragging my claws through his jeans at the backs of his knees.

The man dropped to the ground, muscles, tendons, ligaments shredded, but registering no pain. Kneeling in a pool of blood, he tried to get up, but his legs no longer worked properly. Crumpling to the floor, he rolled over onto his stomach and used his arms to crawl toward me, the knife still firmly in his grip.

"You're going to add this poor guy to your tally? Not even going to bother to try to save him, huh? Typical."

I knew what he was doing. I knew it and yet I couldn't deflect the barbs because a part of me believed what he was saying. A part of me still believed that everyone else's needs should come first. I was working on it, but I wasn't there yet.

I had my aunt's magic, the spells I'd stolen from her when

she'd tried to kill me. I could use her spells. Take this man out of the equation, but he'd done nothing to deserve being used this way, first by a demon and then by me. Oddly, it was Stheno's voice in my head, remembering her annoyance whenever I put myself at risk for what she deemed a stupid reason, that got me moving. *Have I taught you nothing, kid?*

Stepping out of the man's path, I pulled the pain from the wicche glass, combined it with my own magic, and then let them run down my arm and gather in my hand. The homeless man who'd been used to kill my mother had died as soon as the demon left him. It would probably be the same here. He'd already lost too much blood, but still I hesitated. *Damn it, kid!*

Rolling the ball of magic in my hand, I paused, said a little prayer asking someone upstairs to please collect this poor man, and then threw the spell. It hit him straight on. He convulsed and then fell onto his back, his mouth opening and closing, like a fish on a dock. I'd hit him with Abigail's spell to stop the heart and lungs. In less time than I would have guessed, he lay still, eyes staring sightlessly up into the rafters.

# 8

# Come On, We All Knew This Would Happen Eventually

Clive made a quiet grunt of pain. *Damn it.* My brilliant plan of getting him to holy ground did nothing to protect him from Sitri, the demon who used to run San Francisco, who messed with my head, prompting Clive to take his. Maybe I could run over to the cathedral next door and get some holy water. Did stealing holy water negate the holiness? Hmm. Then again, what if vampires reacted badly to holy water? It could be like acid to them. Maybe I should do a holy water test strip.

I was just stepping around the corpse when I heard a sound in the rafters. Bracing, I looked up and found dozens of shiny black eyes staring back at me. After a moment of charged silence a *CAW* rent the air, echoing off the walls. That was followed by a cacophonous, deafening response from the murder of crows crowding the catwalks.

The sound of one crow can evoke a lonely road in the middle of nowhere, isolation, desolation. Dozens, if not hundreds, of crows cawing speaks to imminent death by beak and claw. I'd seen *The Birds*. I went lightheaded. I was about to have my eyes pecked out.

Soon the caws were joined by the flapping of wings. Terrified, I lunged to the side, looking for some kind of protection. Instead, I hit the ground, a hand clamped around my ankle. I rolled, kicking, and then stilled in shock. The homeless man, eyes glazed over in death, crawled after me. Teeth bared, he slithered toward me, smearing a blood trail in his wake.

"Are you fucking kidding me?" I screamed over the cries of the crows. "You're adding a zombie to the mix?"

As one, their wings beat the air as they arrowed through the dim church, straight for me. I rolled the mostly dead homeless man on top of me. If I hadn't been terrified out of my mind, I'd have been sick.

Asshole throws a zombie at me? At *me*? "I'm a fricking necromancer, you dick!" Easily—honestly, far too easily—I severed the demon's control of the zombie and took over, having him cover me from the sharp beaks and claws trying to dig through him to get to me.

I wasn't going to think about the zombie blood dripping on me right now. Nope. Focusing my aunt's magic in my palm again, I shot a hand out, throwing the spell at the crows. More than a few found me with their stabbing beaks, but then the church was filled with the thuds of dead birds dropping to the floor.

Meg was going to kill me.

I shoved the zombie off and ordered him to wait. I'd probably need him again soon. A crow—I scanned the building and didn't find any others still alive—flew down and landed on the back of the couch, watching me.

The crow opened its mouth and the demon's voice floated out. "How is it I didn't know you were a necromancer? Interesting. Secrets, secrets everywhere." It lifted its head and cawed. The sound, amplified a hundred times, felt like a spike to the brain.

Clive hissed, the pain no doubt amping up as he was wearing down.

Head pounding, I stood, covered in blood—some mine, some the zombie's—and considered my options.

"I don't believe your aunt was one. Or your mother, for that matter. I wonder—"

A soft *coo* cut him off. The crow looked at the wall behind the used-to-be-altar. A snow-white dove was perched on the end of a long metal pipe, part of an organ that no longer played. The crow —I was almost positive—rolled his eyes. A moment later, he disappeared. The dove flew up to the rafters and disappeared as well.

I couldn't be sure, obviously, but it *felt* like the demon was gone. I meant, truly gone from the building. Clive was silent. I ran to Pew Mountain and shoved the end pew back into place. What I wanted to do was crawl in and check on him, but I knew I'd be endangering him if I did. The tunnel hadn't been built for two.

My gaze dropped to where the homeless man had just been. The floor was smeared with blood, but empty. Glancing back up to where the dove had been perched, I wondered if my earlier prayer had been heard. The man had had a difficult enough life, living on the streets. He didn't deserve to end it as a demon's puppet.

Dead crows were everywhere. Feeling more than a little queasy, I went in search of garbage bags. Now that the adrenaline was wearing off, I realized my injured hand was still itching. A score of tiny spiders seemed to be struggling to extricate themselves from the layer of salve they were caught in.

In the throes of a full-body cringe, I ran to the bathroom and washed my hands, watching the spiders swirl down the drain with the soapy water. My right hand now had a thin layer of skin, but it was covered in painful red bite marks. Of course, my traitorous mind went straight to spiders laying eggs beneath that thin layer of skin, but I told my thoughts to keep that shit to themselves. Like I wasn't dealing with enough over here.

I wasn't sure exactly what Dr. Underfoot's ointment was supposed to cure, but I hoped it included demon-directed spider and crow attacks. Meg had a first aid kit under the sink in her bathroom, which was odd as I hadn't realized Meg could be hurt. Regardless, I made use of her antibiotics and Band-Aids to cover where the crows got me.

I was desperate to use Meg's huge powerful showerheads, but

I still needed to clean up her home, so that'd have to wait. After locating garbage bags, I set to work cleaning up all the dead crows.

As I filled bags, I piled them to the side of the church. I'd have to wait for Clive to rise to get them out. Once I was finally done with bird duty, I started scrubbing Meg's floors, cleaning up the blood—of which there was an alarming amount. Mind you, all of this was done with minimal help from my right hand.

Once reasonably sure I'd found every blood droplet, I went in search of her vacuum. Using it, I went over every inch of her home, finding dark corners with pockets of spiders. I didn't think my body had stopped itching since I'd felt the first spider, but I was powering through, telling myself I'd be in the shower very soon. I even opened Meg's trapdoor, leading to her tunnel exit and vacuumed up all the cobwebs and a few more pockets of spiders. Yes, fine, spiders are important and do good things. Talk to me again when you've been covered in the little bastards.

Once I'd wiped down all the surfaces with Meg's lemony cleanser and bagged the garbage, I looked around the former church. Other than Mount Pew, everything looked in order. Finally, at long and overdue last, I ran to the bathroom, stripped, and jumped into the shower, the showerheads on full force and the temperature just short of scalding. Holding my head under the pounding spray, I washed and rewashed my hair at least four times, shuddering at the memory of tiny spiders crawling across my scalp.

I'd been in the shower for quite a while when I saw movement reflected in the glass. Shouting, I spun, claws out, and found Clive watching me, blood staining his clothes, a towel in his hand, my overnight case on the floor by his feet.

"It's okay, love." Voice gentle, he added, "Come on. You're all clean now. Let's get you dried and dressed."

I turned off the jets and lost it. Clive wrapped me in a huge towel and held me while I sobbed on his shoulder.

"What the Hell!" Meg roared from the living room.

"Shitshitshitshitshit," I chanted, drying off my face and securing the towel under my arms.

Running out of the bathroom, I held up a hand, trying to stave off the inevitable and understandable rage. The woman had loaned us her home for one day and returned to find all of her pews in a jumbled mess and a dozen garbage bags filled with dead birds and another one undulating as spiders tried to find a way out. Just the thought of them had me scratching my already abused scalp.

"There was an incident," I began, "and if you give me a minute to dress, I'll explain it all."

Clive wrapped an arm around me. "It's been a rather horrific day for her, Meg."

"I wasn't throwing a kegger. You can see; I spent hours cleaning everything." My smile registered somewhere on the desperation scale.

"Fine." Meg made a shooing motion and I ran back into the bathroom. I heard her wings flap, but I was busy dressing.

Clive stood in the doorway and watched whatever Meg was doing. "You needn't race. She's dealing with the crows."

With Clive giving me updates on time, I was able to brush my teeth and dry my hair while he set the pews to rights. We were sitting on the couch as I braided my ponytail when Meg dropped back in.

"I love crows," she fumed. "They're intelligent, loyal, clever little pranksters and I just dumped them in a landfill. I'm not happy right now." She walked to her sideboard and poured herself a glass of whiskey. She downed half where she stood and then carried the rest back to her chair and sat. Pinning me with a hard stare, she led with the obvious. "What the hell happened?"

Clive opened his mouth, but I patted his knee. She was asking me. "Clive already told you about the demon after him, right?"

Meg nodded. "It's why you wanted my church."

"Exactly. Well, demons may not be able to walk in here, but they can possess people to walk in for them"—I glanced up at the cat walks—"or drop in, I guess." I explained to both Clive and Meg what had happened while he was sleeping and she was away.

Meg absently tapped a finger on the empty glass, sitting on the arm of her chair. "An angel?"

Shrugging, I said, "No idea, but when the dove showed up, the demon crow left. And when the dove disappeared, it took the homeless man with it."

She sighed and stood, walking the glass back to the sideboard. "My home isn't safe for you, so we never need to repeat this. You cleaned up after yourselves." She turned to glare at Clive. "If I find you damaged any of my antique pews, I'll be sending you a bill."

"Understood."

Giving us her back, she said, "Fine. Go away. I'm going to lock this place up and stay in my apartment." She paused. "You might not see me for a while."

I glanced at Clive, who seemed to share my concern.

"It's been a long time since I've seen my sisters. They're both back in Greece right now, so I'll visit."

"I see," I responded carefully. It felt like I was missing a ton of subtext in this conversation, but then I really didn't know that much about Meg's life. She may have been visiting my bar for seven years, but the woman kept her lip buttoned.

If Ancient Greek mythology was correct, she and her sisters had sprung from the blood of Uranus, father of the Titans, when it fell to earth. His son Cronus had castrated him and chucked his junk in the ocean. The Furies, giants, and nymphs were born of his blood.

Even if all of that was only symbolically accurate, it still made Meg ancient. Since Meg had sprung from bloody dirt, the age-old quandary of which came first, Meg or dirt, had been answered. Dirt.

Months ago, when my aunt was trapping me in visions and none of us could figure out who was attacking me, Meg knew. She'd kept the information to herself, but she knew. When I confronted her, asking why she'd never told me, she'd said she'd been ordered not to. So, given Meg was an ancient goddess, a little younger than dirt, who the hell was giving her orders?

She normally took everything in stride, as she'd seen and done it all a million times. She'd run out of fucks to give thousands of years ago. Which begged the related question: Why had my crow-filled encounter with a demon unnerved her so?

9

# Wherein Clive Comes Dangerously Close to Being Pantsed

"Go. I need to pack," Meg said, dismissing us.

"Thank you for allowing us to use your home." Clive stood, pulling me up with him. "We appreciate the hospitality and regret the difficulties."

Nodding, she kept her back to us.

Clive swung me onto his back, picked up my overnight case, and handed it to me. Flexing his legs, he leapt straight up, through the bell tower trapdoor that Meg had left open. Pausing, he scanned the neighborhood.

"Do the look-away spell."

I did—no idea if it worked—and then he jumped, landing right beside his car. I threw my bag behind my seat and slid in. Thankfully, the narrow drive was still only partially blocked, so Clive was able to maneuver his way out.

In all the hubbub of the day, it had only now occurred to me that I hadn't called The Slaughtered Lamb to say I wouldn't be arriving until after sundown. I checked my phone. No messages. Apparently, Owen hadn't been looking for me. I wondered—

Clive patted my leg. "We'll be there in a few minutes. I'm sure everything is fine."

"Sure, but is that good or bad? Is it an everything's-going-great-and-there-are-no-problems kind of fine or is it a we-don't-even-bother-to-look-for-Sam-anymore-as-we're-clearly-on-our-own kind of fine?"

Shaking his head, Clive waited for the light. "I believe it is more of a we're-adults-who-have-been-doing-this-sort-of-work-for-years-and-have-it-handled kind of fine."

"Ha! I'm rubbing off on you."

He glanced over and then executed a perfect turn, cutting through oncoming traffic. "Bite your tongue, darling."

Okay. Fine. Clive was right. Owen and Fyr had everything under control when we arrived. Fergus raced over and pounced on my boots, waging war on the laces before giving up and biting the bottoms of my jeans. All four of his legs were splayed, trying to stop my forward motion. It was a good effort, but he was forced to slide along in my wake all the way to the apartment.

Dropping my bag, I scooped him up and then sat on the couch, feet up on the coffee table. I put Fergus on his back in my lap and then gave him a full-body scratch. His rear paws waved until I found the magic spot, and then one paw went nuts, scratching at the air.

"Did you have the best time hanging out with the dragons? Did you and Alec have a fun playdate?"

Clive walked in, pocketing his phone. "Somehow I doubt Alec would care for that characterization."

I shrugged and continued scratching puppy tummy, which was the perfect antidote to spiders, demons, and crows.

Clive leaned over the back of the couch, dropping a kiss on my head and scratching under Fergus' chin. "I'm going to visit the nocturne this evening, help Russell plan the—do you remember when I reclaimed my nocturne by sharing blood?"

"Sure. The blood thingy." Fergus was like a turtle on his back, trying to flip over.

"Precisely. He'll be doing something very similar, making the nocturne and all who dwell within it his own. I said I'd assist in any way he sees fit."

"Coolcoolcool." When Fergus' teeth clamped on my scritching hand a little too hard, I growled, and he quickly released. Yes, I was initiating all the play, and no, he hadn't bitten me hard, but he'd be well over a hundred pounds as an adult, probably closer to one-twenty or one-fifty. I needed to make sure he'd be safe for others to be around.

"You're not actually paying attention to me, are you?" Clive sounded so put out, I had a hard time not laughing. Gesturing to my ear, I said, "Sorry. Men talk at a vocal range that's hard for women to hear."

He snatched me up from the couch and hung me upside down by my ankles. I gently put Fergus down on the floor. "How about now?" he asked. "Can you hear me now?"

Fergus jumped on Clive and barked. My sweet warrior was giving my vampy significant other what for.

"You tell him, buddy." I grabbed Clive's trouser legs, as they were right in front of me, and yanked. Unfortunately, he seemed to be wearing some kind of super belt. Fergus stopped barking and clamped onto the hem of Clive's pants, helping me pull. Good boy.

"Dare I ask?"

"You're going to feel pretty darn silly when we pants you." Fergus growled, his oversized paws slipping on the wood floors. I patted Clive's leg and pushed the pup back. "Could you flip me over now? My head's really starting to pound."

Before I'd finished asking, he had me righted and was sitting on the side of the bed with me in his lap. Fergus gave a panicked yowl and then came running into the bedroom. Clive moved so fast, it must have looked as though we'd disappeared.

Clive kissed my temple, pulling the pain away. "Better?"

Nodding, I rested my head on his shoulder. "Yeah, better. The demon was messing with my head, so it was ouchy to begin with. I'm okay now."

"I don't need to leave right away." He held me close and then lowered a hand to scratch the top of Fergus' head.

Kissing his jaw, I pushed up and patted his shoulder. "Go play with your pointy-toothed friends. I've got a whole bar full of magical people to back me up."

"All right. While I'm at the nocturne, I want to meet with Gregory. He was a theologian in life. His understanding of demonology might help us." Leaning over, he gave Fergus another scritch under the chin. "You're on duty, young man. Take care of her." He gave me a tender kiss, one that had my heart flipping over in my chest, and then left.

"Come on, little dude. We have work to do." When we passed through the kitchen, my throat tightened. What if Dave really wasn't coming back? I'd half hoped he'd be stomping around in here, bitching under his breath while cooking us dinner. Instead, it was empty.

My hollow stomach rumbled, causing Fergus to bark. Ducking my head out of the swinging door, I found Fyr tending bar. "Has Fergus eaten?"

Nodding, he came around the bar to deliver a pot of tea. "Yeah. Fed and walked."

"Great. Be right out. I need to eat too."

He shooed me away and picked up empties on a nearby table. "We're fine. Go eat."

Fergus had gone back to patrolling, so I was on my own as I scoured the fridge for anything edible. It was embarrassing how much I'd relied on Dave to feed me.

I didn't know what he was planning to make before he stormed off, but there were fresh eggs, ground chorizo, onions, peppers, mushrooms. If nothing else, I could make an omelette. Once I started cooking, Fergus nosed his way back in, sniffing madly at the island and stove.

Fyr swung open the door. "Whatever you're cooking, the people out here are hoping you're serving it as well."

"Oh. Um." I supposed I could. "I'm not Dave. Make sure they know it won't be as good as what he makes."

When Fyr nodded and turned to leave, I called, "Wait. Don't you have to go?"

He shrugged. "I don't have anything planned until later. I can hang for a while. And it does smell good, so I want one too." He paused again. "You eat first though."

I went back and flipped the omelette before stepping out into the bar. "I need a head count. How many am I making?" Twelve people raised their hands. "Okey-dokey."

The omelette slid right out of the pan and onto my plate. I took it and a fork and sat at Dave's desk to eat. Mmm, not bad. It worked for me, but if I was serving it to my customers, it needed something. Still eating, I stood in front of the open refrigerator. Cheese. Sour cream. I glanced over at the fruit basket on the counter and found avocados. That worked.

When I finished my meal, I got to work on everyone else's. Just in case, I went out into the bar again. "Does anyone not want sour cream or avocado?"

One little wicche raised her hand. "No, thank you."

Another one piped up, "Sam, can I get an order too?"

"Lucky thirteen. You got it." I went back in and set to work. Considering, I went into the cold storage room and found a large container of salsa, more eggs, and chorizo.

After I finished the first one, I called Fyr and he delivered it for me. When he came back in to get the next, he said I had four more orders. Dang. There was no way I was going to keep track. I grabbed a notepad and pen from Dave's desk and scratched out seventeen marks. As I served one, I crossed out that line. I made the plain one next so I could get it off the books and not worry I'd forget.

Dave said cooking was relaxing for him. It was the opposite for me. Luckily, what I was making was pretty simple, but I still had multiple pans all going at once, one to brown the chorizo, one to cook the onions and mushrooms, and one to put it all together in the omelette. I decided not to cook the peppers first, thinking a bright crunch might be good, but who the hell knew? I needed to learn how to cook. More than a handful of dishes, that was.

Once everyone was fed—including Fyr who got a double-sized

meal—I went into the bar, made myself a cup of tea, and sat on my stool. I needed to get Dave back, maybe hire an interim cook until Dave cooled off and forgave me for whatever I'd done.

Fyr checked his watch. "Are you good? I need to take off. George and Alec are watching rugby tonight. If I leave now, I can make the drop kick."

"Go. Go. I'm fine. Thanks for staying late."

He took off his apron and tossed it in the basket I kept under the bar for soiled towels. He pounded the bar twice with his fist and then gave a quick wave to the people who looked over, nodding their goodbyes.

It was a quiet evening, with only six people scattered around the bar, talking quietly or reading. I unboxed an order for the bookstore, loading up a cart. I'd need to add the books to my inventory tomorrow before we opened.

I took the cart into the back before someone tried to shop off it. When I returned to the bar, a man had taken a stool, a man who made my heart stop. Irdu. I remembered him from the demon-owned strip joint Demon's Lair. Golden brown skin, he had features so perfect, so stunning, he seemed molded by the gods. The light hazel eyes, though, were pure predator. He was a jungle cat, hypnotically beautiful and deadly.

I was pretty sure Dave had said Irdu was an incubus, the male version of Tara, the succubus who worked at the Tiki Room at the Fairmont Hotel. Incubi and succubi were a flavor of demon who used sex to lure in humans and then feed off them, body and soul.

Only a few patrons remained in the bar, including that odd elf who Fergus hated. My trusty warrior pup was sitting on the third stair, as had become his habit. I think he liked the perspective, seeing everything at once. Right now, his gaze was going back and forth between Irdu and the elf.

Screwing up my courage, I walked behind the bar. "Can I help you?"

Irdu had had his eyes on me ever since I'd appeared from the back. He had to know my heart was in my throat and beating a mile a minute.

"It's good to see you again." His voice was deep and warm, inviting me closer.

When I felt myself tip forward, I took a step back, leaned against the counter, and crossed my arms over my chest. "Are you looking for Dave, because he's not here." Nothing to see here. No reason to stick around.

"Who?" His eyes twinkled, his sensuous mouth kicking up in a soft, knowing grin.

"Dave. My cook. Part demon?" Please, just go now.

"You have a Nephilim employee? How open-minded of you. But, no, I was looking for you." His gaze smoldered and I felt sweat gather at the base of my spine.

This wasn't like the homeless man or the crow. Sitri had been possessing them, but it was still a man and an animal I needed to best. This time, an actual demon was standing in my bar. He could've probably wiped us all out if he'd wanted. Against this guy, I had nothing but cold sweat and nausea.

"You may have heard that I took over when Sitri disappeared—and that was quite the mystery," he added, leaning on the bar, his muscles bunching beneath the fabric of his shirt.

Everything he did was designed to make me want him. Thankfully, my contrary nature was working for me. He was inhumanly gorgeous, sure, but he mostly made me sick to my stomach.

"You don't know anything about that, do you?" His warm molasses voice tried to glue me in place.

I shook my head, mental blocks up and reinforced as best as I could.

Nodding slowly, his expression was one of patent disbelief. "When you're in charge of a city, you're given access to info on all its residents." His fingertips glided over the bar in a caress, his eyes warm on me.

Throat tight, I forced out, "Everyone, or all the demons?"

He placed a finger over his lips before using his fingertip to ghost over his full lower lip. "I'll never tell. I'm quite discreet." He winked and my stomach recoiled.

If he didn't quit the seductive shit, I was going to hurl. All over him.

He gave a slow blink and then straightened, the fingers of one hand drumming on the surface of the bar as he studied me, all flirtation gone. "I learned something very interesting about your cook, something that made me question whether or not you knew."

"I thought you said you didn't know Dave." I kept my arms crossed tightly over my chest, needing any kind of barrier between us.

When he smiled this time, it turned feral and deadly. "I lied."

"Why?" Why the hell was he even here?

He shrugged one shoulder, looking me up and down. "It's fun. Anyway, I heard you've been leaving messages, looking for him," he said, glancing around the near-empty bar. "He's working at the Biergarten of the Damned, beneath the Demon's Lair. When I heard your voice mail, I thought, I should get these two crazy kids together and see what happens. I do so enjoy stories of betrayal, teary recriminations. You should ask him why he works here, why he showed up as soon as you opened, looking for a job. It's a good story. I think you'll like it."

He tapped the bar, an echo of how Fyr had said goodbye. "Ta." He turned and walked up the stairs and out of The Slaughtered Lamb.

Thankfully, he was out of sight before my knees buckled.

# 10

# Spun Glass

Unfolding my arms quickly, I grabbed the counter I was leaning against. I wasn't going down. There were only a couple of people left in the bar who witnessed the bobble.

"Was that really a demon?" Dermot, a selkie friend of Liam's, sat by the window, an open book on the table before him.

Nodding, I said, "Yeah, that really was."

"This isn't going to become a demon bar, is it?" Iris, an older wicche, took a sip of her tea. "That happened to me once before. A lovely little tea shop along the coast. The crone who owned it sold it to her nephew. Soon the flowered tea pots and lace curtains were replaced with pint glasses and leather shades." She shook her head in disapproval. "The last time I went, I didn't even get out of my car. A rather rude young man with pupils like a goat's banged on my hood and told me to fuck off, so I did."

"I'm sorry." Hearing the very proper Iris say *fuck* was quite jarring.

She made a sound of disappointment in the back of her throat before taking another sip. "The nephew wasn't terribly promising. Probably why he turned to sorcery. Well," she said, picking up her handbag and pushing up from the table, "that's enough excitement for me. I need to go home and burn some sage." She was muttering to herself about the demon horde as she walked up the stairs and out into the night.

I'd have offered to escort her if I hadn't known it would offend her. I had a few incredibly powerful crone wicches who were regulars here. I'd made the mistake of once offering to walk one to her car. The pitying look I was given was one I will recall with perfect, cringe-inducing clarity every time I make a magical community blunder. The crones knew how to take care of themselves, thank you very much.

Dermot stood to leave as well. "Goodnight, Sam."

"Goodnight."

He returned his modesty robe to the hook by the water entrance, donned his seal skin, and dove out into the ocean.

"Fergus?" Where'd he go? I needed to take him on a potty walk. He might have already put himself to bed. He'd done that once before. Closing down my wards, I headed to the apartment.

When I stepped into the kitchen, I found Fergus. He was being crushed under Poldo's arm—the strange new fae guy, the one Fergus rightfully distrusted. The elf had a hand wrapped around Fergus' muzzle. My pup struggled to get free, growling and whining, but he was no match for the fae.

"You need to come with me." It was all so matter-of-fact. He wasn't angry. He had a job to do and wasn't putting up with a difficult dog. Fergus scrabbled wildly, one of his claws managing to draw blood. The elf, who had exuded quiet confidence, became less so. He clamped down harder and my poor little guy's cries became louder.

"Put my dog down or I will rip off your head."

He started to laugh and then, recognizing something in my expression, stopped. "You will come with me now or I will snap this animal's neck. You choose."

"Wait. Wait." I held my hands up, raising the white flag immediately while I pulled magic and readied my aunt's spell. "Just, please, put him down. He's just a puppy. I'll go with you."

A sly smile pulled at his lips. "I don't think so. He drew blood.

There are consequences." He glanced down at Fergus. "He's the perfect size for a soldier's snack."

I didn't even know if the spell would work on the fae, and I was pretty sure if my aim was off, I'd end up killing Fergus myself. Something had to be done, though.

Grinning, the elf moved to grab my arm. I dropped and went for my patented claws to the groin move that I'd used on an elf in Wales. The current fae assassin roared, dropping Fergus. Hoping for just that to happen, I caught the pup and slid him toward the apartment door. The wards guarding my apartment were stronger than the bar. That must have been why the elf had been waiting for me here, in a room full of sharp cooking implements, instead of in my apartment where he could have taken me out as soon as I walked in.

Fergus hit the ward and then bounced off it. *Damn it!* The elf must have spelled the kitchen to lock us in. That had to have been why I hadn't heard Fergus whining until I'd come through the door. Fucking fae were made of magic. I had no idea what they could do.

The fae stood taller, vengeance and rage all over his sweaty face. Thinking time was over, I hit him with the heart-stopping spell. He flinched like I'd slapped him but kept moving toward me. *Shitshitshitshitshit.*

I dove away from him, rolling once and popping up by the knife block. Yanking the biggest one free, I opened the drawer under the counter and grabbed the first thing I touched, a meat tenderizer. Sliding to the side, a weapon in each hand, I kept him in front of me.

"You will die very badly now, and I will present your broken body to my king, who will honor me greatly."

Still circling, I was working out contingencies. "Super. Very exciting. For you, that is." Thankfully, his focus was on me, not on the pup getting painfully but quietly to his feet behind him.

Poldo leapt across the divide, grabbing me, the arm around my middle trying to split me in two. Moving almost as quickly, I drove down with the knife in my right hand, running it through his thigh while striking up with the tenderizer, bashing him as hard I could in the side of the head.

He flung me across the room and I hit the concrete counter, cracking ribs. My head bashed against the tiled backsplash before I slid to the floor.

Pouncing, he landed on top of me, straddling my stomach and stealing what breath I had left. Blood ran down his face. He wrenched the weapons from my hands, his expression turning triumphant.

Fergus lunged forward and sunk his teeth into the elf's ankle, shaking his head back and forth. A moment of distraction. That was all I needed.

The elf swung back with the knife, but Fergus jumped out of the way. I waited for him to turn back to me. When he straightened his neck, I raked my razor-sharp claws viciously across his neck, sending his head spinning across the kitchen floor. Spattered in fae blood, I shoved the asshole off me and dragged myself away and into a sitting position, leaning against a cabinet.

Fergus came to me on shaky legs and then crawled up into my lap with a whine. The elf's remains disappeared, returning to Faerie.

Clive flew in the door a moment later. Eyes wild, he took in the scene before kneeling beside me. "Where are you hurt?"

"He hurt Fergus. We need Lilah." I ran my hand gently over the pup and he whimpered. "Can you call her? George too. He's a vet. Maybe he could help." Everything became blurry as tears filled my eyes. "He's in a lot of pain."

Clive ran a hand over my hair. "What about you?" His phone was already out, tapping screens to call Lilah.

"Ribs, I think. And my head."

His fingers found a knot forming and I hissed.

"Lilah, I apologize for the lateness of the hour. Sam was attacked." At my glare, he added, "And Fergus. She believes she has broken ribs and may have a concussion."

I'd had concussions before and recognized the nausea and dizziness, the horrible pain and light sensitivity. Closing my eyes, I cradled my hands around Fergus, wanting him to know he was safe and loved without causing him additional pain.

Clive sat beside me and rested his hand on Fergus' head. "George? Yes, my apologies for waking you. Sam was attacked and —yes, she's going to be okay. Lilah is on her way. Sam is quite concerned about Fergus, who was injured as well. We're wondering if you would be kind enough to check on him?" He listened a moment. "Of course. I know you're used to working with far larger animals, but if you wouldn't mind…Good. Thank you."

Clive pocketed his phone. "The troops are coming. Now, while we wait, can you tell me what happened?"

I told him about the new elf who had been visiting and Fergus' very astute distrust of him before relating what had happened tonight, including the visit from Irdu.

Clive retrieved a dish towel, wet it, and then brought it back, wiping the elf's blood from my face. "I was in the study at the nocturne, discussing logistics with Russell, Godfrey, and Audrey when I realized that the reason I was feeling anxious was because I'd stopped hearing your heartbeat. I called for you." He tapped his forehead. "But you weren't there.

"I tore out of the nocturne and raced here." He shook his head. "I forgot the car. I didn't think. I had to find you, had to make sure you were okay. I was coming down the steps when you popped back into my head. Your heart was racing and you were in pain, but you were back where you belonged."

"Can you turn off the l—"

Clive had turned off the overhead lights before I'd finished the question. He left the soft, under-cabinet lights on, though, so we weren't waiting in complete darkness.

"I want to move you somewhere more comfortable, but I'm afraid of hurting you."

"Maybe the couch in the bookstore? We'll have moonlight

through the window and no one has to walk through all the blood in here." Looking through my lashes at the blood pool, I said, "That better not leave a stain or Dave'll be…" Right. Forgot.

Clive kissed my forehead gently. "He'll be back, love. We'll figure out what's happening and we'll help him. Okay?"

When I didn't respond, he gave me another soft kiss and then picked me up, Fergus in my lap, and cradled us like we were made of spun glass. As he glided across the barroom floor, I remembered the last time he'd done this.

"Don't remind me," he murmured.

Resting my aching head on his shoulder, I said, "But I fell a little bit in love with you that night?" I felt his surprise and it made me smile.

"Is that so?"

"Powerful, aloof, Master vampire making sure the blanket covered me, knowing how I felt about anyone seeing my scars. Just like now, you carried me like I was precious and breakable."

"You were and are."

"And you told me the story of meeting Shakespeare to distract me from the big, sharp, pointy things Dr. Underfoot was using to get the bullets out. And when I got scared, you wrapped your hand around my foot." I felt the tears that had been threatening to fall trail down my face. "I wasn't alone. Even though I mostly annoyed you, you stayed."

"May I tell you a secret?" He gently kissed my sore head.

I watched him, waiting.

"I wasn't that annoyed."

# 11

# The Heart Rattling Around in Clive's Chest Is Mine

It wasn't long before I felt a push on the ward. George. I opened it and heard three sets of footsteps on the stairs.

"Sam?" Owen had come, of course.

"We're in here," Clive called, trying to keep his voice low so as not to hurt my head more than necessary.

Owen, George, and Alec rushed into the bookstore and found me lying on the couch, the pup on me.

"Sorry to pull you guys out of bed." I knew poor George had to get up before the crack of dawn for his work at the zoo.

Alec crouched down beside me and laid his hand gently on Fergus' back. The pup whined. "I know. It hurts."

George dropped down as well, crooning softly to Fergus while he worked, gently but thoroughly running his hands over the pup. Fergus licked George's fingers and my eyes filled again.

"What happened?" Owen asked, sitting in the chair closest to me.

"You know that new elf that's been showing up the last couple of days?"

Owen's expression clouded for a moment. "Oh, yeah, okay. I haven't really dealt with him much. I think he's only been in the last day or two. He arrived as I was leaving. The bar had been busy all afternoon and I was just thinking about getting home and showering before our dinner reservation. I'm sorry. I wasn't paying much attention to him."

"He's been arriving at the same time as Sam?" Clive asked.

"Yeah. A little before, maybe. I hadn't put it together like that. It's when the after-work crowd shows up, so it didn't seem odd." Owen's gaze traveled over Fergus and me. "He attacked you?"

I started to nod and then stopped when my head pounded and my stomach swooped. "One of the king's assassins."

George and Alec's gazes snapped to me.

I tried to smile, but given how crappy I was feeling, it probably looked more like a grimace. "You guys are looking so much alike these days."

Alec nodded seriously. "That happens with twins."

"Hardy har."

George ignored us, his focus on Alec. Talk of the fae king plotting had him scowling. After searching for twenty years, they'd finally found and rescued Alec. Finvarra put everyone on edge.

Proving twins were attuned to one another, without looking at him, Alec patted his brother's shoulder, reminding him that he was okay now.

"Did he get away?" Owen asked.

"No," George responded.

"How could you know that?" Owen asked.

Alec nodded toward the bar. "We can smell the blood. A lot of it. And if the person who'd attacked his wife was still breathing, I think Clive would be hunting right now."

"Astute," Clive responded. "In this case, though, I was superfluous. Sam had already taken care of the threat."

"The kitchen's a mess, but I got him."

"Where are your weapons?" Owen asked.

"What?" I'll blame my messed-up head for this one. I'd assumed he meant my claws, so it seemed an odd question.

"You came back from Wales with a new axe and sword." Owen leaned forward. "And you already had the one Clive gave you.

You need to start wearing weapons if you've still got fae bad guys after you."

"Yes," Clive agreed. "We can resume our sword training as well."

More footsteps.

"In here," Owen called.

A moment later, Lilah came in. Owen pulled over the other chair so his sister could sit right beside me. She held her hands close to my head, almost cradling it the way I had been almost holding Fergus.

"Concussion. Mild this time." Her hands moved. "Two cracked ribs. They're starting to knit. I can help with that. Your hand is getting better. Good. Some internal bruising. No bleeding. Okay, I'll get started."

"Wait. Can you check Fergus first?" At the quiet sound of impatience from Clive, I said, "I understand what's going on. He doesn't. He's hurting."

George sat on his heels. "Broken ribs, just like Mom."

Lilah held her hands over Fergus. "Oh, poor little guy. Just a minute." Her eyes flicked to George. "This is going to hurt, and I need him not to squirm. One of the breaks is—" She stopped speaking abruptly.

"What?" I tried to sit up but my head swam and Clive pushed me back.

"One of the breaks is near a lung," George answered.

"Right up against it," Lilah clarified. "Give me a sec."

"I've got him," Alec said to his brother, holding Fergus still. "Do that thing."

George nodded and then leaned forward, touching his head to Fergus'. After a moment, Fergus stopped shaking. George softly crooned words of comfort. My pup may not have understood the language, but he understood the message. He relaxed in my lap with four people doing their best to help.

When Lilah was done with Fergus, she slumped back in her chair. "Okay, I had to do more. You can't tell a dog to take it easy and get rest. I think he's all right now. Scared, but his bones have knit together." She ran a hand down his back. "Do whatever you can to keep him quiet."

Owen lifted a black doctor's bag from the floor by his feet. I hadn't noticed him carrying it in, but my focus had been on his boyfriend, the veterinarian.

George nodded. "I could give him a mild sedative to help him rest, give his body time to heal." He patted my leg. "He'll be okay."

I held Fergus with one hand, the other gliding from head to tail over his wiry coat. His eyes closed, the rhythm of my fingertips becoming hypnotic. When the needle went in, he flinched but quickly settled.

"Now you," Lilah said.

"Do you need to rest longer? Maybe some tea?" Healing took a lot out of her, and I didn't want her to push herself. We'd dragged the poor woman out of bed to help us.

"I'm fine," she said. "Although I wouldn't mind a cup when I'm done."

Owen rose silently while his sister concentrated on me, to brew her a pot of tea.

It always felt strange having Lilah work on me. It was a little like invisible fingers prodding me. Clive was siphoning off most of the pain while I channeled the remnants into the wicche glass around my neck.

Soon, I could breathe more easily and the pounding in my head was downgraded to an irritating thump. Clive relaxed beside me. "Thank you, Lilah. Thank you, everyone, for rushing over to help."

"No problem. We were just sleeping," Owen deadpanned as he handed his sister her tea.

George shook his head while Alec grinned. "We're happy to help. If you notice problems tomorrow, give me a call and I'll come back after work, okay? The sedative I gave him should let him rest for the next four or five hours, though he may remain a little groggy for the next day or so."

"He's okay, though, right?" His great big paws hung over either side of my lap while he nestled his snout between my knees.

George stroked the velvety edge of one of Fergus' ears. "He'll be back to patrolling the bar in no time."

After our friends left, I locked down the wards. Clive picked up Fergus and we walked back to the apartment.

"How's the blood thingy planning going?"

The corner of Clive's mouth kicked up before he leaned over and kissed the side of my head. "Well. It's scheduled for tomorrow evening."

Nodding, I pushed through the kitchen door, pleased that nodding hadn't set off new pains, and then spotted the drying blood. "Damn, I forgot."

When I paused to start cleaning, Clive nudged me along. "Let's get you two to bed and then I'll come back and deal with the mess."

I raised my eyebrows at that, clearly questioning his domestic abilities.

"Did you think I was born wealthy and in charge? Farmer, darling. I've done all manner of unpleasant tasks."

After gently laying Fergus in his bed, Clive walked me to our bed, had me sit, and then hunkered down to untie my shoes and slip them off, tucking them under the bed in their usual spot. He helped me undress, grabbing a set of pajamas from my bureau, before leading me into the shower to wash off the blood spatter.

"I'm okay now. You don't have to do all this." Lilah knew her stuff.

He ignored that comment and waited for me, helping me dry off and dress afterward. "What you seem to forget," he said, "is that I can't do without you either." He took my hands in his and kissed my fingers. "You disappeared, love. Again. It was like Canterbury all over. Your heartbeat has become my constant companion. Whatever it was the fae did tonight, he hid you from me. There and gone."

He flipped the comforter back so I could slide in. "I know you didn't need my help to dress or wash, but I needed it." Crouching beside the bed, he brushed stray hairs off my face. "I needed it."

"I wish I could hear yours."

At that, he laughed. "Mine stopped beating long ago. You, my dear, are walking around with my heart." He gave me a soft kiss and then headed back to the kitchen. "Try to get some rest, you two."

My poor abused head could not have been more thankful for a soft pillow, so much so, I almost fell asleep before I remembered. Throwing back the covers, I stood too quickly and abruptly sat back down again. Taking a breath, I tried again, successfully getting to my feet and padding to the kitchen.

Clive's sleeves were rolled up as he mopped. He paused as I entered, eyebrows raised, waiting.

"We still have a daytime demon problem." Thoughtlessly, I began to push myself up to sit on the counter but felt a sharp twinge and stopped. I settled for leaning instead. "I had a thought tonight, but I don't think it was my thought. I may have been eavesdropping on one of yours."

He leaned on the handle. "Oh? And what did you hear?"

"That the nocturne has protections that will keep you safe during the day."

Shaking his head, he began mopping again. "I'm not leaving you when Finv—"

I hissed.

"When the king is still sending assassins. I'll be fine."

"Clive," I began.

"No. Even if he works on me all day again today, I'll survive. I'm already dead—"

"Ish."

Nodding, he tried to smile. "Deadish. All he can do it hurt me and as I'm almost completely dead during the day and feel nothing, it's a rather ineffective form of torture. Not to worry, darling," he said, slopping the mop back in the bucket and churning it in the soapy water. "I'll be perfectly fine."

I wasn't taking no for an answer and so crossed to him.

"Sam."

"Shut up, you." Framing his face with my hands, I went up on my toes and kissed him, tenderness quickly turning to heat. When I finally came up for air, I was staring into vamp black eyes. "I accept that for whatever reason you love me, *but* you have to accept that I feel exactly the same way about you. I can't just go about my day knowing you're being cut up in our bed."

When he opened his mouth to argue, I slapped my hand over it. "No. I can't sit back and allow you to be hurt. What I need—are you listening—what *I* need is for you to be safe in the nocturne where he can't reach you.

"I'll call Stheno," I rushed on. "I'll ask her to hang out with me. I'll wear my weapons. Worse comes to worst, we'll have some new garden sculptures. Because in gorgon versus fae, gorgon wins. Every time."

"I won't risk your life on a hope. Yes, by all means, have Stheno stay with you. I'll hire her as your bodyguard again. She was taken out once before, though. Only one of her eyes is working, and she has it behind a patch. One of the king's people could snatch you away to Faerie before she has time to lift the eye patch. You were there and gone in Canterbury." He shook his head and began to pull the mop out of the bucket.

Staying his hand, I turned his face back to me. "Have you looked in the mirror lately?"

"It's nothing."

"It's very much something. You look older, my love. Whatever the demon is doing, it's wearing you out and aging you." When he opened his mouth, I pressed on. "What will happen when I desperately need you but you no longer have the strength and speed to save me? How long did it take tonight to realize my heartbeat had disappeared?"

He stopped, the immediate rebuttal dying on his lips.

"As you said, it's an ineffective form of torture, to attack you while you're sleeping. If, that is, the point is to cause pain. If instead the point is to wear you down, to age you, to weaken some of your truly formidable powers, then he's doing a pretty good job."

"Damn." In that one word was a combination of frustration, acceptance, and no small amount of defeat.

12

# In Which Sam Seeks Stheno's Advice

"I'll call Russell." He left the mop in the bucket and pulled out his phone.

"I'll be fine," I promised. I was asking a lot of him, and I knew it.

"See that you are or I'll be quite put out." He rested his forehead against my own. "A nice, quiet life for us. That's all I wanted."

"Someday." I kissed the tip of his nose.

Nodding wearily, he tapped his phone screen. "Russell, I have a favor to ask..."

While he spoke to the new Master of San Francisco, I finished cleaning the floor. I felt his eyes on me, knew he worried, but I couldn't have him stay here when it meant being preyed on all day.

I'd meant what I'd told him. In all the time I'd known Clive, he'd been heart-stoppingly gorgeous. For years, he'd drop by the bar every few weeks for one drink. He rarely said a word, but I never felt threatened. It felt more like he was checking up on us. On me, Russell had once told me.

I hadn't been ready for romance—honestly believed I never would be—but he made me wonder and dream. It wasn't as though he had suddenly become unattractive. It was that he looked tired. He had shadows under his eyes. If the demon had changed his outward appearance, even this much, what was happening to his strength and abilities?

He stayed with me until the dawn, holding me close, protecting me while I slept. When I woke hours later, though, I was alone in the bed and Fergus was whining to go out.

"Okay, buddy. Give me a sec." I ran to the bathroom and quickly dressed in jeans, a hoodie, and slipper boots. Grabbing his leash, I headed to the doorway between our apartment and The Slaughtered Lamb.

Fergus raced ahead. I could see him sniffing around past the wards in the kitchen and had a moment to worry he'd lift his leg inside. My weapons had been left on the living room coffee table. Clive was making sure I didn't go anywhere unarmed.

He was right. It would have been stupid for me to go outside with Fergus without gearing up. It wasn't as though the king's minions would wait for me while I ran back to get what I needed.

The axe sheath had what amounted to backpack straps, with the weapon laying between my shoulder blades. Clive had given me the sword, its sheath wrapping around my waist and thigh. Hurrying after my pup, I got the sword partially strapped on before pushing through the swinging kitchen door into the bar.

I stopped short at the same time Fergus howled.

"Jeez, you two are jumpy." Stheno sat at a table next to the window, a glass of red wine and a book on the table in front of her.

Blowing out a breath, I tried to concentrate on slowing my racing heart. "Are you trying to kill me?" Shaking my head, I jogged with Fergus across the bar toward the stairs. "Potty walk. We'll be back." Before Fergus bolted ahead, I got the leash attached to his collar.

We kept climbing up to the top of the bluff overlooking the ocean. Heading to the left, away from the parking lot, we started down a tree-lined path parallel to the water. Fergus relieved himself almost immediately, but it was such a crisp, clear morning, we both wanted to keep going.

I was considering going back for the proper shoes so we could take a good, long run, when I heard heavy breathing behind me. Spinning, I reached for my axe and then stopped. "What are you doing?"

"Your husband is paying me a great deal of money to guard you. How am I supposed to do that from the bar?" Waving her hand forward, she added, "Go ahead. Walk the dog. And while you do that, tell me why you need a guard this time."

While I caught Stheno up, Fergus was in heaven, sniffing, strutting, and piddling to his heart's content.

"Demons, huh? They're a nasty lot." The sun broke through the gray clouds and Stheno pulled sunglasses from the top of her head, where they were holding back her long dark corkscrew curls, and placed them on her nose. "Why does the day have to be so damn bright? You know," she said, elbowing me, "most civilized people are still asleep at this hour."

"Civilized people who don't want to clean up their puppy's accidents aren't." I'd been watching Fergus, looking for any signs of pain. His gait had been a bit stiff at the beginning, but he was trotting along nicely now. He wasn't showing a hint of pain. Looking over his shoulder, tongue lolling, he seemed to be telling me the same. He was fine and I needed to send flowers to Lilah and George.

"Are you listening to me?" Stheno stuffed her hands into the pockets of her long, flowy dress.

"Um, you were bitching about the sun, I think. Look," I said, pointing to my dog. "He's not showing any distress. Good as new, huh, buddy?" I pulled out my phone and took a picture to send Owen, George, Alec, and Lilah. I wanted everyone to know my boy was all better.

When Fergus' pace began to flag, I turned us around. "George said he might be a little groggy from the sedative. We'll head back so he can nap."

"Thank the gods. Exercise is overrated."

"Speaking of which, how are you coming on deflowering my new bartender?" Tall grass swirled in the high winds.

Stheno shivered. "Damn. Just the memory gave me a phantom orgasm." She smacked my elbow. "And that flower was lost long before me. Dragons, man. They know how to direct heat with their mouths and"—she shivered again—"oh my. Plus, I don't think there's anything hotter than when smoke billows out of their nostrils." She laughed, shaking her head. "Good times."

When we returned to The Slaughtered Lamb, she picked up her glass of wine and followed us back into the kitchen. I refilled Fergus' bowl with fresh water and rained a scoop of kibble into his food dish.

While he ate, I got a glass of water and Stheno sat at Dave's desk, sipping her wine.

"Got anything in here you can turn into breakfast for us?"

Hmm, good question. I looked through the refrigerator and then cold storage. "I made chorizo omelettes for customers last night. I'm not sure what I have left."

"I'm not picky, kid. You could hand me a bag of chips and a banana and I'd call it good."

"Did your sisters leave town?" I called from the storage room.

"Yes, and not a moment too soon. I was close to wrapping Euryale around Medusa's neck and pulling. A homicidal two-for-one deal."

"Look at it this way," I said, picking up an apple and our last carton of eggs—shit, I was going to have to do the marketing now. I had no idea where Dave bought our food. "You are now enjoying the longest amount of time before you have to see each other again. You've got ninety-nine years, eleven months, and however many weeks before you have to start worrying about it again."

"Good point," she said on a laugh.

When I walked back in the kitchen, she had her wine glass tipped up, finishing the last of it. "I swear, no one can get me as worked up as those two. They are truly, deeply assholes. They're family, though. What are you going to do?"

"Coffee?"

"Yes, please. Oh, while you cook, can I see that chess set you were telling me about? I want to know who I'm guarding you against."

"Good call." I went into the apartment, Fergus on my heels. When I ducked into the bedroom to get the carved wooden box off my dresser, the pup headed straight to his bed and flopped down with a deep sigh. Leaning over, I gave him a tummy rub and then headed back to Stheno. I heard his collar jingle and knew he was following me again. "Stay and sleep, little man."

Opening the lid and revealing the pieces, I placed the box on Dave's desk. "This is the queen—no names as we don't want to draw their attention—and this is her side of the board. Now, the fae can change their appearance, but, in general, we shouldn't have to worry about anyone on this side."

I sensed movement to my right and tensed. It was Fergus, sliding down in the doorway. Most of his body was hidden behind the ward in our living room. His head and front paws, though, were in the kitchen so he could keep watch.

I replaced the delicate, light blue-gray chalcedony queen and picked up the onyx king. "And this is the asshole who keeps throwing his assassins at me."

Stheno nodded. "You can tell. He looks like a dick."

"Right? His side of the board are the ones we need to look out for."

Stheno picked up a blank. "What's with the creepy faceless ones?"

"That's a—what—knight? It just means no one has taken up the mantle yet. The pieces change to reflect the current combatants. Once someone has been drafted into service, their face appears."

"Well, this is a handy bit of magic. Where did you get it?" Stheno continued to pick up pieces and study faces.

"I think a wicche put it in my path, or—which is totally

disturbing—where she knew my path would take me long before I'd set out on a journey." I shook my head, not comfortable with the implications. "I'd been living alone in the back, working seven days a week, not venturing out into San Francisco, let alone the rest of the world, when she placed a magical object in an art gallery in Canterbury, England for me to find while wandering by."

Stheno leaned back in her chair, Finvarra in her hand, her thumb covering his face. "Is that so?" At my nod, she asked, "And do we know who the wicche is?"

"Arwyn Cassandra Corey, artist living somewhere in the UK."

"Cassandra, huh?"

"Yep. My first thought as well. Clive met her. Well, okay, he put the fear of Clive in her, trying to get information to find me." I glanced over my shoulder as I started preparing breakfast. "I told you about being abducted into Faerie, right?"

"You didn't, but I got the story from Owen. Keep going."

"Anyway," I said, chopping the apple, "he was hunting down anyone who might have a clue as to what happened to me. They found the chessboard's creator and he said she was a powerful wicche who was also a psychic."

"And family," she added, replacing Finvarra in the box, facedown.

"Do you think that helps?" I asked, gesturing to the box.

She shrugged. "Couldn't hurt." She watched me for a moment. "I'm not a picky eater, but an apple omelette doesn't sound good to me."

Pulling a face, I said, "It really doesn't. Thank goodness I'm making cinnamon apple pancakes instead."

"Ha." She slammed the lid on the pieces. "I knew there was a reason I liked you."

"Because I consistently feed you?" I dumped in the minced apples into a small pan with butter and cinnamon to brown.

"Sometimes, that's all it takes."

When the apple pieces were soft and fragrant, I added them to the batter and mixed. Once the first batch of pancakes done, I gave Stheno a stack and some syrup so she could get started while I made my own.

"Okay, now tell me about Dave. Is he a part of whatever is going on with the demon poking at Clive?"

I almost said no and then realized I wasn't sure. "Would you mind if I ran it all by you? I'd appreciate your take."

Stheno gave me a hurry up hand wave while she stuffed in another bite.

"Okay, condensed version: Owen said demons were stopping by the bar to see Dave while we were in Europe. Apparently, Dave got angry, rushing them out and going with them. Then he started missing work. By the time we returned home, he was missing more shifts than he was making, usually showing up late or leaving early. And he was really surly."

I slid a couple more pancakes onto her plate. "I know some people think he's always surly, but he isn't. I mean, yes, fine, fiery temper, but beneath that, mostly hidden from view, he's secretly kind. He always makes sure I eat, bakes my favorite cookies, taught me to drive. He's done all the banking since I opened. He's on the front line when people come at me." I shook my head, eyes filling with tears.

"What else?"

Turning off the stove, I doused my pancakes in syrup and then hopped up onto the island to eat. "He quit. Showed up late. Went off when I tried to get him to tell me what was going on. I followed him up the stairs, trying to get him to talk to me." I looked down at my hand, strangely absent of lines. "I touched his arm to get him to stop and he burned the skin off my hand."

Stheno's fork clattered to her plate. "The fuck he did. Let me see that." She grabbed my hand and studied it, expression thoughtful. "Son of a bitch," she said under her breath, not quite believing it.

"It was my fault. *I* touched *him*. I thought maybe he and Maggie broke up or something. He didn't answer but it felt more like he was worried about her rather than angry with her. Then he said some horrible things to hurt me so I wouldn't follow him.

"Yesterday, the top-ranking demon in San Francisco dropped by to harass me. When I asked about Dave, he said Dave was in trouble and I should go to the Demon's Lair strip club. He said through there I'd find the Biergarten of the Damned—and Dave."

I hadn't touched the pancakes, but I wasn't hungry anymore. "So what do you think?"

"I think that demon loves you and if he was being that much of an asshole, it was because he was trying to keep you away from him. I think he was also trying to keep demons away from your home. If these demons are after him, he's trying to stay far away from you. Probably why he looked nervous when you mentioned Maggie. At a guess, he's distanced himself from her too."

Stheno paced the room. "I don't trust the guy who stopped by yesterday, especially as he's trying so hard to draw you into demon shit, but I bet he's telling you the truth about where to find Dave. That's exactly the kind of shit-disturbing demons love. Set up high-drama situations and then sit back to watch the fireworks."

I slid off the island. "Then that's where I go. The demons can't have him. He's mine."

"We."

"What?"

"We. Friends don't let friends go to demon bars alone. Clive's going to fire me for this, but you're right. Dave's your family. My sisters might bug the ever-living shit out of me, but if either one was in trouble, I'd be there to lay waste to thousands."

"Aww."

"Shut up and eat. How do you plan to battle demons on little sleep and no food?" Stheno picked up her empty plate and took it to the sink, running hot water over the syrupy sludge.

I took a bite, thinking. "If we left now, we'd probably get back before opening."

"Finish and we'll all nap before opening. Then—"

"But—"

"Don't be an idiot," she said, cutting me off. "Do you know a lot of strip joints open this early in the morning? Not to mention this hellish biergarten we're headed to; they probably closed up a couple of hours ago. Now, if it was Satan's Waffle House, I'd say, sure, let's go."

She was right. I knew it. Still, I hadn't anticipated her agreeing with me, so I wanted to jump on it before she came to her senses. I finished eating and rinsed off my plate as well.

"What kind of waffles do you think they serve at Satan's Waffle House?" I wondered.

Stheno thought a moment. "Mushy, undercooked ones. Made with spoiled milk and expired eggs. Motor oil as syrup."

"And they get repeat customers?"

"It wasn't a stellar business plan." Stheno handed me the chess set box and pushed me toward the apartment doorway.

Fergus hopped up, took a few steps into the kitchen, and then circled behind me to herd me into our home.

"I'm taking your couch. I'll set an alarm to get you up before opening. Go lie down and take your dog with you."

As much as I wanted to work on inventorying the order that had just arrived, the siren call of sleep was already dragging me down. Kicking off my shoes, I put the box back on my bureau, unstrapped my blades, and crawled into bed. Wrapping the comforter around myself, I settled in. A moment later, I was out.

## 13

# A Communiqué from Faerie

I woke to the sound of knocking. Trying to get up, I almost hit the ground, trapped in a bedding cocoon. "Just a minute." What time was it? I checked my phone.

"Stheno! You said you'd wake me."

I got a grunt as I rushed by, and then she rolled over and continued sleeping.

Fyr was standing on the other side of the door, Fergus by his side. When we'd left the country, I'd given Owen control of the wards. He'd had to open and close them every day. Now that I was back, he only opened them when necessary. I still found it jarring, though, when I didn't realize people were in my place.

Fergus' tail began to wag madly.

Fyr watched the pup's excitement and then said, "Sorry to bother you, but we can't find Fergus' leash. He needs to go out."

Opening the ward, I waved him in. "Sorry! I didn't realize I hadn't left it on the bar." I gestured to the couch as I went back to the bedroom. "You remember Stheno." The leash wasn't on the bureau. Where the heck had I left it? I mentally retraced my steps and then smacked the kangaroo pocket on my hoodie. Yep. I'd stuffed it in my pocket and then forgot about it.

When I returned to the living room, Fyr was sitting on the

couch with Stheno straddling him, her mouth fused to his. "Oh, come on. You were sound asleep thirty seconds ago."

When she finally came up for air, she said, "But then you brought me a dragon." She was talking to me, but all her attention, and both her hands, were on my new bartender. "How could I sleep with this much heat in the room?"

"Boundaries, Stheno. We've talked about this."

Fyr looked over his shoulder, a grin on his face. "I don't mind."

"Fine," I said, going back into the bedroom to grab shoes. "I'll walk Fergus."

"Oh, it's Nathaniel's turn. We just needed the leash." His hands slid up Stheno's thighs and she swooped in to claim his mouth again.

"Fine, fine. I'm going," I grumbled.

"Blades," Stheno moaned.

I almost kept walking, just to get away from those two, but knew she was right.

Axe and sword in place, I went out to the bar and handed the leash to Nathaniel, a quietly kind and very proper wicche. Fergus was a good boy and dropped his butt to the floor so Nathaniel could snap on the lead. "Behave," I called as they left. I was pretty sure Fergus knew I was talking to him.

I got some strange looks from my patrons because of the blades, but gossip being what it was, they probably already knew I'd been attacked last night. Ignoring the glances, I joined Owen behind the bar, where he was brewing tea. Afternoons mostly meant small groups of wicches drinking tea. "Sorry. I overslept."

Owen waved away my apology. "How are you feeling today?"

"Mostly fine, especially after the nap. My head was still aching first thing this morning, but it's fine now."

"Good." He slid a cup of tea in front of me.

I was lifting the cup to my mouth when I felt something strange and powerful pass through my ward. Putting down the cup, I changed places with Owen, who'd been standing closest to the stairs, and pushed him toward the kitchen.

"Go get Stheno and Fyr." Taking a deep breath, I centered myself and began uncoiling magic, right hand on the hilt of my sword.

A moment later, a fae warrior appeared at the bottom of my steps. Tall, broad shouldered, he wore a tunic and breeches. Ignoring the rest of the bar, he kept his eyes on me.

"You are Sam." His voice was clear and confident, completely absent of rancor.

"I am."

Nodding in acknowledgment, he said, "I have a message from my queen." He scanned the bar. "Is there somewhere we might speak?"

I heard three sets of footfalls behind me. "It's okay." We were finally meeting the light king on the chessboard.

"I know. I recognize him," Stheno said.

When I glanced toward Stheno, I realized multiple wicches were standing, their fingertips readying spells. Aww, my customers were the best.

Pointing to the bookstore entrance, I said, "We can talk in here." I led the way. The warrior tried to let Stheno go first, but she wasn't having it.

"I'm the guard. You go first."

Nodding, he followed, with Stheno bring up the rear. Thankfully, I didn't have to ask anyone to move. The couch and chairs by the window wall were empty. There was a moment of awkwardness as both the warrior and Stheno seemed to be determining which seat was tactically best.

The warrior took one of the chairs, angling it so he could see the couch, chair, and bookstore doorway, with only books behind him. Stheno moved to the other chair, so I took the couch, and we all sat at the same time.

"Thank you for meeting with me. I am Algar, captain of my queen's guard."

"That ain't all you are," Stheno snarked.

The warrior turned to her, his head tilted as though trying to understand the remark. "May I know who you are?"

"Stheno," she said.

I could see him trying to work out if he should know the name. Raising my eyebrows in question, she gave a quick nod. "Algar, Stheno is one of three gorgon sisters. She is ancient—"

"Watch it, kid."

"—and very powerful, much like yourself."

"Gorgon." He said the word carefully, as though trying to find context for it. His expression didn't change, but his gaze snapped to her eyepatch. He bowed his head once, acknowledging her threat, and then returned his attention to me.

"I don't believe my queen has visited your establishment. She would have mentioned something so unusual."

"No. She came to our local nocturne and then to the Palace of Fine Arts for my wedding."

Smiling, he nodded. "She was pleased to be invited and thought the ceremony quite diverting."

"Good. I'm glad." This was such an odd conversation.

"I'm here because my queen has learned of the attack on you. She wants you to know that this was not sanctioned. She thanks you for discovering what was poisoning Faerie and has accepted your information as payment in full for saving your life."

I was waiting for a shoe to drop but said, "Great."

"She requests that she might call on you in the future." The warrior paused, waiting for a response.

After a quick glance at Stheno, I said, "Not knowing what I might be called upon for, I will say that I support the queen and, barring any threat to me or mine, would be open to hearing what Gloriana needs and would consider helping." Out of the corner of my eye, I noticed Stheno nodding so I figured I must have worded that response properly.

The warrior gave one decisive nod. "My queen thought you should know that the king has been imprisoned, though she has not routed all his supporters, as you are aware. She is concerned that you will be the focus of retaliation since they are no match for our queen."

Stheno scoffed. "Meanwhile, the king has sent how many against you now?" She was addressing me but glaring at the warrior. "Sam's still here, unlike the bodies of all those dead fae assassins who were returned to Faerie. So, let's not discuss my girl here like she can't hold her own."

Shaking his head, he said, "No insult was intended. In fact, if I might borrow the dwarf's axe on your back, I have a gift for you from my queen."

I glanced at Stheno, who shrugged. Good point. If his intent was to kill me, he wouldn't need my axe to do it. I unsheathed it and handed it to him.

He studied it a moment and then ran a finger over the blade. The metal axe head shone blindingly for a moment. When he handed it back to me, there was a silver cap at the base of the handle.

"The queen has given you an advantage over any of her people who attack you against her orders. What I have done ensures that this blade will be deadly to any fae who harm you."

Holy crap!

"She warns, though, that if you were to raise this weapon against a peaceful member of her people, it is you who will forfeit your life."

Stheno nodded in approval. "Good boon."

"Please convey to Gloriana my immense pleasure with her gift." The fae could be so tricksy with language, I was doing my best to make statements that couldn't be twisted to another purpose.

"I will," he said, rising from his chair.

"If I might ask a question."

He paused, considering, and then nodded.

"Can you tell me anything about Arwyn Corey?" As I'd said to Stheno, I was fascinated—or perhaps disturbed—by a wicche who could not only create a magical object as powerful and precise as the chess set, but also one prescient enough to leave it in a spot she knew I'd find a year later.

"My queen is aware of her." After a lengthy pause, I realized that was all he had to say on the subject.

I remembered the conversation I'd had with Dave's dad. "Is there something special about Corey wicches?"

Algar paused a moment, as though deciding how much to share. "I believe my queen already told you she considers you one of hers, yes?"

I nodded.

"The same could be said for all Corey wicches. Now, I have someone I'd like to properly introduce you to, if I may?"

Stheno and I exchanged a look. "Of course," I said.

"Good." He looked toward the doorway to the bar just as heavy footsteps thundered down the stairs.

I heard shouts from the bar and then an Orc walked in the bookstore, Fyr racing in behind him.

## 14

# I Guard!

I held up a hand to Fyr. "Wait."

"May I introduce Fangorn to you. This soldier was one of the prisoners you freed from the vampire Aldith. As you saved his life, he has sworn to protect yours."

Standing in the doorway, devotion shining in his dark eyes, was seven and a half feet of muscle. He had a bald, blockish head with ears like balloon knots, sitting atop massive shoulders straining to break free of a tunic belted at the waist with a leather cord. His breeches, like his shirt, had stretched seams. His boots were a scuffed worn leather that reached his calves. A large, heavy sword hung at his side. With thick, rough, light green skin, he was terrifying but appeared far less vicious than the last few Orcs I'd battled. Eyes a dark gray, bordering on black, he watched me, waiting.

Unsure of what was happening, I looked past the Orc and discovered that both Fyr and Owen were blocking the doorway, waiting for my cue to attack. While I appreciated their courage, I didn't want anyone to die today.

"Hello, Mr. Fangorn. It's very nice to meet you. I'm pleased to see you up and around. You're looking quite healthy." When we'd rescued him, I wasn't sure if he'd live long enough to escape the dungeon.

He gave a grunt of agreement at the healthy comment and struck his chest to prove it.

"Fangorn is an excellent soldier. He's served our queen for an age. He's requested of her that he now be allowed to protect you. Our queen has granted his request." Algar nodded to Stheno. "Fangorn, this is your lady's captain of the guard, just as I am our queen's. They will let you know how you might serve your lady."

Fangorn nodded decisively, crossing bulging arms across his massive chest. "Good." He had a deep foghorn of a voice that was oddly soothing.

Owen and Fyr gave me identical what-the-hell looks and I was right there with them.

"I'm honored by your generous offer, but you don't owe me anything. I was happy to help in any way I could. I wanted you to be free to live your life as you wished, not to make you indebted to me."

The Orc's brow furrowed rather impressively.

"Your lady is releasing you from your debt. You are not obligated to serve her," Algar translated.

Fangorn's confusion changed to defiant anger. "I guard."

Algar turned to me. "We've had this discussion and he has remained adamant. If you insist, I can take him with me, but that won't alleviate his need to do this. He'll be in Faerie, angry and unfulfilled because, for him, this is now his duty."

"I guard!" he said again, more forcefully.

"I can add that Fangorn is one of our queen's most loyal and trusted soldiers," Algar said.

Fangorn nodded with a grunt of approval.

Stheno smacked my arm. "Looks like you've got your own soldier, kid."

"Yes, cap'n," Fangorn rumbled.

Grinning, Stehno said, "I don't hate that."

Glancing at Algar, I gave a quick nod before returning my attention to Fangorn. "I accept your offer of service."

The Orc gave a happy grunt. I was starting to hear the tonal differences in his grunts.

"If, however, your queen needs you, I grant you your freedom to return to Faerie."

Slamming his fist against his chest again, he said, "Must guard queen."

"Yes, exactly." Algar laid a hand on Fangorn's shoulder. "If the queen has need of you, I will call you back."

Fangorn gave a quiet grunt of approval.

"I must return now. You remember the location of the doorway?" he asked the soldier.

My new guard gave one decisive nod.

"Thank you for seeing us. If you have a need, I believe you have a way"—he glanced down at Gloriana's ring on my pinky—"of contacting our queen." Patting Fangorn's back, he moved to the doorway as Owen and Fyr stepped to the side. The queen's captain was up the steps and gone a moment later, leaving us with our own Orc.

Unsure of how to proceed, I went with the mundane. "Can I get you something to eat or drink?"

He shook his blocky head. "I guard."

"Right. Okay." I glanced back at the couch. There was no way he was fitting on that thing. "I'm sorry. I don't have a room for you right now." I gestured to the couch. "And I'm afraid the couch will be too small. I can get—"

"Sleep outside," he rumbled.

"You prefer sleeping outside?" That made it easy. "What about when it rains?"

"Get wet."

I'd read somewhere—maybe a Chinese proverb—that if you save a life, you become responsible for it. I was definitely feeling that responsibility right now. Although I knew Clive would understand why I didn't send Fangorn away, and agree with me even, I was pretty sure he wouldn't be happy about an Orc roommate. Speaking of which…

"Fangorn, I know the fae hate vampires, but my husband is a vampire. If that's a deal breaker for—"

"No deal broke. Vampire chained me. Vampire rescued me. Fae," he said, disgust on his face, "betrayed me. Gave me to vampire."

Yeah, I totally understood the resentment. "Is there anything you need right now?"

He shook his head.

Okay then. I checked the time on my phone and then looked at Stheno. "It's gotta be open by now, right?"

Fyr stood in the doorway, his eyes on the Orc. Owen was picking up empties.

"Owen, can I borrow your car? Stheno and I are on a mission." I had a moment to wonder why everyone was staring at me until I realized Fangorn was standing directly behind me.

Turning to him, I said, "Stheno and I are going out for a little while."

He nodded. "I guard."

"Oh, we don't need—"

Stheno smacked my arm again. "We're going to a demon bar. Take the soldier."

"Demons," Fangorn grumbled, a sneer on his lips.

How the heck were we getting a seven-and-a-half-foot tall Orc into a vehicle? Turning to Fyr, I said, "You were going to buy some kind of big truck. Did you do that yet?" Dragons are very large, even in human form. Poor George had to fold himself painfully to fit into Owen's compact car.

Nodding, he pulled the keys from his pocket and threw them to me.

"Thank you!" I said. "I have my license now. It's all legal."

The side of Fyr's mouth kicked up. "I'm not worried. If you wreck it, your husband will buy me a replacement that's nicer than the one I have now."

I couldn't argue with that logic.

"It's the used white Ascent in the parking lot."

"Perfect." I looked down at myself and realized I'd never gotten cleaned up, as Stheno's sexcapades had kept me out of my own apartment. "I need fifteen minutes. I'll be right back."

After a quick shower, I tied up my wet hair, put on clean clothes, and stepped into a pair of boots. I was just about to head out when I remembered my blades. Humans would be in the strip club, but I was sure the demons wouldn't care about my weapons. I couldn't hurt them with the blades, and I doubted any customers would be looking at the fully clothed women when there were mostly naked ones dancing on the stage. Not to mention the demons would probably get a kick out of my hacking up humans. My soul would be up for grabs, which was kind of their deal.

When I returned to the bar, I found Fangorn sitting on the steps with Fergus in his lap. My pup was straining to lick the soldier's smiling face. I glanced over at Owen and found him grinning, watching the whole thing play out. Fergus: Orc slayer!

"I'm ready." I checked my pockets to make sure I'd remembered to pocket Fyr's keys. Keys, phone, wallet; I was good to go.

Stheno walked out of the bookstore and Fangorn stood, putting Fergus back on the floor.

"Good luck," Owen said. We were both missing our grumpy cook.

Fyr's SUV was easy to find. The parking lot was scattered with smaller cars—San Francisco was notoriously difficult to park in—so an oversized one stuck out. I hit the key fob and his rig chirped.

When Fangorn emerged from our secret stairway, he wore a glamour to hide his true nature. He now appeared to be a 1920s gangster. Still huge, he'd shrunk to six and a half feet, had slicked-back black hair, olive skin, and a navy pin-striped, three-piece suit. All he needed was a violin case with a Tommy gun to complete the look. I had no idea where he'd seen this image to copy, but I loved it.

Stheno and Fangorn both reached for the front passenger seat door. Stheno could have ordered him to the backseat, but instead she gave way and took it herself. He was bigger and needed it. I wasn't sure how much time he'd spent in the human realm, so I went to his side and adjusted the seat for him.

I'd only been driving a short time, and this was a large SUV. It had the power to go up and down steep hills, but it was a little wide for crowded, narrow streets. Letting my phone direct me, I cautiously made my way downtown.

A delivery truck pulled away from the curb two doors down from the Demon's Lair. Thanking the parking gods for the huge spot, I was able to drive straight in. No parallel parking for this girl. When we got out, heads turned at Fangorn's glamour and my weapons. If anything, though, we probably looked like we were cosplaying.

The soldier stepped in front of me as we approached the large, padded double doors of the Demon's Lair. The last time I'd been here, Sitri, the former head demon in town, had screwed with my head, making my body respond to his every word. His voice had left me desperately, painfully aroused. Clive had battled Sitri's influence, clearing away the manufactured lust until Sitri spoke again and my mind was filled with intense images of hot, sweaty couplings with various demons. And then Clive would fan the images away and I'd be left feeling helpless, sick, and used.

Sitri'd had a discussion with Clive while keeping a sly eye on me. I was sure he knew about my past, the torture and rape, the helplessness and humiliation. He'd known and he'd been making my body a traitor to my mind, making me want what I reviled. And then Clive would brush the influence away again. I'd wanted to kill Sitri then. I'd wanted to sink my wolf's teeth into his throat and tear it to shreds, to feel the life drain out of him so I could keep myself safe.

Once we'd determined we didn't need Sitri in order find who was trapping me in visions, Clive had apparently come back and killed Sitri for what he'd done to me. I hadn't known it at the time, but learning it, I breathed easier. Until, that is, Dave told me demons couldn't be killed.

And now here I was, walking back into the Demon's Lair. This time, I was stronger. I knew how to protect my mind. At least, I hoped I did.

Taking a deep breath and steeling myself, I patted Fangorn's back. He opened the tall door, ducking under the lintel and then waited for Stheno to grab it, thereby keeping me between the two of them. I was about to tell him that this level of concern wasn't necessary, that I could take care of myself, but then my newfound bravery drained away.

The shadowy entrance held a large, muscle-bound bouncer, but my soldier was bigger and stronger. It wasn't that. The hard-driving beat, the dark club, the raw, pervasive miasma of violence and sex in the air had me going light-headed.

I felt Stheno's hand on my arm and realized I must have stopped walking. I could do this. Dave needed our help, and I was stronger now.

The same creepy guy from last time appeared out of the shadows to loom over me, though his gaze cut to Fangorn. The foolish man completely ignored Stheno. "Mr. Irdu said to expect you. If you'll follow me?"

## 15

# Is That Ted Bundy?

We followed Lurch through the back of the club. To Fangorn's credit, he kept his attention focused on the demons, never once gawking at the woman swinging around the pole. As an aside, the dancer's core strength was impressive. She was like a Cirque du Soleil acrobat in eight-inch platforms and a G-string.

Lurch led us past the bar and down a dark hall with *Employees Only* signs. I tried unsuccessfully to not think about my boots sticking to the floor and why. The music changed with a beat drop. Anemic applause punctuated by hoots followed us from the main room.

When we reached the end of the hall, our guide extended his hand toward a blank wall. Assuming this was an optical illusion to keep the humans away, I reached for the invisible doorknob.

Fangorn pushed me behind him and nodded to Stheno. Looking Lurch up and down, she tapped her eyepatch and then shooed him away. Smirking, he retreated down the hall.

"What are you thinking here, kid?"

"It's probably invisible so humans don't wander in the Biergarten looking for a bathroom." I tried to reach out again at doorknob height, but my soldier blocked me.

"Cap'n do it." Fangorn nodded to Stheno.

She touched the back wall and a door shimmered into view. As we might have been walking into an ambush, Stheno flipped her eyepatch up before opening the door. She stepped out into the alley behind the Demon's Lair, Fangorn and I following.

I almost turned to comment on the weird stench when I remembered her eyepatch was up. "Dude, cover yourself."

"Oh." She snapped the patch over her eye. "I hate having a blind side, especially when we're walking into a nest of demons."

"Is that the collective noun for demons?" I wondered aloud. "Like a murder of crows or a flamboyance of flamingos?"

Fangorn gave me an annoyed hiss to shut me up.

Holding up my hands, I mouthed *sorry* to both of them. I was terrified of what we were walking into and was distracting myself with stupid stuff.

Stheno patted my shoulder and then pointed down the path at Fangorn's back, seeming to understand but also telling me to haul ass.

The alley didn't open to the street. A narrow, poorly lit path filled the space between two buildings. An ancient, rather forbidding door stood ajar at the end of the alley. I looked into every darkened window we passed, every padlocked door, and found nothing, heard nothing other than the scratch of rat claws scurrying up drainpipes and under doors.

Fangorn pointed to his ear and then the open door, shaking his head. Yeah, I didn't hear anything either. His sword appeared in his hand and he used it to push open the door. I wasn't sure what I was expecting, but it definitely wasn't a shiny elevator. Next to the elevator door was a plaque reading *Biergarten of the Damned* with an arrow pointing down to a call button.

We all stared a moment and then I leaned forward and pushed it. It dinged and I flinched. Damn it. I had to shake off the nerves. I was going to stroke out in a minute. Pulling my phone out of my pocket, I shot off a quick text to Clive, letting him know where I was. If this visit didn't end well, I needed him to know who to drain.

Fangorn seemed unclear on elevators. When the door slid open, Stheno went in first. Patting my soldier's arm, I stepped in as well. Clearly uncomfortable, he followed, barely avoiding the closing door.

"It's an elevator," I explained to him. "Essentially, it's a box on a rope going up and down a shaft cut deep in the earth. When it stops moving, the door will open, and we'll be somewhere else."

I glanced at the panel. Three buttons: DL, BD, and A. I got Demon's Lair and Biergarten of the Damned, but what the heck did the A stand for?

Pushing the BD button, I turned to Stheno. "A?" There was a momentary drop and then a smooth glide deep underground.

She shook her head. "No idea." Smacking my arm, she said, "Wait a minute. I thought you had a ghost helper. Why aren't we sending her in first to check the place out for us?"

"Charlotte? I haven't seen or felt her since before the wedding. I tried calling her once, but she didn't come. Martha made a big deal about never calling the dead back once they've crossed over." I shrugged. "Maybe she just wanted to sort of even the score, help me like I helped her, before she moved on? I mean, good for her."

"Okay, but there are a shit ton of ghosts around. Why didn't you call a different one?"

I shrugged, guilty. "Mostly because I hadn't thought of it."

Stheno threw her hands up in the air. "Are you shitting me right now? You have weapons at your disposal. We're walking into a murder of demons and it doesn't occur to you?" She shook her coiled curls. "I like you, but there are times I really want to smack you upside the head."

"Sorry. It's this place. I know what they can do to me, what Sitri did last time. I have problems with the loss of control." I felt like a cowardly asshole. I was letting fear fuck me up.

"Yeah, I get it. What the hell is with this elevator, anyway? How far down are we going?"

The elevator finally dinged and the door slid open, Fangorn blocking the entrance. Expecting to see the same Hell from the vision I'd been trapped in a few months ago, I was pleasantly surprised to see grass and flowering bushes, soft sunlight moving toward dusk, the air redolent with the scent of jasmine. Apparently the demons had access to magical builders as well.

I knew we were Hell adjacent and all, but this was really nice.

Fangorn stepped out and we followed. Hummingbirds danced around a bush blooming with hot pink flowers. The soldier, still wearing his 1920s gangster glamour, used his sword to point at a path cutting through the tall trees canopying the flower-laden clearing. Yes, I heard the voices now too.

Circling around white wisteria blossoms that dripped from high branches, we found another clearing, this one much larger, that held perhaps twenty picnic tables also shaded by the trees above. At the far end was a wooden building with shutters pushed open to reveal a long counter filled with taps. The bartender, who looked disturbingly like Ted Bundy, gave us a little wave and motioned us over.

I scanned the tables, looking for Dave. Some patrons sat together, but most alone. Heads had turned when we'd arrived, but they'd quickly lost interest and had gone back to talking, playing on their phones, or staring into their beers.

Some of the demons looked like regular people, like someone you'd pass on the street and not even notice. Others were walking nightmares. One was skeletally thin, skin the gray of death, with a trail of blood tears running down his face. Another wore what looked like a filthy toga, his mouth filled with broken teeth, his body covered in pustules of varying sizes, most appearing to be one stiff breeze from rupturing. There was even a demon who looked exactly like an old illustration in a book: red skin, vertical pupils, big horns, fur from the waist down, cloven hooves for feet.

Chills ran down my spine at the sight of the demon with a mop of dark, curly hair and dead eyes. Beside him sat a pasty-faced man, who lifted his right hand to scratch his face. On the back of his hand was what looked like a homemade tattoo of a circle bisected by two lines, a rifle sight.

My stomach dropped as I realized who they were. The dark-haired man put on aviator sunglasses and did something approximating a black-toothed grin that made my blood run cold. The Night Stalker and the Zodiac Killer were hanging out in a San Francisco demon biergarten.

I took an involuntary step back and bumped into Stheno.

"What?"

"Serial killers straight ahead," I whispered.

"Honey, I hate to break it to you, but the joint is filled with nothing but serial killers. It's a fucking demon bar."

Right. Of course. Got it. This was a really bad idea. And then I thought of Dave, explaining how payroll worked or sliding a plate of cookies down the bar to me each night. Turning on my heel, I arrowed straight to Ted Bundy, Fangorn and Stheno on either side of me.

"Oh, good," he said as I approached. "I was afraid you were going to change your mind and leave. We so rarely get visitors." He wiped down the bar. "So what can I get you?"

I assumed the rules for eating and drinking in a demon bar were not the same as those in Faerie, but as I had no intention of being trapped here, I erred on the side of caution and shook my head. "We're looking for Dave. Can you tell us if he's around?"

"Hmm." He leaned his elbows on the bar, moving closer to me. "Dave who? Do you have a last name?"

Demons had last names?

"You know," he continued, "if you wore your hair long and parted in the center, you'd look dynamite."

"Knock it off," Stheno said, pushing me out of his line of sight at the same time Fangorn held his sword to Ted's neck. Someone behind me giggled, making my hackles rise.

Stepping back, he held up his hands. "Just an observation." Moving farther into the shadows, he said, "Let me go check if Dave is in the back."

Fangorn's hand dropped and I glanced to the right to identify the giggler and found a man in clown makeup watching us. Oh, so not good… A door slammed and I jumped.

"What the fuck, Sam? How did you even get in here?" Dave's shark black eyes darted around the room before landing on me again. "I told you. I quit."

"I know, but—"

"But nothing. Go home." When I didn't move, he sighed. "Listen, I was getting paid, okay? Someone wanted me to keep an eye on you, so I did. *I* don't care. Never did. I got paid a lot to pass on info. Simple as that. My job there is done, so I left."

He shook his head, frustration and annoyance clear in his expression. His gaze finally fell on Fangorn. The look of confusion he wore was priceless. "Take your friends and run along home, will ya? I've got shit to do that thankfully no longer involves you." He turned away and bellowed, "Bundy! You're on the stick." He slammed the door and it burst into flames.

"Well, that was quite rude, wasn't it?"

I startled at the voice directly behind me, not having heard his approach. The fire was, as you'd guess, pretty distracting. When I felt Stheno flinch at the same moment, I knew I wasn't the only one who hadn't heard him. Turning, I found a dark-haired man with golden brown skin and black eyes glowing with fake concern.

"You'll have to excuse him. He's always been an odd one, keeping to himself, crying to daddy when he gets caught in a lie." He shook his head. "Forget about him. What can *I* do for you?"

"Nothing. Uh, you might want to…" I pointed to the flames running up the door and now spreading across the ceiling.

"Oh." Waving a hand, he put out the fire without taking his eyes off me.

"We're going now." He'd done nothing threatening and yet his standing so close was making me sick to my stomach.

His hand was suddenly around my wrist. I hadn't seen him move. "Don't go. We're just getting acquainted, you and I."

Fangorn's sword was at the demon's neck. He glanced down at it and then back up into the mobster's impassive face.

The demon tsked and then Fangorn's arm began to shake. Good soldier that he was, he didn't give in to whatever the demon was doing to him. Teeth gritted, he kept his sword at the demon's neck. A moment later, the other demons in the biergarten stood and as one moved toward us.

"All you assholes know who I am," Stheno said, reaching for her eyepatch. "Unless you'd like to start a statue garden down here, you'll ease off and have a seat."

The demon who had my wrist in a vice-like grip squeezed harder. At my yelp of pain, Stheno's curls whipped out, small snake heads emerging from each coil of hair to bite the demon's neck and face. Fangorn pushed forward with his sword and the demon disappeared.

Clearly done dealing with demon shit, Fangorn picked me up, threw me over his shoulder, and then tore off for the elevator. Stheno followed, walking backward, her hand still on her eyepatch, staring down the rest of the demons. "This has got nothing to do with you. Relax and have another beer."

Fangorn pushed the button, having learned that trick, and the door opened immediately. Stheno came around the wisteria a moment later, running for the open door. She skidded in and jabbed the DL button. As the doors closed, the demon appeared, snake bites and sword cut healed. He waved at me, a terrifying smile on his face.

## 16

# There Goes Another Phone

Fangorn sheathed his sword and it disappeared again, before putting me down. When he reached for my wrist, I almost pulled away from him but stopped myself. It hurt, but I was pretty sure nothing was broken.

Nodding, he grunted, "Good," and then crossed his huge arms over his muscular chest, waiting for the box to open again.

"Please tell me we learned something." That I hadn't just made a new demon enemy for no reason.

"Sure we did," Stheno said. "We learned that serial killers end up where they should. We learned that demons come in all shapes and sizes. Remember the horned one—half man, half goat—sitting at a table of three?"

"Hard to forget."

"Exactly. The guy stood out. Guess who I didn't see as we were leaving?"

*Shit.* Where did that one go? What was he up to now?

"Grabbed you," Fangorn said, gesturing to my wrist. "Wearing glamour," he added, pointing to his own disguise.

Just thinking about it made me break out in a retroactive cold sweat. "Are you sure?"

He nodded. "Saw change."

The elevator finally dinged. Stheno reached for her eyepatch as Fangorn's hand hovered at his side, ready to unsheathe his sword. He stepped to the front of the car when the door slid open and… nothing. Fangorn got out first and searched the area, Stheno and I jumping out before the door closed again.

"Let's get the hell out of here," Stheno said, striding down the alley.

It was just as ominously quiet on the return trip, except for the sudden caw of a crow that made my heart stop. Perched on a fire escape above us, he watched our progress. The oppressive silence had my hackles rising.

Stheno reached the back door of the strip club first. When she touched it, a doorknob appeared. She checked over her shoulder to find us right behind her, so she readied her patch and opened the door. Lurch, who'd shown us to the door, was just moving out of the hall, returning to the main room. Wait. I checked my phone. No time had passed. This alley and the biergarten apparently existed outside of time.

Fangorn took the lead again. When we passed through the bar, a man sat at a rear table all alone. He wasn't facing the stage. The demon who'd grabbed me was watching us. Wearing a suit now, he was Fangorn's twin, his dark hair slicked back, a drink in his hand. When we strode by, he took a sip and winked at me.

I couldn't be positive, but it felt like all my internal organs liquefied on the spot.

When we were all back in Fyr's SUV, I locked the doors, started the engine, and took a minute to freak the fuck out. A truck honked, adding another layer of anxiety, as I'd completely forgotten how to drive.

Stheno rolled down her window and flipped off the truck driver. Okay. I could remember how to do this. Check the mirrors. Take off the emergency brake. Check rearview. Put it into reverse. Roll back a couple feet to give myself room. Check mirrors again. Look over my shoulder. The truck was blocking oncoming traffic. Put it in drive. Turn the wheel. Gas. Check mirrors. Go.

I had to coach myself the whole way back. When my thoughts drifted to the demon's wink, I shoved it out, reciting in my head each step of the driving process. When I finally returned Fyr's rig to its parking space, I let out a long, slow breath.

Fangorn jumped out and walked around the front of the vehicle, waiting at the driver's door to guard me, all the while scanning the bluff, looking for threats.

"I gotta say," Stheno began, "that soldier is handy to have around."

"You're telling me." I slid out, waited for Stheno to open her door, and then locked up Fyr's rig.

Once we were back in the Slaughtered Lamb and Fangorn had dropped his glamour, I returned Fyr's keys, slid a tankard of mead to my bodyguard, and pulled out a shaker to make Stheno and myself cocktails.

I was watching the soldier out of the corner of my eye. He was just about to push the tankard back when Grim, the dwarf who'd been sitting on the last stool at the bar since the first day I'd opened, said something to him. Fangorn nodded and lifted the tankard, downing the mead in one.

Grim patted him on the back and waved Fyr down to fill their tankards.

Carrying a pitcher of margaritas to Stheno's table, I put down the glasses I had in one hand and then filled them. Fergus was still giving us a wide berth. When we came down the stairs, he ran to me and then skidded to a halt, sniffing the air around us before backing away. Not going to lie; That hurt.

The sun would be going down soon. I needed to let Clive know we were fine. When I checked my messages, though, my text to him had never been sent. Right. I'd texted in the alley, before entering the elevator. We must have stepped off the human plane when we'd entered Hell-adjacent areas.

Clive needed to help Russell tonight. I didn't want him racing back to stay with me when I had a soldier, a gorgon, a dragon, and a wicche at my disposal. Russell and the nocturn needed him.

"What are you thinking?" Stheno asked.

Deleting the unsent text, I said, "I'm thinking I need a good long run with my boy here." I took a gulp. "With one notable exception, I've never been so scared in my life."

Like Fangorn, Stheno downed her margarita in one before refilling her glass. "I hear ya, kid." She paused. "I have to admit," she added, lowering her voice, "I did not enjoy that." Like the first, she drank her second one down like a shot and refilled.

"I'm a jangle of nerves. I need to burn off this nervous energy." Fergus turned to Fangorn and growled. We all needed showers to get the stench of demon off us. I finished my drink and stood.

"Remember to bring your weapons and take your soldier." Stheno stood with me. "I need to go shower and then sit on my balcony, watch the ocean, and drink a crate of wine." Shaking her head, she headed up the stairs grumbling, "Fucking demons," under her breath.

Curious, I stepped behind the bar to check something. I sidled up to Fyr and asked under my breath, "Are you responsible for today's fashion choice?"

He looked down at me, brows furrowed.

I shot a glance at Fangorn and Fyr grinned unrepentantly.

"He asked what human bodyguards looked like. I showed him a few pics." He pulled a pint glass down and drew from the tap. With a shrug, he said, "I like watching old gangster movies."

Given Fyr's dislike of the fae, it could have been worse, I supposed. I headed back to the apartment, Fergus trailing at a distance. After sending off a quick text, wishing Clive luck with the vampy blood thingy, I headed to the bathroom to scrub myself with scented soaps and shampoos. Showering before a run sounded stupid, true, but I needed the pup to run with me, not away. Plus, I wondered how much of my nerves were due to the lingering scent.

Cleaned, dressed, and ponytailed, I grabbed my pup's leash. He jumped up from his bed and danced around me. I'd almost left before I remembered what Stheno had said. Running with a sword strapped to my leg was going to be miserable. The axe wouldn't be great, but marginally better than the sword. It would have to do.

I unzipped my sweat jacket, strapped on the axe sheath, and then hid it under my jacket. No point in scaring the people lounging on the beach.

When we got back to the bar, Fangorn and Grim were still chatting in grunts and grumbles, full tankards before them. Grim rarely said anything. Ever. It would be nice if they each found a friend.

Patting Fangorn's back, I said, "Fergus and I are going for a run."

He slammed down the tankard and stood, swaying a bit. Grim pulled him back down and waved us on. All three of us were dealing with the aftereffects of demons, it seemed.

After letting Fyr and Owen know we wouldn't be too long, I snapped the long leash on Fergus and we headed out. I was pleased to see that my pup was keeping up with me on the path to the beach. When we hit the sand, he took a moment to sniff madly and dig furiously. Once that was out of his system, we went down near the water and started to run.

The sheath banged against my back, so I zipped up the jacket to my neck, giving it less room to bounce. After a few miles, I could feel the straps chafing, but that would heal. The freedom and exhilaration of running, the scent of the ocean, the give of the sand, Fergus keeping me company, all of it helped to relax me by degrees.

When we got to Funston Beach, I knew we needed to turn around. The pup was slowing. He was still too young to be running so far. Remembering there was a water fountain at a long carpark by the beach, I ran us in that direction.

I let the water arc past the fountain and into my cupped hand, which I held at Fergus height. He drank and I got splattered, which was fine. Once he'd had his fill, I carried him for the next mile or so of my run. When he squirmed to be let down, I figured he was ready to put paws to sand again.

We were getting close to home when we hit a patch of beach that was completely deserted. It was beautiful, though a tad eerie. The ocean seemed to call to me, but I ignored it. I had a pup I needed to get home. I considered taking Fergus off leash, but then a surfer emerged from the water.

His dark hair was slicked back, light amber eyes locked on mine. As we ran past, I had a moment to think it odd he wasn't wearing a wetsuit, before he shot forward, out of the surf, and grabbed me. Fingers like a steel trap, he pulled me into the water with a strength that said he wasn't human.

Eyes flashing red, he gnashed a mouthful of sharp teeth and made a strange triumphant sound that reminded me of a neigh. Fergus raced forward and tried to bite him, but the man kicked him back to the beach. I let go of Fergus' leash so he could get to safety.

Claws shooting out, I swung, trying to separate his arm from his body before I separated his head from his neck. He could bleed to death in the water for all I cared. I needed to get this fucker off me and get Fergus to a healer. He'd just had his ribs broken. He didn't need more injuries.

Even though my claws should have taken him apart, he moved too fast to track. There and gone. When I tried to scramble away, he was pulling me under again, his fingers squeezed like a vice on my hand. I hadn't had a chance to fill my lungs. Scraping my claws over the wrist of the hand that'd shackled me, I had the satisfaction of hearing him squeal before he let go. Struggling to the surface, I gulped air and then was dragged back down again. I swung over and over, my claws finally tearing through flesh. When he recoiled again, I swam for shore. A roar echoing down the beach had me clearing the salt water from my eyes. My soldier was coming.

My soldier. My axe. *Shit.* The damn demons had my head all messed up. I reached for the axe as he latched onto my foot and yanked me back under. The thing trying to kill me was shifting and changing, long past holding a human form.

Wrenching with enough force to shred my jacket, I had the weapon in my hand. Sharp teeth bit down on my other hand, pulling me farther from shore. Clutching the axe for dear life, I swung at the fae trying to drown me. It moved like quicksilver, and I missed.

My lungs were ready to explode when I finally made contact with the thing. I got it right in the snout, blood billowing in the water, and then it winked out of existence in a flash of light.

I was fighting my way to the surface when something snatched me up and held me aloft by my sheath. Lifting the axe again, I almost killed my soldier before I recognized his blocky head, fierce expression, and three-piece suit.

"I guard!" he roared into my face.

Exhausted, I hung limply from my sheath straps and nodded.

17

# Seriously, Though, What Did I Do to Make the Kelpies Hate Me So Much?

Fangorn dragged me out of the water, Fergus racing back and forth, barking. After I checked the pup, who didn't seem hurt, we walked up the beach, Fangorn in wet black wingtips. As the adrenaline waned, I realized my hand was throbbing. I held it up, horror-struck. The kelpie had shredded it while dragging me down. Fucking kelpies. The bastards had it out for me.

Fangorn, who had been scanning our surroundings for possible threats, glanced over and grunted in annoyance. He appeared to grab the bottom of his suit jacket and rip, but what he handed me was a piece of fabric off the bottom of his tunic.

I wrapped it around my hand. "I have a healer I can call."

He made an annoyed sound in the back of his throat. "I guard, you not hurt."

"True. But in my defense, I did tell you I was going for a run. You stayed in the bar with Grim." Fergus was starting to flag and appeared to now be limping. He whined once when I picked him up with my good hand. I kissed his head. It looked like he was starting to feel his injuries too.

I reached for my phone to call Lilah when I remembered that it had gone into the ocean with me. Damn, I'd never live this down. Wait. We didn't live in the nocturne anymore. Russell and Godfrey didn't have to know anything about this. Of course, now I didn't have access to the spares Russell had purchased for me and kept in Clive's desk. I couldn't ask Norma to get me one anymore either. Double damn.

"I kill him," Fangorn said.

I stopped moving, confused. "You killed who? Wait. Grim?" At his shrug, I took off at a run. Was it good to run with a bleeding wound? No, no it was not. But that surly dwarf had been sitting on my barstool for almost eight years.

I was lightheaded by the time we returned to The Slaughtered Lamb. I put Fergus down and held on to the stair rail. Fangorn was directly behind me, but he hadn't said anything more.

Foot sliding off the last step, I held myself up by grabbing the wall. Everyone in the bar turned to watch my ungainly entrance, but my focus was on the last stool at the bar. Grim sat with his tankard of mead, not bothering to turn his head toward me.

"Sam! You're bleeding." Owen ran around the bar and helped me to a chair while he pulled his phone from his pocket.

"Fangorn said he'd killed Grim." Damn, I was about to pass out. *Shit, shit, shit.*

"No," Owen said. "He killed fake Grim. I was wondering why the old guy was so talkative today. That was one of the king's assassins trying to take out your bodyguard. Luckily, the real Grim walked in and then the imposter was minus his head. Your soldier took off at a run to find you."

He dialed his sister, while putting a bar towel down on the table and helping me move my hand. "Right before the fake Grim disappeared," he continued, "he lost his glamour. He was still a dwarf but looked nothing like Grim. I cleaned up the blood and the real Grim took his seat."

I almost went to get the chess set so he could tell us which one he'd seen, but I remembered that the piece would now be faceless. Just as well. I didn't think I could stand.

Clive appeared in front of me, taking away the pain while I was still trying to process yet another assassin waltzing into my place.

Finvarra was really pissing me off. Oh, dear. Black spots were starting to crowd out the bar. And then Fangorn's sword was at Clive's neck.

"Darling, who is this and do I need to kill him?"

"Stop! Fangorn, this is my husband Clive. Clive, this is Fangorn. He was one of Aldith's prisoners. Since we rescued him, he came to guard me."

"I guard!" The soldier sheathed his sword but slammed his fist against his chest to make his point.

"Fine. We'll get to that later." Clive unwrapped my hand. "Fyr, bring me a basin of clean water." He stared into my eyes. "And a glass of juice. She's lost a lot of blood." He turned to Owen. "Is Lilah on her way?"

Owen was still on the phone but nodded.

Fyr returned with a bowl of water, which Clive guided my hand into before washing sand and grit from the wound.

"At least it's my left hand this time," I said. Of course, now both my hands were messed up.

"Small favors," he said to me. "We need bandages."

I nodded toward the end of the bar. "I put the kit back under the bar near Grim."

Clive lifted my hand and ran his tongue over the wound, helping to heal it. "Still salty," he said, brow furrowed. "Fyr, please clean this out and get me fresh water."

Bumping him with my other hand, I whispered, "Nice job with the 'please.' "

Shoulders relaxing, he looked up into my eyes, cupping my face with his left hand. "How are you feeling?"

"Still lightheaded, but mostly okay." I gulped down the juice Fyr dropped off when he brought Clive fresh water. "Wouldn't it be easier to use the sink and let the water run over it?"

"It would. Are you able to stand?"

I shrugged. "Probably."

"Good enough. We'll give it a try." Considering Clive all but carried me to the kitchen, I didn't think my ability to stand made much difference. Once in the kitchen, away from the others, the water running over the wound, he spoke to me, mind to mind.

*This bite pattern looks familiar. What's been happening, and how was a kelpie involved?*

*No idea. The bastards really hate me. You know, I just realized we haven't considered a fae-demon alliance.*

*Don't the fae hate demons?* He was so gentle, cleaning the last of the salt and grit from my wounds.

*Sure, but they hate vampires too, and that didn't stop Finvarra from using one to weaken Gloriana.*

*True. We'll keep that option open.*

I gave him an abbreviated recounting of Algar and Fangorn, of the Biergarten of the Damned, Dave, and the other demons, and then the run and the kelpie. Told all together, it had been a pretty busy day. I didn't want to go into too much detail, as Clive was already upset and he needed to go back to the nocturne to help Russell.

*Did it work? Did the nocturne keep you safe from Sitri?*

*Not sure, but I did awaken feeling stronger than I have in while, so most likely.*

*Good. You need to stay again after the blood ceremony until we figure out what to do about Sitri.*

Clive had already begun shaking his head. *No. They'll be fine without me.* Concentrating on my hand, he finished washing it clean.

*Clive—*

*Damn it, Sam, do you actually expect me to hide, leaving you vulnerable to a demon or fae attack?* He licked the wound again. *Clean.*

*You can't ask me to trade your safety for mine.*

*Right back atcha, darling.* He stared me down a moment and then pulled his phone out and tapped the screen. "Russell, might I impose on your hospitality and ask that I be allowed to bring my wife with me?"

"Of course. Is there a problem?"

I missed Russell.

"When isn't there a problem?" Clive said, shaking his head.

I smacked him in the abdomen, but he didn't flinch.

"Russell?" As I could hear both sides of the conversation, I decided to jump in.

"Yes, my lady?"

Ha! Now I had two people calling me *my lady*. "Also, if you wouldn't mind, could I get another one of those spare phones? Mine went in the ocean."

"They were purchased for you."

"Great! Oh, and can you not tell Godfrey? I'll never hear the end of it."

"While I would love nothing more than to help you in any way I can, I'm afraid I can't do that."

My stomach sank. "He's listening, isn't he?"

"Both Godfrey and Audrey are with me and now aware you've destroyed another phone."

"He's laughing, isn't he?"

"I'm afraid so."

Sighing, I thunked my head against Clive's shoulder. He pulled me in close and kissed my head. *Shit.* I just remembered. "Russell, there's one more thing."

"Yes?"

"I'll need to bring my Orc with me." I looked up at Clive. "There's no way he'll stay here without me."

Clive closed his eyes a moment and then nodded.

"I'm sorry your—what do you need to bring?"

"A soldier, one of the queen's guards. I don't know if Orc is a real fae designation or something Tolkien created. He reminds me of one, though, so—anyway, he's the one we rescued from Aldith's dungeon. He's sworn to protect me now. There's no way he'll stay here if I leave."

Fangorn pushed into the kitchen and roared, "I guard!"

Godfrey's laughter was crystal clear through the phone. Perfect.

Luckily the blood ceremony didn't begin until midnight. I took over at the bar so Owen could leave. Lilah came and worked on my hand, rebandaging it when she was done. She said the right one looked like it was coming along fine. Fyr was nice enough to stay and work late with me. We took turns breaking for dinner, after Clive went out to get us food. At eleven, though, I booted the last few patrons and closed early. Clive needed to help Russell get ready.

While Clive had been out picking up our dinners, he'd swung by the nocturne and switched his roadster for a Land Rover. There was no way Fangorn was fitting in his sports car. As it was, we had to move the front seat all the way back and then tip it to give the soldier more room. At least it wouldn't be a long drive. I put the backpack I used as Fergus' overnight bag on the floor of the vehicle and held the long-legged pup in my lap while Clive drove.

When we pulled up, the vamps on the gate still inclined their heads to Clive, though the soldier and I were getting a heavy dose of side-eye as he drove past. Instead of leaving his SUV parked in front, like a visitor, Clive drove around back to the garage.

Okay, I'll admit it. I missed the place. Not most of the vamps, but the mansion, the stocked kitchen, Russell, Godfrey, Audrey, Norma, our rooms, the library, the closets, his office… I was glad it was okay for us to visit.

We were met in the hall outside the garage by Godfrey, who scooped up Fergus and held him under his arm. Godfrey's grin was a mile wide as he took in my seven-and-a-half-foot tall protector.

"Welcome to the nocturne. It's nice to see you again, Missus." He looked me up and down, taking in the axe and sword. "Nice blades. I must say, it's been a right bore without you."

"Don't let Russell hear you say that." I'd missed them so much. Maybe this was part of why Clive was feeling off. He still talked with them all the time, but it wasn't the same.

Godfrey returned Fergus to the floor. "Go find the Master." As Fergus wandered away, sniffing madly, Godfrey said, "Now that you're not the Master's woman, can I have a hug?"

I leapt forward and hugged him as hard as I could. It was good that vampires didn't need to breathe.

Godfrey patted my back. "And are you going to introduce me to your new friend?"

"Sorry, sorry." I pulled away and motioned to my soldier. "Godfrey, allow me to introduce Fangorn, one of the queen's most loyal soldiers. Fangorn, this is Godfrey. He is the Master of San Francisco's…second? Third?" I looked to Godfrey.

He held up three fingers.

Shaking my head, I said, "The Master of San Francisco's third. He's dead useful in a pinch, but other than that, isn't terribly into it."

Nodding, Godfrey said, "Fair. Come, I'll take you in."

We were brought to the study. Much of it was the same, but all the little treasures on the shelves were different. They reflected Russell now. Audrey nodded to us; gone were the days of the hesitant curtsy, thank goodness.

"Audrey, it's lovely to see you." When I held out my hand, she shook it and smiled.

"And you, Mrs. Fitzwilliam. I'm told you'll be staying with us tonight. Please let me know if you'll be needing anything."

Nodding, I turned to Russell, standing behind his desk to greet us with Fergus under his arm.

"My lady." His voice, a deep, comforting rumble, brought tears to my eyes.

I didn't check to make sure it was okay. I went to him, and he thankfully held an arm out for me, the pup getting squished between us.

"Godfrey is correct. It's been rather dull without you bringing home trouble all the time." He gave me a squeeze and then let go.

"To be fair," I answered, wiping my eyes, "only half the trouble was mine. The other half was his." I pointed at Clive, who looked happier than I'd seen him in weeks. Oh, no. He was regretting leaving his position and the nocturne.

*No, love. I'm just happy to spend time with my wife and my friends.*

"Oh, Russell, Audrey, this is Fangorn, one of the queen's soldiers who's acting as my bodyguard until the queen needs him back. Fangorn, this is Russell, the Master of San Francisco, and Audrey, his second in command."

"Yes, of course," Russell began, "you may not remember but—"

"You carried me," Fangorn rumbled, referring to his rescue from Aldith.

In Aldith's dungeon, I'd questioned whether or not to release the Orc, as the ones I'd met before had all tried to kill me. I couldn't leave him the way he was, though, tortured horribly, so I took the chance and broke him out. Russell had picked up the mountain-sized fae and carried him to freedom while I'd moved on to the next cell.

"Yes, and then Sam supported you and got you through the doorway back into Faerie." Fergus pawed the air, so Russell put him down.

His gaze cut to me at my quiet intake of air. "I do know your name, my lady." Russell's smile was a rare and powerful thing.

I felt a tug of emotion behind me. When I turned, I found Audrey staring at Russell. Aww, she still had it bad for the big lug.

"Shall we sit?" Russell slid behind his desk while Audrey and Godfrey moved to the chairs before it. Clive joined me on my bench by the wall and Fangorn stood sentry by the door. Opening the backpack, I pulled out a chew stick for Fergus. He dropped to our feet, pinned the stick between his paws, and chewed contentedly, ignoring us.

"Perhaps you should catch us up on what's been happening, so we can help," Russell said.

I ran down most of what had been going on the last few days. It never hurt to make allies aware, so they'd know when we needed them to jump in.

"Sire," Godfrey began, "we should really ask them to move back in." He shook his head, clearly delighted. "When was the last time we had a good demon throwdown? Why should *they* have all the fun?"

I had to admit, it was jolting to hear Godfrey call someone other than Clive *Sire*.

*I'm still getting used to it myself.*

# 18

# Pick a Color

"Clive and Sam should know they will always have a home here, though I imagine we'll soon be the ones asking to move into theirs," Russell said.

"Too right," Godfrey responded. "Have you had a peek at the construction yet?" He adjusted his chair to have both Clive and Russell in his sights.

I'd imagine the change in management was even more difficult for Godfrey. He and Clive had been friends for four or five hundred years. Godfrey had gone off to live elsewhere in the world, like when he lived in York at Bram's nocturne, but he always eventually returned to Clive. Swearing his allegiance to Russell rather than moving on again said a lot about Russell, and Godfrey's loyalty to him. Still, it had to be odd.

"The house on Seal Rock," Clive began, "yes. Our new folly? No. The dragons don't like to be reminded that they're working for a vampire and a werewolf."

"I've sneaked peeks."

Clive turned, eyebrows raised. "You never said."

"You said you didn't need to know the step-by-step, that you were looking forward to seeing the finished folly." I shrugged. "So, I didn't tell you."

"Well?" Godfrey leaned in. "How is it looking?"

"The first area closest to The Slaughtered Lamb is the Shire." I had a hard time holding in the giddy trying to bubble up. "I took a couple of pics because I didn't see any of the workers, but…"

Godfrey had just reached for the phone when he remembered. "Sire, can you hand me one of her spares? I'll begin setup. The photos should be in her account. Tell us while I do this," he said, tearing open the phone box Russell had slid across his desk.

"Rolling hills of tall grass, a dirt path cut through the countryside, a cart with what absolutely looks like a live horse. He tossed his head and stamped a hoof during my extended peek. A beautiful, clear pond near the door, so I was looking over that to the hillside." I couldn't stop smiling. "Round wooden doors in different colors were dotted along a tall hill topped by a huge tree, its branches so long they shaded all the hobbit holes."

"Blue," Godfrey said. "I've always liked blue. I claim the blue door."

"Okay! We get the green one, because that's Bilbo's door—and it was the grandest one on the hillside." I turned to Clive. "We even have this incredible door garden with every manner of flowering plant." Looking to Russell, I asked, "What's your favorite color?"

"Blue, but it's already been claimed."

When Godfrey opened his mouth, no doubt to offer it to Russell, I cut him off. "There are two blue doors, one light, one dark. There was also red, yellow, brown, and what looked to be more of a purple."

Russell said, "Light," at the same time Godfrey said, "Dark."

"Perfect." I looked at Audrey. "And which color do you want?"

She waved a hand and shook her head. "Oh, no. It wouldn't be fittin', ma'am."

"Audrey." Russell said the word quietly, and she straightened her spine.

"I like yellow."

"Then yellow it shall be!" I said, laughing, trying to smooth over her brief lapse back into servitude. I glanced over at Godfrey, who appeared to be scrolling through my pictures. "Hey, don't you need my password or something to get in there?"

Scoffing, he shook his head. "We all know your passwords, Missus. You're not exactly sneaky. The dog lives with you. Do you really need this many pictures of him?"

When I stood to retrieve it, he waved me back down. "Found them. My word. This is enchanting." Standing, he went behind the desk to show Russell. "Look, Sire. Our homes are on opposite sides. Audrey, yours is beside our Master's."

Audrey moved to stand beside Godfrey, both looking over Russell's shoulder as he scrolled through the pictures.

I nudged Clive's shoulder with my own. "Do you still want to wait or do you want to see?"

"Well, I can't very well have this lot know more about my folly than I do." He nodded to Russell, who tossed him the phone. Scrolling through, he picked up my hand and kissed it. "It's perfect, isn't it?"

"It really is!"

"Have you noticed," Godfrey began, "is there a time when all the little dragons go home to sleep? I'd love to wander through the other rooms."

I shook my head. "They have crews working around the clock."

"Do they come through the bar to get to the worksite?" Audrey asked. It was lovely to have her participating.

"They don't come through at all. They have their own magical entrance and I have no idea where it is. I've only heard of one dragon coming out on my side to have a beer with Fyr and George before going back to work. From what George has said, they only agreed to the job because both Benvair and Clive were paying them. For double an already exorbitant fee, they'll ignore who they're building for."

Clive stretched out his legs, crossing them at the ankles. "Ah, well. It's only money."

Russell leaned back in his chair, watching Clive. "So, this business with the demons—"

"No names," I jumped in.

He nodded. "The one who took an interest in you today at the Biergarten, his connection was to Dave?"

"I'm not sure," I said. "I don't know if he approached us because of Dave or if he used Dave as a reason to approach."

Tapping his fingers on the desk, he considered. "When we were in Wales, George said Dave was having issues with demons coming in to harass him and that Dave escorted them out, often not coming back himself, right?"

I nodded.

"And today the demon said something about Dave crying to his daddy. Is that correct?"

"Yes."

"So," he asked, looking around the room, "do we know who Dave's father is?"

"One would assume a demon," Clive said. "I believe, much like vampires and werewolves, there are more male than female demons. Just playing the odds, if it's Dave's father who is the demon and this one you met used the phrase, 'Crying to daddy,' I'd assume he's known Dave since childhood."

"Which would indicate," Godfrey began, "there are toddler demons. Adolescents with spots on their chins and hair sprouting on their bodies."

Pushing aside the horror of a childhood in Hell, I tried to find an error in Clive's logic and couldn't. "It is an odd phrase for an adult to use. I could see it if Dave were an infantile man-child, but he's not. So if it's not Dave acting childlike, it's the goat-man using a phrase from their childhood?"

"Stands to reason," Godfrey volunteered.

"Which brings us back to who's Dave's dad?" I asked.

"No idea," Clive said. "He came to me when we were still building The Slaughtered Lamb and asked for a job."

I grabbed Clive's arm. "You didn't already know him?"

Clive shook his head. "No. Demons don't fall under the Master's purview. When he asked to work with you, I was suspicious. How did he know about your bookstore bar? I asked and he said he knew a workman. I asked one of my people to check it out."

"Who?" Russell asked.

"Stephen."

"Okay," he nodded, still considering.

"Stephen reported that one of the construction workers had talked about the job with a bouncer at a South of Market nightclub. He said he hadn't given specifics, but the description of the bouncer sounded like Dave. We checked the nightclub—which is demon-owned—but they had a new bouncer. The people there said they couldn't remember the last guy's name or where he went."

"Payroll?" Russell asked.

"No paperwork," Clive responded. "But if it's demon-owned, they're not going to inform on one of their own."

"Well, that sounds pretty shady," I said, pulling my feet up to the bench and wrapping my arms around my legs. "Was it really all a setup? He said today that he'd been paid to watch me. The job ended, so he left." I turned to Clive, whispering, "That's not true, is it?"

Clive rested his hand on my knee but didn't answer. "He seemed trustworthy. I can't say now why I felt that way, but I did then and have since. As you recall, I sent a vampire to guard you as well, in case I'd read him wrong."

"I remember. Fucking kelpies," I muttered, staring at my bandaged hand.

"Couldn't agree more, darling. Dave was consistent and helpful, in his own angry, profanity-laden way. And then you hired Owen. Looking back on it now, I have no idea why I trusted him with you." He shook his head. "There was an earnestness there that I believed."

I took his hand in my mostly good one and squeezed. "I

believed him too. Right from the beginning. He's a surly SOB with anger management issues, but I loved him. Still do." I dropped my legs to the floor and pulled Clive's hand into my lap. "My banking accounts are connected to yours, right? He's been doing my banking right from the start."

Clive pulled out his phone and swiped through screens and accounts. Finally, he shook his head. "Our personal accounts are correct." He continued to tap. "The Slaughtered Lamb runs pretty close to the bone, as I recall. You make enough to pay everyone and cover expenses, but not too much more than that."

His brow furrowed and he tapped again. "Well, this is odd."

"Am I broke? I mean more broke than usual?" This didn't feel real, any of it. Dave had been my cranky friend from the beginning. How could I have been so wrong about him?

"On the contrary. You have about seven million more in your account than you should."

Godfrey whistled.

My head snapped back like I'd been hit. "I what?"

"A deposit was made about the time we were married. There's a note attached to the deposit that says, 'In case you need to survive on your own.' " Clive studied me. "That's not the act of someone spying for an employer."

"That's assuming Dave was the one who made the deposit," Godfrey said.

Staring down at Clive's hand in mine, I said, "We need answers."

"We do," he agreed.

Godfrey popped up. "Yes! Let's go storm this demon bar and get some answers."

Stomach in knots, I grinned at Godfrey's excitement to stir up shit. "You guys have a vampy blood thingy starting soon."

"Really, darling," Clive murmured. "You know how I feel about that word."

I grinned and, out of the corner of my eye, caught Russell smiling too.

"Oh." Godfrey dropped back into his chair. "Sorry, Sire. I forgot. I've never visited a demon biergarten before. It sounded like fun."

Clive pulled our entwined fingers into his lap. "We need to prepare for the ceremony now. Our room is on the third floor again. At the top of the stairs, turn right, rather than left. We're in the first room on the right."

Turning to Russell, I said, "Thank you again for letting us stay here."

"Of course. You'll have the nocturne to yourself this evening. There are still some foodstuffs in the kitchen cabinets, if you get hungry. You can check the progress of the library reconstruction, if you'd like."

I jumped up. "Yes! You guys go do whatever you do. The books call."

Clive stood with me and pulled me in for a hug. *I'm nearby if you need me.* He gave me a soft kiss. *Have fun with the books. I'll join you before dawn.*

"Okay. Have fun vamping out. Stay safe, Russell."

He rose, saying, "I'll keep them all safe."

"I know you will." I grabbed the backpack and left, Fergus at my heels, Fangorn bringing up the rear. Deciding a snack wouldn't hurt, I detoured to the kitchen before exploring the library. I hated thinking about how much of it had been blown to bits. Stupid Aldith sending stupid assassins with bombs. And stupid Liang redirecting the freaking bomb right at me while I read in the library. I mean, okay, sure, she wanted Clive back and me out. I got that, but enough to destroy a library? P'fft. Psycho.

## 19

# Speak of the Devil

I loved Norma! Even when I didn't live here, the woman was hooking me up. I found an unopened package of the chocolate caramel shortbread cookies I loved. There was even fresh milk in the fridge, maybe for her coffee. Didn't matter.

"Are you hungry?"

Fangorn glanced at the packaged food and made a face, shaking his head.

"Listen, it's late and I'm just going to hang out in the library before going to bed. Why don't you go outside and rest? The grounds are extensive for San Francisco. I'm sure you can find a nice spot to sleep."

He gazed out the window and then back at me. He nodded once, said, "I sleep," and then left.

I grabbed the cookies, poured a tall glass of milk, and went down the hall, Fergus trotting along, exploring open doorways. I was nervous about opening the library door. How much had they been able to do in a month?

Gathering my courage, I mentally prepared myself for the scorched floor, the missing shelves. At least the hall wall had been replaced. I ran my fingers over the carved wood door. It was exquisite. Good. They were taking their time and doing it right.

When I walked in, I almost dropped the milk and cookies. They were done and it was perfect. Little changes here and there, but perfect! The shelves with little brass tags identifying the subject matter were back and the damaged books replaced, but there were subtle changes as well. The marble fireplace I'd been thrown into was now an echo of the main door. Vines and blossoms had been carved into both the door and fireplace. The craftsmanship was staggering.

The furniture had been replaced, including the overhead lights. Instead of the glittering crystal chandeliers that had been here, he had oversized blown glass light fixtures, like the ones Benvair had in her home. Again, they echoed the vines and blossoms of the door and fireplace. My heart hurt, it was all so incredibly beautiful. Our new library at our home needed to look like this.

Even my window seat had been given a makeover. The cushions and pillows were now done in a variety of greens, the curtains continuing the vine and blossom theme, with delicate embroidered flowers in whites and peaches and yellows and pinks, all against a mossy background.

I put the cookies in the crook of my arm and then pulled out my phone. I wanted to record it all. I spun in slow motion, not wanting to miss a detail. When I circled back around to the conversation area, there was a man sitting in one of the chairs.

Yelping, I dropped the phone. My heart stopped; just flat-out seized. All the vamps were downstairs. I'd felt it when they'd moved en masse. I didn't know who this guy was, but he wasn't a vamp. *Shitshitshit.*

Fergus stood between my legs, barking wildly at the strange man. When I leaned over to retrieve the phone, he said, "Don't spill the milk." He didn't appear angry or vengeful, just a powerful man in a pleasant mood who didn't want me to accidentally make a mess.

Rising, he came to me. Eyes, dark and magnetic, tried to draw me in. He wore his hair shorn close, his skin tone darker than

Irdu's. His dark gray suit was perfectly tailored, a small red silk square in the chest pocket.

"Let me help you." He gently relieved me of the cookies and milk, bringing them back to the coffee table, before resuming his seat. When Fergus continued to bark, the man put a finger over his lips and my pup went silent.

Head spinning, I bent to grab my phone, closing my eyes and finding his blip in my head. Unrelieved black, like Dave. A demon. "I thought the nocturne's magic kept demons out."

"It does," he said.

"But…" If he wasn't a demon, what the hell was he?

"Nothing keeps me out, child. Come," he said, waving me over. "Let's chat."

I took a step back. *Clive!*

"He can't hear us. You've nothing to worry about, I promise. There are rules, you know." He crossed his legs and studied the library. "I wouldn't mind having a library like this myself."

"What rules?" I couldn't keep the tremble from my voice.

"Hmm? Oh, let's see… Far too many to go into tonight, but the most important from your perspective is probably that we can't hurt innocents." It felt like his eyes were boring into my soul. I tried every mind block I'd been taught. Nothing seemed to work.

Clearing my throat, I said, "I beg to differ."

"From what I've been told, Olivier didn't do much today. Nothing more than scare you, anyway. Your wrist only hurt when you were in Hell-adjacent places, as you refer to them. It doesn't hurt now, does it?"

Oh. I hadn't even realized. I'd been so freaked out by the whole thing, I hadn't noticed that the pain had disappeared when we'd walked outside. "What about Sitri?"

"What about him?" he asked, mildly curious.

I remembered my first visit to the Demon's Lair, how he'd played on my trauma. It was like a different kind of rape. And now his torture of Clive, his attempt to kill me in the church. As I tried to find the right words to explain what we'd been going through, the man's face became a mask of rage.

Walking slowly backward, I tried to make my escape. Mid-step, I'd been transported across the library, my heel hitting the base of the couch. I plopped down to sit across from a very angry demon. *Shitshitshit.*

Fergus yelped and then raced across the rug to sit on the floor by my legs, protecting me from the well-dressed demon.

Drumming his fingers on the arm of his chair, he said, "We have rules, as I said. One look at you should have told him you were off limits. I will see to Sitri, and in a way that will keep him out of your lives."

"Thank you." If he did it, that is. He was a demon, after all. He could be promising exactly what I wanted to draw me in and more easily manipulate me. "I'm not an innocent. I mean, I've killed lots of people." I was feeling pretty queasy about that right now. "And I swear. I've had sex. Um—"

He raised his hand. "Let me stop you, though your list is adorable. You've killed supernatural creatures who were trying to kill you and your loved ones."

"But—"

"You might get dinged for murder upstairs—they're all about turning the other cheek up there, which is idiotic. If someone has already proven they can't be trusted, why in His name would you give them another chance to hurt you?" He shook his head. "Regardless, downstairs we take a more tolerant stance on killing in self-defense. It's not evil, it's smart.

"As for swearing." He flicked his fingers. "In word or deed, did you denigrate or demoralize another? Did you push someone into devaluing their gifts and talents, their life? Did you hurt another and feel a thrill at your power to do so?"

I began to scroll back through my life, considering how my words may have hit someone in a way I hadn't intended. Perhaps I'd—

"I'll save you the trouble. You haven't. As for sex, don't be ridiculous. First of all, sex is our main selling point. It's usually the reason people want to join us. And the only person you've had sex with, you married. All of that means you're off limits. We know when we look at humans which of them are open to seduction and manipulation, are willing to sink into cruelty and depravity in order to get what they want. In short, who will sacrifice another's safety and well-being for personal gain.

"Your husband, now that's another story. While he does have his own brand of ethics, he's never shied away from a fight. Most of his long life, he's been more of a *kill now and ask questions later* kind of guy. Like us, he doesn't hurt innocents, though." He paused, studying me. "Shall I tell you what I know about Clive?"

Shaking my head, I said, "No. I know my husband. He's a good man. And if, at the end of this rollercoaster, I end up in Heaven, I'm making sure he gets in with me. He might think he's soulless, but I know better."

"And if that doesn't work?" he asked, expression curious.

"I guess I'll be petitioning to move into your place."

A glass with two fingers of whiskey suddenly appeared in his hand. He took a sip. "I had wondered if my son had some sort of romantic attachment to you, but I don't think that's it."

His son? Sitr—no. "You're Dave's dad."

"I am," he said solemnly.

"No. There's nothing like that between us. He has a—" I shook my head. "No romance." *Shit.* If Dave didn't want his dad to know he had a girlfriend, assuming he did in fact send her away from all the demon drama, I didn't want to be the one to spill it.

"A girlfriend? There was a banshee he was seeing years ago… He's still with her or is there a new one?" He tilted his head, watching me.

Slapping a hand over my forehead, I said, "I get this is total comeuppance, since I can do this to vamps, but please stop reading my mind. I have too many people's secrets up here. Shouldn't this be part of the not-preying-on-innocents thing?"

"Hmm, perhaps." His fingers began drumming again as he

seemed to be trying to figure out how to get around the rule. "I want to know about my son's life."

"You could ask him. And Dave is more like my cranky uncle. He's been my cook since I opened the bookstore and bar. He always makes sure I'm fed and take breaks. Just recently, he taught me how to drive. Your son's a good person, though he'd prefer people didn't know that."

"Didn't he recently quit, walk out, burn you, tell you that friendship you believe exists was a fantasy?"

Slapping my other hand over my forehead, I said, "No." We stared each other down a moment. "Okay, fine. He said those things, but he didn't mean them. I'm almost positive. And the burn was my fault."

"Didn't he try to choke the life out of you while, again, burning your neck a short time ago?"

"Jeez, do you have a nanny cam stuffed in the corner of my bar?" Cringing internally, I thought about that time Clive and I…I *really* hoped there were no cameras. "The choking thing was my aunt's fault. She was on the homicidal sorcerer branch of my family tree. She worked on him until she broke through his defenses.

"Hey, it was one of your guys who took her away. She should be living in your neck of the woods now." *Damn.* That meant I *had* to get Clive into Heaven. There was no way I was dealing with Abigail for all eternity.

"And," I continued, "I was the one who grabbed your son's arm when I knew he was super pissed. I shouldn't have touched him."

"Your aunt was a sorceress? Quinn isn't a wicche line I'm aware of. It is the original werewolf line, though." He finished his drink and the glass disappeared.

"Corey," I said.

He became laser focused. "Is that so?"

Dropping my hands from my head, I nodded. Who was I kidding? I couldn't keep him out. At least if he was grilling me about me, he wasn't forcing me to divulge information about my friends. "My mother was a Corey wicche, my father a Quinn wolf."

"Aren't you the little rarity. A wicche-werewolf married to a vampire."

I shrugged.

"The Corey wicches are one of the oldest and most powerful wicche lines in the world, along with Waterhouse, Liu, Lemnos, Hemmah," he trailed off. "Coreys have unique gifts, even amongst wicches," he murmured. "It has to mean something. Fifteen hundred years. Another continent. But still a Corey." He drummed his fingers on the armrest, studying me. "And why do you wear a fae ring on your finger?"

"How did you—but the fae aren't a part of your religious tradition. Or did you just pluck that out of my head?" Dave's dad was a super scary dude, but he wasn't like Sitri or Olivier. Being near him didn't nauseate me. Scared the shit out of me, sure, but didn't nauseate me.

"Why?" he pushed.

"I had to go into Faerie to deliver a message."

His eyebrows went up at that.

"Gloriana took a liking to the opal engagement ring Clive had given me, so she asked to exchange rings. I mean, it's not like you tell the queen no when she's got a dozen of her warriors with very big swords surrounding you."

He glanced over at the fireplace, and it burst into flame. Tapping his finger on his chin, he wondered aloud. "But why give you her own ring? She could have just taken yours. Why bother with the exchange?" He turned back to me, resting his chin in his hand, as though waiting for a story. "You know why, don't you?"

I didn't know what to do. He was a demon and seemed to be a pretty high-ranking one if he could take care of Sitri for us, so demon but not a total dick. He was Dave's father, but Dave hid details of his life from him. He could easily pluck the answer from my head but seemed to be giving me some privacy. Or he was faking all this not-knowing business to screw with me and try to forge some kind of imaginary bond in order to get what he really wanted.

I knew if I asked any of my friends, they'd tell me to keep my trap shut, but he seemed trustworthy. Yes, a demon, but...not evil? Or I was a trusting moron who deserved everything coming my way.

# 20

# Villain Origin Story

"The queen said the wicche who created the first werewolf used fae magic to do so. She took an interest in me, as anyone with a drop of fae blood is one of hers. Or so she said."

He held his hand out to me. "Might I have your hand?"

I shook my head. "No, thank you."

Waiting, hand held out, his power swamped me like one of the waves that tried to take me under earlier today. He might have been waiting, but not patiently.

I tucked my hands under my arms and shook my head.

Dropping his hand, he said, "You're infuriatingly cute."

"Thanks?"

His head fell back and he released a deep gust of breath. "Perhaps if I explained some of my story as it relates to my son, you'll understand why I'm here."

"As much as I would love answers, I'd rather get them directly from Dave. I don't like talking about him when he isn't here. And respectfully, sir, if Dave doesn't trust you, I don't think I should." As my fingers hadn't stopped trembling since he arrived, I kept my hands jammed in my pits.

"Noted. Many years ago, in the Dark Ages, there was a woman living in a hovel at the edge of a village. She was young and beautiful and therefore suspect. The villagers weren't sure what to make of her, as she was a widow with a young son and yet quite content on her own, much to the frustration of local men.

"Years earlier, you see, her husband, a cruel, brutal man, had purchased her from her father, a man very much like himself. She'd been twelve and had a spark that drew people to her. She had long, dark hair and big green eyes, like your own, and she had a way with plants and animals.

"Her mother had passed the previous winter in childbirth. Both mother and babe were barely in the ground when her father started watching her. As one thing led to another and she was, after all, his property, he began to use her as he had his wife, forgetting the difference between a wife and a daughter.

"She lost her light, lost that spark that drew others, that made them feel special to have been singled out by one so extraordinary. The villagers knew or suspected what was happening, but what was there to do? She belonged to him. When she was seen in the village with dark bruises or a split lip, the villagers mumbled behind their hands. It wasn't right. The beautiful child who had captured their hearts had been dulled and broken. In the same way nasty little boys pull wings off butterflies, the father destroyed the extraordinary because he could, leaving behind the damaged and ordinary.

"When the child had missed her courses three months in a row, the father knew something had to be done. He made her clean and dress in her mother's best dress, hitched up the cart, and drove them a day's journey away, to a village where he was not known. He left his daughter sitting on the cart bench, on display, while he visited a tavern. There he found a man in need of a wife and plied him with liquor until he presumed the man ready to negotiate a bride price.

"Now, some of the other men in this village observed what was happening, but as the probable groom was universally despised, they didn't intervene. The villagers had studied the girl sitting atop the cart outside the tavern. They discerned beauty under the bruises, but they also noticed the skittish way she turned her face away at a friendly word, the way she ducked her head, kept her fingers knotted tightly in her lap, knuckles white. They knew a kicked dog when they saw one. The probable groom was rich and powerful, relatively speaking, and had cheated the other farmers on crop prices at harvest, so the villagers were hoping he'd be duped, as they had been.

"When the man stumbled out to get a look at the child, he beheld only the young willowy body, ripe for the taking. The hunched shoulders and fading bruises meant that she wasn't headstrong. A biddable wife was a man's greatest treasure.

"A price was agreed upon and the child was left in a new village of strangers with only the clothes on her back. Whatever hopes the child may have had of a better life were stripped and beaten out of her that first night. Soon, when she began to show, the new husband knew he had been cheated and beat the girl within an inch of life, because she was at hand and her father long gone."

The demon shifted his focus from the fire to me. I wasn't sure what he recognized in my expression, but he leaned over and patted my knee. "The villagers whispered behind their hands and laughed outright in the tavern. The husband took his humiliation out on the child, as she was the root of it.

"Thankfully for her, the husband was away from home working much of the day. When alone, the child found solace in the garden, helping young plants to grow and thrive. Far too soon, though, he would return, and her life narrowed to subservience and pain.

"After walking into the tavern to raucous laughter, for it only to be pointedly hushed upon seeing him, the man returned home in a rage. He found his wife, heavy with child, chopping vegetables for the midday meal, and exorcized that stinging humiliation with his fists, leaving her bloody and broken on the floor, her uterus contracting.

"Terrified, broken, in horrible pain, she lay on the floor in labor.

One and then two village women who'd heard the screaming cautiously came to help, always looking over their shoulders at the open door, afraid her husband's shadow would darken it.

"When the tiny babe arrived, still and silent, the women made signs to ward off evil, knowing their own husbands would see the young woman as cursed and themselves now in danger of suffering the same fate. They left a cup of water and placed a rag between her legs, but left as quickly as possible, both looking guilty for having run to her aid.

"The child, who had been looking forward to the babe, to having someone to love, curled in on herself and waited to die. It couldn't be long. Instead, she slept. When she woke in full dark, she realized her husband had not returned and that the women had left the dead babe wrapped in rags beside her.

"Hoping she'd soon be dying of her injuries, she eventually got unsteadily to her feet, legs covered in dried blood, and picked up the roll of rags, stumbling out the door to her garden. Using a small spade, she slowly dug a hole. Unable to stand for long, she dropped to her knees and continued to dig down with her fingers. When she knew she was close to losing consciousness again, she placed the small bundle in the hole and covered it as best she could, saying a prayer for her little one to be received into God's arms.

"She awoke in the warmth of midday to a kick. When she stirred, he complained the meal hadn't been prepared. Lost in pain and grief, she pushed herself to her knees and discovered a plant had grown where her babe had been buried. It wasn't possible. It had only been a few hours. She knew, though, looking at the unfamiliar plant, what needed to be done.

"Breaking off a stalk, she carried it into the cottage, one hand on walls and table to stay upright. The stew she had been making the previous day had been simmering all night. She stirred it, not caring if it had scorched or spiders had dropped in, not caring about anything but the plant in her hand.

"She used a mortar and pestle to grind the plant into a thick paste. Once the stew was bubbling again, she ladled up a hearty serving and stirred in the green paste. She found him sitting on the porch steps, dark sweat stains on his back and under his arms.

"The child handed her husband his death and then shuffled inside to lay on her mattress. When she woke hours later, it was dark and relievedly silent. No snores, no grunts, no heavy breathing, no boots stomping, no curses shouted, no smacking lips, no gas passing, no doors slamming, no fists landing. Silence.

"She lay in a haze, contemplating the noise of a life. As Death had chosen yet again to overlook her, she got out of bed to clean up her mess. She went first to the porch and found her husband lying on the ground, dried blood on his lips, a pool of sick under his head.

"She'd known what the plant would do. It didn't matter that she'd never seen it before or been taught its properties. She'd known." He broke the trance and looked at me. "A murderer, yes? Did she deserve Hell?"

I wiped my face dry, shaking my head, my throat too tight to speak. Fergus crawled up into my lap. Already too big to fit, most of him slid off to the couch cushion, but I had my pup to hold.

He turned back to the fire. "She got her spade and began to dig near her husband's body. She knew she'd never be able to drag him anywhere, but she thought she could roll him a short distance. In her fragile state, she struggled, needing to take frequent breaks. Eventually, though, she finished her digging and kicked him in, finding some small satisfaction in that final act. She covered him over and dragged herself back into the house to once again collapse into sleep.

"The following day when she rose, she had a plan. It wouldn't take long for the village to brand her a murderer as well as a wanton. She needed to start over where no one knew her. She set out to clean herself in the stream. When she went down the front steps, she found a large shrubbery with dark green leaves and delicate white blossoms stood over the spot where her husband had been buried.

"Running her fingertips over a petal, she set off for the shady stream. When she arrived, she looked down into the water and was met with her reflection. Had she not known she was seeing herself, she would have screamed at the horror looking back at her. She took off her boots and stepped into the stream, sliding on rocks and sinking into silt, until she reached the middle. There she laid down and submerged herself.

"Cold, clear water rushed over her, from head to toe. The depth was such that her mouth and nose remained above the surface. While the cold water was a shock at first, she soon became accustomed to it, even welcoming the cold.

"Each moment she lay there, the water washed away the hurt and derision, the neglect and cruelty, left on her by others. When she finally stood, impervious to the cold, she knew what she was capable of and how far she was willing to go to keep herself safe.

"She spent the day collecting seeds and slips of plants she wanted to take with her, including the one that had changed her life. She hitched the horse to the cart, drove it close to the front door, and then began sorting through the cottage, looking for what she'd need in this new life. She kept much of what had been in the kitchen and ignored that remaining in the bedroom. As much as she would have liked to walk away clean, she understood that wasn't sensible. She took blankets and clothes, a small table and two chairs. When the sun began to set, she took one last look around and wiggled the brick in the fireplace she'd spied her husband move a time or two. Behind it, she found his leather pouch weighed down with the coins he'd taken from her father and cheated from his neighbors.

"The world can be a dangerous place for a woman alone, but not quite alone enough. The child knew that better than most. She drove the cart, and what were now her belongings, far from the village under the cover of night. Following the stream as best she could, she slept during the day before continuing west at moonrise.

"Ever alert, she listened intently to any sound not the clop of hooves or the bump and jar of the cart. She knew if she were caught, she'd feel fists again, hear the pant and grunt in her ear. In the wee hours of the third night, she knew she needed to hide. She didn't know how she knew, but she knew. Pulling the reins, she directed the horse off the narrow path, deep into the woods.

"When she heard the clop of two horses in the distance, her heart stopped. She wasn't sure why, but what one man might feel hesitant to do, two men reveled in. Not wanting to be caught all alone by two men, she eased herself out of the cart, in case she needed to run, and spotted the ruts in the tall grass from the cart's wheels. Dropping to her knees, she dug her fingers into the ground and called upon that connection she had with plants and animals, asking them to hide her.

"She opened her eyes to tall grass standing unbroken and a large hare racing from underbrush toward the road. A moment later, the horses on the path raced by in pursuit of breakfast.

"And in this way, she traveled far from her original home and settled in a small seaside village. She'd changed her name, claiming more years than she'd lived, and survived by selling herbal remedies. Her home was little more than a hovel. She found that the solitude agreed with her, the silence soothed. Her reputation as a healer grew and she found contentment." He glanced my way again. "For a time."

21

# For a Demon, He Wasn't a Complete Tool

"As she healed and matured, her loveliness returned and with it, the men. She'd spun a story of a beloved older husband who had taken ill and died. When it was suggested she should marry again, she refused, claiming heartbreak. As there was no husband or father to force her to marry, it worked for a time.

"Now, as I believe you're familiar, some men are not to be put off. She knew it would have been wiser to pack up and leave, but she'd found contentment there. She remained polite for as long as she could, but when one man in particular became relentless, she resorted to spells to keep him away, which, again, worked for a time. For a certain type of man, though, refusal is not to be borne. Fascination and lust turn quickly to resentment and violence.

"One evening, feeling cheated of something that should rightfully be his, he broke down her door and pinned her to the wall. He would take what had not been given.

"It was at this point I entered the story," he intoned with a nod to me. "I'd already delivered her father and husband to the Abyss. Even now, I can't explain what it was about her that drew me. She was being smothered under the weight of others' wants. Instead of being dragged down, though, she did her best to survive this new life on her own terms. When they wouldn't allow that, she found a way to fight back.

"So when this man decided to brutally force what had been withheld from him, I intervened, dragging him screaming down where he belonged. I later went back and introduced myself, explaining how I could help her protect herself. They'd never stop, never allow one they perceived as weaker than themselves to make her own decisions. I offered what I believed to be the best way to keep certain men from claiming her. I offered to teach her sorcery.

"I allowed her to draw on a fraction of my power when she needed it. In time, though, the power changed her. She gloried in being untouchable, in finally having the upper hand. I, like the men before me, destroyed what I loved."

He sighed, closing his eyes. "I knew better. Ageless, and still I made mistake after mistake. I'd wanted to help and instead, my influence had twisted her beyond recognition. When she bore our child, I'd had dreams of a different life." He shook his head. "Impossible. I felt a huge pull of power one day and went to check on them. She was tied to a post, fire engulfing her, four men dead on the ground before her.

"Consumed by the flames, she screamed my name. I snatched my son out of the bonfire as the life left her body. His skin was dark red, his eyes full black, like my own." He dropped the glamour and I beheld the most beautiful being I'd ever seen, ever imagined. My vision blurred and tears filled my eyes. Like his son, his eyes were shark-black, but where Dave's skin was dark red, his father's was almost pure black. Firelight danced over his perfect features, making my head pound, my heart lose its rhythm, and my lungs seize.

The glamour was back in place a moment later and I took a deep, shuddering breath, closing my eyes and trying to steady my galloping heart. In that moment, I knew he was nothing like Sitri or Olivier or any of the demons in the Biergarten. This was no mid-level demon. This was a fallen angel.

"The villagers backed away, dropped to the ground in fits, and cried out. My son would never be accepted there, so I took him home with me. As you might assume, Hell is a horrible place to raise a child. The only ones who had any experience with taking care of children were the last ones any sane parent would want near a child. As he got older, I tried to protect him from his tormentors, but he asked me to stop, as that seemed to make things worse. He was half demon, half wicche in a world of petty, vicious demons who loathed him simply because I cared for him. He suffered horribly but wouldn't talk with me about it."

He glanced over. "I'm sure you're wondering why I didn't pluck the answer out of his head, as I did with you. He'd made me promise not to do that. I understood what it was to have another dip in at will to read that which was held close and secret. The loss of privacy, of identity, can annihilate. If your thoughts are not your own, do you exist at all? Or are you the self-aware thought of another thinker?" He shook his head. "I gave him the space he wanted. And then all that was left between us was space."

Sighing deeply again, he returned his focus to the fire. "Something happened perhaps a decade ago. Something that changed everything. He left, returned to the human realm, and never contacted me again. I'd heard he was working in one of our nightclubs for a while and then that he'd come to work for you." He lifted one shoulder. "I had no idea he enjoyed cooking." It felt as though he was talking to himself before he lapsed into silence.

Leaning forward, I started to reach out to him before I remembered myself and tucked my hands under my thighs. "Can I ask why you're trying to find him now, if this has been going on for a while?"

He flicked his fingers and the fire went out. I hadn't realized the overhead lights had slowly been dimming as he spoke until they snapped back on. The spell was broken.

"He's requested to return home. I need to know why. He's in turmoil. I can feel it. I don't know what happened today, but I do know that he spoke with you and then lost his temper. You were able to wring some emotion out of him besides indifference."

He studied me a moment. "I'm here to ask a favor, to be repaid when and how you see fit. Talk to him again, please. Find out what's going on and why he's returning to a home he despises. You may not believe me capable of it, but I love my son. If staying far away from me is what will make him happy, then that's what I want for him."

He tapped the arms of the chair again. "And he has been happy. I've felt it. I've given him the privacy he wants. I haven't pried, but I've felt his contentment, even happiness at times. This is where he belongs."

I knew he was a demon, that all of this could have been invented to manipulate me, to play on my heartstrings and bargain for my soul. It didn't feel like that, though. God help me—seriously—but I believed him.

"I'll talk to him again because I was already planning to do that. I won't tell you what's said and I'm not doing you a favor. We have no arrangement or agreement. I want to make sure my friend is okay, so I'll do whatever he needs, not you."

"Understood. I'll leave you now." He touched the forgotten milk glass and it frosted.

"Um."

He paused, raising an eyebrow.

"You're not going to forget about Sitri, right?" When no answer was forthcoming, I continued, "Also, what happened with the girl, Dave's mom. That wasn't your fault. That kind of trauma is hard to come back from. She may have seemed content, living alone in the little seaside hovel, but she wasn't. I bet she spelled the doors and windows every day, trying to keep people out. I bet she flinched at strange noises and dreaded having to talk to others. She spent all her time cultivating plants because plants can't sneak up on you in the dark. They can't put their hands on you and strip away your power and control. Plants can't reduce you to gibbering fear and unending pain because they were bored and felt like it.

"I get that you think the sorcery put her over the edge, and maybe it did. I wasn't there. But I think it more likely you gave her the power to get the upper hand on her fear. And when she did, when she realized that no one could ever hurt her again, she started using that power every time she witnessed anything that felt like an echo of before because she had never healed from what had been done to her. Inside, she remained that brutalized twelve-year-old who had no one to run to, no one to trust. She wasn't content. She was broken and unable to heal. She may have gotten there, eventually, but she wasn't there yet when the match was lit."

He stared at me a moment and then disappeared.

The sadness that had consumed me moments ago lifted. Fergus barked once and then slid down to patrol the room. I reached for the package of cookies and ice-cold milk, feeling hungry again. I took a sip and put it down, thankfully, as I would have dropped it a moment later when the sword at my side shone bright enough to blind me. As the light faded, the shadow of a fingerprint blazed, and then it was gone along with the glow.

What the ever-loving fuck was that? Scanning the library, I tore open the cookies, checking over my shoulder to make sure no one else was in here with me. I popped a cookie in my mouth, washing it down with milk, and considered. It felt just like what Algar had done with the axe, giving me a weapon against the fae. Perhaps Dave's dad had given me a weapon against demons. Chewing another cookie, I hoped against hope I was right. And I hoped even more he was telling the truth about Sitri.

When I was done, I put the rest of the cookies away and washed out the glass, too restless to read. I'd tried but my mind kept wandering off. That never happened to me. I could always lose myself in a book. Tonight, though, there was too much jumbled up in my head. I wanted to go for a run but knew I couldn't. We'd need to settle for a walk on the nocturne grounds.

*Hey, what's the alarm code? I need to take Fergus for a walk around the grounds. Oh, and after your ceremony, I've got a story for you.*

*Don't leave the grounds, please. The code is the same and I look forward to your story.*

It was a beautiful night, cold and clear. Fergus dashed to the nearest tree and squatted to pee. He'd spent his formative months with a female dog, so he copied her style. When he was done, he ran to the gate and right through the wrought iron. *Damn it!*

He stood, looking in all directions, quivering with freedom and excitement. "Fergus, you get your butt right back in here." I gave my words an Alpha push that had him slinking back through the gate, his tail between his legs.

I patted my leg and he ran to me. I gave him full-body scratches that had him shivering and squirming. "Let's go, bud." I took off at a jog, having already forged a path when I'd lived here. Strangely enough, as I don't think I'm an asshole, at least not a huge one, random powerful creatures have been after me, messing up my daily runs for a while.

When I was single and living at The Slaughtered Lamb, I ran along the cliffs and down on the beach every night after closing. The nocturne was in Pacific Heights, a wealthy, rarified neighborhood. Even so, it was often too dangerous of late for me to run out in the open. All that was to say that I had a preset route on the property, one I was now teaching Fergus.

On our sixth circuit, I heard chittering in the trees beside a tall wall. Fergus' ears went up and his steps faltered, so I knew he'd heard it too. I kept going and he caught up. When we came back around, I studied the walls and trees as we approached the same spot.

Three pixies stood on a tree branch, small swords in hands. Pippin, the pixie who lived beside The Wicche Glass Tavern, had taught me a very important lesson. When it came to the fae, size didn't matter. Pixies could be just as deadly as Orcs.

Which reminded me. "Fangorn!"

## 22

# I Could Eat

I pulled the axe out of the sheath on my back. It was getting ridiculous how often I needed a blade. "Fergus, go!"

Ignoring my order, he barked at the pixies and stayed right by my side. First thing tomorrow, I was teaching him a run-away-from-the-melee command. Right now, though, I had three armed pixies scampering along tree branches. Could I have just run away from the tree? Yes. But then I'd have to always be looking over my shoulder for the wee assassins. I wanted them dealt with now.

Impact tremors shook the ground. Either Fangorn was coming or someone had cloned dinosaur DNA. Not wanting to take my eyes off them, I hoped for an Orc.

When the first pixie dropped, sword first, I feinted left and then came up swinging, slicing the creep in half. With a bright flash, he disappeared. The second dropped as Fangorn appeared. Turning the axe, I swung hard, bashing this one in a line drive to my soldier's hand. Roaring, he squeezed his fist, turning the second one into pulp. I was afraid that since he wasn't killed by my blade, the whole well-and-truly-dead gift wouldn't work, but when Fangorn shook pixie pulp off his hand, it again disappeared in a flash of light.

Fangorn and I silently moved beneath the branches, heads

raised, searching for the last pixie when we should have been looking down. The little fucker cleared his squeaky throat, and Fangorn and I spun. Our attention snapped to a trembling Fergus, who had a pixie holding on to his collar, riding him like a horse. The little bastard had his very sharp sword against my pup's throat.

"Youneedtocomewith—"

Clive suddenly stood before us, stretching the pixie taut between his hands. When the pixie struggled and kicked, Clive jerked his hands apart and the pixie squealed in pain. A moment later, the pixie fell silent. He was still obviously screaming his head off, but the sound had been cut off.

"He was giving me a headache." Clive looked between me and Fangorn before settling back on me. "Why is this pixie trying to murder our Fergus?"

"Because he's an asshole!" I flicked the little shit in the forehead. Hard. Sheathing the axe, I plopped down on the grass beside Fergus, who hopped into my lap.

"I smell blood, darling. Check his neck."

Pushing his fur this way and that, I found the spot. "Looks like a shallow nick." I held the pup aloft. "Can you check?"

"Fangorn, can you hold him for me?" When the soldier put out his bloody hand, Clive said, "Don't kill him yet. I have questions."

The pixie struggled frantically and Fangorn gave him a quick squeeze that made the pixie turn a sickly purple color.

When Clive raised an eyebrow, Fangorn said, "Not dead."

"Fair enough." Clive picked up Fergus and held him close, slowly dragging one of his hands down the pup's back. Sometimes I forgot that Clive had been a farmer in life, one who cared for animals as well as crops.

Fergus tucked his head under Clive's chin. He'd been brave for as long as he'd needed to be. Now he was a scared pup seeking safety. While Clive held him, I checked his neck again.

"It's just this spot. Give me your tongue?"

"Pardon?"

I wiped my finger clean on my hoodie and then held it up in front of his mouth. I'm pretty sure I caught an eyeroll before he licked my finger. Whatevs. I pressed my wet index finger against the cut and then gave Fergus a snoot kiss. When I lifted my finger, the cut was gone. "All better, buddy."

Clive put Fergus down and then took the pixie back. Our prisoner looked unconscious, but Clive didn't seem to believe it. He crouched beside the pup and held the pixie under Fergus' nose. "You don't have to talk, if you'd prefer not. I will, however, be feeding you to my dog. Choose wisely."

Fergus sniffed the blue feathery hair on the pixie's head and the little creep's eyes flew open as he cringed away.

"Why did you ambush Sam?" Clive asked.

"Don'tknowwhatyou'retalkingabout."

"Give," Fangorn said, holding out his massive hand again.

Clive looked down at the pixie and smiled. "Poor choice, mate."

Fangorn grabbed the pixie and ripped off an arm, tossing it in his mouth and chewing. Shaking the bleeding, wailing pixie, Fangorn trapped the other arm between his thumb and forefinger before bellowing, "Why?"

Clive laughed. *Oh, I like this one. Can we keep him?*

*As long as the queen allows it.*

A flood of high-pitched words came flooding out of the pixie, but I didn't understand a word of it. When he finally stopped, Fangorn bit off his head. Jolting, I grabbed Clive's arm. In three bites, the pixie was gone and the soldier was looking quite pleased.

*Did you understand anything the pixie said?*

*A few words, at most. Hopefully your soldier with explain once he's swallowed.*

*Does this change your mind about wanting to keep him?*

*On the contrary.*

After a rather large belch, the soldier turned to leave.

"Wait, Fangorn." When he paused, I went on. "We didn't understand what he said. Can you tell us?"

Huge sigh, small burp, and then, "King sent. Waited at bar. Followed. Watched. Dwarf take you to Faerie."

Clive kissed me and then leapt over the wall. In almost no time, he was back with a sagging dwarf under his right arm and an axe in his left. Passing me the axe, he said, "For your collection." To Fangorn, he said, "Still hungry?"

The Orc grunted with something approximating a shrug.

"Perfect. I'll keep you on the back burner." He dropped the unconscious dwarf on the ground and pulled a thin rope from his pocket.

"Where'd that come from?" Did he just walk around with rope, and how had I not noticed that before?

"I stopped by the gatehouse before I came back." He threw one end over a low branch and then picked up the dwarf and tied him, so he was dangling in Clive's line of sight.

"In the minute and a half you were gone?" Can he stop time too?

Clive grinned at me in the dark. "I'm very fast." He returned his attention to the dwarf, who woke swinging a burly arm that no longer held an axe.

The dwarf took one look at us and snapped his mouth shut.

Clive spun the fae assassin. "I don't know if you noticed, but we have a soldier here who's feeling a bit peckish." When the dwarf swung back around, Clive put out a hand to stop the rotation. "We know the king sent you. What was the plan?"

He remained belligerently silent.

"I have an idea," I said.

Clive inclined his head, allowing me to take over. He was an equal opportunity interrogator.

"By the way, do we need to worry about neighbors calling the cops about strange squealing happening over here?" That was all we needed, a raid when we've got vamps downstairs biting each other and a seven-and-a-half-foot Orc out here with pixie bones stuck in his teeth.

Clive shook his head. "It's part of the spelling of nocturnes. No sound makes it past the walls." He drilled a finger into the dwarf's chest. "You should remember that. No one will hear you scream."

"Okay, so, this may not work." I'd felt a strange flash of emotion when I'd killed the pixies with my axe. This was a working theory and I needed to experiment. Putting the head of the axe against his stomach, I listened, using that part of my mind that allowed me to hear vampires. I was a necromancer. I knew vamps, the mostly dead, were not the same as the fae, the eternally alive. I knew that, but I'd felt something, so I wanted to try.

After a long, silent moment, no thoughts, no emotions, I was about to give it up as a fail, when the dwarf smacked my sword away and I felt his anger and disgust.

"Ha! Skin. It needs to touch skin."

Fangorn grabbed the dwarf's hands, holding them at his side so he couldn't swat the axe away.

I pressed the blunt top of the axe head under his chin. "Give me a minute," I said to Clive.

Anger and resentment throbbed in my head. Funneling the pain of invading another's thoughts into the wicche glass around my neck, I pressed harder, trying to work my way into his bubble of fury. I felt a pop and then a spike of pain that Clive washed away. I couldn't hear words, not like I did with vampires. I felt emotion, though, and could discern hazy images.

Eyes closed, I patted Clive's arm to continue with his interrogation.

"Who sent you here?" he asked.

An image of Finvarra came to mind. "The king, but what's interesting is that he doesn't feel any loyalty to the king. There's fear there, but also a recognition that he made his choice and now is stuck with it." I opened my eyes and studied the dwarf, whose expression was closed off, his face turned away. "You aren't actually. You could return to the queen's service, tell her who's working for the king."

An elf appeared in my mind. She had long, golden hair and bright silvery eyes. Wrapping my hand around Gloriana's ring on my pinky, I concentrated on the image. *This person is in the king's employ. She's betrayed you.* The ring pulsed once.

"What were you planning to do with my wife?" Clive's voice took on a dark, sinister edge.

The dwarf didn't want the job. He hated this realm. It stank. Humans were stupid and ugly. A guard in the palace where Gloriana was keeping the king had passed along a message. *Dang.* The dwarf was trying to put up stronger mental blocks.

"He was told to grab me—violence encouraged—and bring me back to Faerie. The queen is closing doorways, but they still have quite a few she has yet to find. He just had to get me to the palace where the king is being held. A guard—" Clutching the ring again, I pushed the image of the green-haired elf with the cold brown eyes into the ring. *He's your guard but one of the king's men.* The ring pulsed again. "A guard will take me to the king to"—torture horribly—"deal with."

I opened my eyes. Clive was watching me, not the dwarf. He knew what I'd left out. *I'm fine. It didn't happen.*

*I know. But while you're sending messages to the queen, make sure she understands that if anything happens to you, and I do mean anything* —He cupped my face with one hand, his thumb brushing over my cheek—*I will burn it all down.* His eyes had gone vamp black as he stared into mine. *It'll be war and they'll soon understand why the world trembles before my kind, why we invade their nightmares even as we lay waste to their villages.*

My ring pulsed, the band hot.

*She's powerful, but so. Am. I.* He leaned in and kissed me softly. *I have thousands at my command. I will suck Faerie dry if she allows anything to happen to you.*

The ring didn't throb, but I knew she'd heard.

Clive nodded, gave me a quick, hard kiss, and then yanked the dwarf off the tree and threw him to Fangorn. "Bon appetit."

23

# If I Do This...

I grabbed my new axe and strolled back to the nocturne, holding Clive's hand, Fergus racing ahead and then running back to us as I related the highlights of my meeting with Dave Sr. to Clive. "Are you guys done with your vampy blood thingy?"

"One. You know how I feel about that word."

"Thingy?" I said, swinging our arms.

"And B. No. I'm done. They're not. They don't need me anymore, though. Are we assuming Dave's dad to be truthful?"

I shrugged. "Hard to say. On one hand, I absolutely believed him. On the other, he's an ancient demon who's probably been lying longer than the world has existed."

"I'd rather take the chance and sleep in our own bed. If it was a lie, you can lay your demon sword on me."

"If protection was a lie, who's to say the sword glowing was anything other than a light show?" I didn't want to take chances with Clive's well-being.

"I'd prefer to go with your gut. Besides, we still have that stealing holy water idea in our back pockets." He grinned, pulling my hand to his lips and kissing the fingertips not covered in bandages. "Shall we go home?"

Dave's dad really did seem pissed off at Sitri. It might have been stupid to believe a demon was going to right a wrong, but I did. "I'd like that."

"Good." Raising his voice, Clive said, "Fangorn, we'll be leaving in a few minutes. When you finish your meal, please meet us at the front gate."

We went in, collected our things, and then headed for the garage.

"How many of these are yours?" It was like a showroom. There had to be forty or fifty cars in here.

Clive barely glanced around. "Most of them."

"Do the contractors at the Seal Rock house know how big the garage has to be?"

"Of course. If you'd like, we can take a run by there and I can show you the progress." He opened the back door for Fergus and me. The pup jumped, scrambling to get in on his own.

"Good boy," I said on a yawn.

"But not tonight. Let's go home and get you in bed." He closed the door behind me and then slid into the driver's seat.

"That's what I'm talkin' 'bout." I could see his eyes crinkle in the rearview mirror, and all was right in the world.

Fangorn was waiting for us by the gate. It took a little work to get him in the vehicle, his stomach distended from the meal that I was definitely not thinking about.

"Captain at bar?"

Captain? "Oh, Stheno? No. She won't be there."

Fangorn let loose a ferocious belch. "Need to report elf, dwarf, pixie attack."

"Elf?" Clive asked. He sought me in the rearview mirror. "You didn't mention an elf."

Shrugging, I responded, "I never saw an elf."

"You call Fangorn. I kill and come." He punched his own stomach, as though trying to knock unconscious something he'd already eaten. Perhaps it was indigestion? Probably best not to consider too deeply.

Clive nodded. "A coordinated effort to get to you. Thank you for your service, Fangorn."

"I guard." But it was said with less enthusiasm than normal. His meal seemed to be paining him at present.

Fergus flopped into my lap for the short drive home. Fog had rolled in, blanketing the water and the neighborhoods along the coastline. We were above it, in the Pacific Heights district, but were driving down a very steep hill, right into a fog bank, streetlights becoming hazy beacons as the world closed in.

The car came to a stop and my eyes flew open.

"Welcome back, sleepyhead," Clive said, sliding out and opening my door.

Fergus stretched and yawned. I handed him over to Clive as I grabbed the pup's backpack of stuff. We didn't put him down in the parking lot if we could help it. Sometimes idiots broke bottles up here. We didn't want the pup cutting a paw.

The passenger door swung open and Fangorn pushed himself out, grunting what might have been a goodbye. He needed to find a spot to rest and digest a dwarf—and possibly an elf. Fergus ran down the stairs before us. When Clive and I passed through the ward, I locked it back up again. From the steps, I heard Fergus drinking from his water bowl in the kitchen.

Peering over my shoulder into the dark recesses of the bookstore, I listened intently for unwanted visitors. Clive took the backpack and shouldered it, wrapping his other arm around me.

"No one's here but us," he assured me.

Sighing in relief, I tipped my head to his shoulder. It was wonderful to return to our apartment, overcrowded as it was. We found Fergus already in his bed, poor tired little guy.

Clive put down the backpack and then helped me out of my blades.

"Oh, I forgot the new axe in the back of your car."

Placing my blades in the top of the dresser, he gave me a kiss. "We can deal with that tomorrow." He drew me into his arms and just held me. It had been a rough few days, and we needed to reassure ourselves that we were okay.

"I must have been mad to think we'd ever have a nice, quiet life together," he said, but I could hear the smile in his voice.

"If you wanted a nice, quiet life," I began, my hands settling on his butt, "you probably should have stayed in your nocturne and ignored the bartending, bookselling werewolf in your territory."

"True. But would I have found elegant nightclubs with gorgeous women as fulfilling as tapping a keg or unboxing books?" He sighed. "Hard to say."

"Seriously, it's like you're begging to be staked." I barely had the words out before I was tossed onto the bed. Giggling, I propped myself up on my elbows and kicked off my shoes, watching him remove his jacket and toe off his own shoes. I pulled my hoodie over my head, suddenly wide awake, while he unbuttoned his white dress shirt.

"I'd appreciate it if you kept all pointy wooden implements from the bedroom, darling." Shirtless, hands on his hips, he studied me a moment. "I see you've woken up." A moment later, the bottom half of my body was feeling far breezier than normal. "Almost," he said, and then my shirt and bra were gone as well.

"Are we in a hurry?"

He unbuckled his belt, his eyes going vamp black. "Not at all. We're just racing the dawn."

Confused, I glanced over at the clock. "That's like five hours away."

Naked, he grabbed my ankles, pulling them apart as he dragged me slowly across the bed to him. "Exactly."

Featherlight, his fingers skated over my skin, up my legs. He had my heart hammering, my breath uneven before his thumb parted me. I jolted as he ran it up and down. Fangs descending, his mouth replaced his thumb. Twisting, trying to catch my breath, I grabbed his hair, needing an anchor.

Pushing my legs up, he gripped the backs of my thighs, keeping me open and tilted up. Head thrown back, I made inhuman noises as he feasted. Torn between the need to pull him closer and push him away, I rode the waves, desperate. His fangs sunk in and I was screaming.

I was still flying apart when he moved up my body and slid in. Mindless, I matched his rhythm and felt it build again, like a wildfire racing through us both. He slipped his arm under me to hold me in place, hammering home while his other hand palmed my breast, plucking at my nipple.

When he came with a roar, I was right there with him, spent and trembling. I clung to him, never wanting to move. Rolling us, he kept one hand on my back and the other on my bum, tracing circles.

"I meant what I said," he murmured.

"About the five hours?"

I bobbled on top of him as he laughed. "Well, yes, that as well. What I meant, though, was that I will dismantle this world if you're taken from me. It's not an idle threat or hyperbole." He ran his hands up and down my back. "I wouldn't be able to stop myself. I almost broke when you disappeared in Canterbury. You could have been lost and hurt, might have needed me, and I wasn't there. Russell and Godfrey did everything they could to keep me in check, but it was a close thing."

"I'm not an idiot. I don't go running headlong into danger."

"No. You mistake me. I'm not chastising. You do what you do because you have a bottomless reserve of compassion for others. You may make horribly selfless choices, but I'd be a hypocrite to berate you for that. Your kindness and empathy are part of the whole, and I'm madly in love with the whole of you." He kissed the top of my head.

"No," he continued. "I meant that I don't trust myself. He's sending fae assassins almost daily. And now demons are taking an interest." He crushed me against him. "What if I can't protect you?"

I made a knot with my hands and rested my chin on them, so I could see him. "Yeah. I get that. I worry about the same thing with you. But then I think there has to be a reason the last five or six months have been so crazy. I mean, think about it. I went from quietly living back here, selling books and pouring drinks, my world the size of The Slaughtered Lamb. And now I'm visiting New Orleans for vampire bloodbaths. Faerie!" I said, shaking my head in wonder. "I visited Faerie. Twice. One was against my will, but still. France, England, Wales. I've been lost on moors, met Geoffrey Chaucer and Bram Stoker, found a magical chess set."

I leaned forward and kissed his chin. "Me. I was hiding for twenty-four years and then *boom*, the world found me. It's been chaotic and terrifying and amazing and more than I could ever have dreamed. All of that has to be for a reason; don't you think?"

He watched me a moment and then asked, "What reason?"

I shrugged. "I don't know but six months ago if the fae had targeted me, no one would have known. I'd have been taken out quickly and quietly. But people started pushing their way into my no-longer-quiet life. I wasn't alone anymore. I had vampires and wicches and demons and the fae. I had dragons and gorgons and a fury. I met the queen and king, a fallen angel"—I drilled my finger into his chest—"I'm almost positive. I have defenses I've never had before. And I fell in love with the best man I've ever known.

"He gave me the time I needed to heal, while making sure I was safe. He let me find my feet, test my skills, and save myself, while waiting in the wings, ready for the assist. It was never about you protecting me. It was about me learning to protect myself. As much as I know you wanted to step in, you didn't. So don't tell me you're not sure if you can be trusted. Crazy shit may be afoot, but we've got this, all of us together."

He shook his head, frustrated. "I've never—you are the one I love more than anything else in this world. If you were taken from me, hurt or...there'd be no coming back for me. Someone—Russell, probably—would need to destroy me."

I put my hand over his mouth. "No one's doing that because you're stronger than anyone I've ever met."

He pulled my hand away. "You haven't met that many people."

I thought about it a minute. "I'll concede that point, *but* you need to concede mine, which is that you'll never go berserker because you love me beyond all reason."

"How does one follow the other?" His brows furrowed as he watched me, tucking a stray hair behind my ear.

"Silly, because you love me, you'd never do something you know would break my heart or make me ashamed. If I go first, you know I'll be negotiating with the powers that be to keep us together. Heaven, Hell, the Underworld, walking the earth as ghosts, wherever, however, whoever's religious tradition, all that matters is that we stick together. If you go psycho bloodsucker on me, how am I going to talk the gatekeepers into letting you in? Maybe we'd have an easier time getting into Hell, but the place is lousy with creeps. I don't want to spend eternity with fricking serial killers and my aunt Abigail, who, come to think of it, is also a serial killer.

"So, knowing you wouldn't want to disappoint me, you'll do the right thing. Plus," I added, tapping my finger on his chest, "I know you. You're no bad guy. Even in the grips of grief, you'll do the right thing."

"You couldn't possibly *know* that."

"Oh, but I do. Just like I know that if I do this…" I let my knees fall to either side of his hips and felt him harden beneath me. "You'll do that. See? I know you."

24

# Tell Me It Wasn't Wearing a Collar

Sometime later, Clive and I showered, changed the linens, and dropped into an exhausted sleep. I awoke briefly mid-morning and watched Clive. No flinching. No pain. It looked like Dave's dad had come through for us. Nice demon, that guy.

After feeding Fergus and taking him out for a quick potty break, I went back to bed, too tired to think about staying up. Having a husband who was only up at night and a puppy who had to go out early and often was wreaking havoc on my sleep schedule.

It was after noon when I finally dragged myself from bed. As Fergus was nowhere to be seen, I had no doubt he was in the bar with Owen. Maybe I could finally work on the book order today. With any luck, last night's leftovers were still in the fridge. Of course, the only reason a werewolf and a dragon had food left over was because Clive knew to buy enough food for ten. Smart vamp.

I hit the refrigerator as soon as I got dressed. Huzzah! Food was my favorite thing to eat. I warmed up some Szechuan beef and rice, excited to see there were more fortune cookies on the counter. I cracked one open while I waited for the microwave. *Meeting adversity well is the source of your strength.* Huh. If you say so, cookie.

Fergus trotted in a moment later and got a full-body scratch, making him quiver and hop. When I heard the ding, I grabbed my food and a fork, sitting at Dave's desk. The pooch attacked my feet while I ate. "Why do you hate these laces?" I muttered, lifting him with one foot while he yanked on the other.

A sticky note above his desk caught my eye. *Stop Sam. I mean it!* Wait. That wasn't there before. That was Dave's handwriting, but the note was new. I rinsed off my plate and then went to the bar in search of Owen, Fergus following, trying to pounce on my heels.

I found Owen ringing up a customer in the bookstore. Once the wicche left, I went to the counter. "Was Dave in today?"

"Well, good morning to you too. Yes, I have had a good afternoon. Thank you for asking." He waited, ignoring my question.

"Good morning. Sorry. I noticed this on Dave's desk." I handed him the note. "I'm sure it wasn't there yesterday."

Owen's brow furrowed as he studied it. "I haven't seen him in a few days."

"Okay." I took the note back. Maybe last night when we were at the nocturne, he came here to warn me off. "Could you cover the bar? I want to work here and get that order done. Our shelves are downright anemic."

"Sure." He started back toward the bar and then stopped. "How was it, being back in the nocturne?"

I thought about it a moment. "Really nice, actually." At his surprised look, I continued, "I was just hanging with Russell, Godfrey, and Audrey. I love them. The shitty ones were downstairs, so it was a great visit. Well, except for meeting Dave's dad and the fae assassins."

Owen shook his head and left the bookstore with no follow-up questions. Odd. I went to the back to roll out a cart of books I needed to inventory. When I got back, Owen had dragged over a chair from the bar and there were two cups of tea on the counter.

"Forget about the books and tell me everything." Owen took a sip of tea from his own mug.

"He just appeared in the library. Scared the bejeezus out of me.

It turned out fine, good even, but, man." I explained my encounter, skating over the more personal stuff, like the details of Dave's mom's life. In the moment, it had felt like the yet-to-be-named demon was doing something extraordinary by opening up and relating the story. I didn't want to turn their tragedy into gossip, so I held my tongue.

I did, however, give him a play-by-play on the fae attack.

Owen made a face and laid a hand on his stomach. "He *ate* them?" he whispered, and I nodded.

Fangorn, who was standing guard in the doorway between the bookstore and bar, looked over his shoulder and grinned. Thankfully, Owen had his back to him.

"And how was your night?" I asked him.

"Same." Rolling his eyes at my ridiculous life, he said, "Alec is still with us, so he and George were in charge of dinner last night. We've been teaching him little things around the kitchen."

"Nice. How's freedom treating him?"

Owen tipped his head from side to side. "Okay-ish. He has horrible nightmares, but he's been more outgoing during the day. He and Lilah did end up going for boba. She said he was starting to sweat, but he held it together and finished his tea, which he liked."

"Good." A short, friendly, no-stakes outing was perfect.

"He swims in the ocean every day."

"He what?" The tide was fierce and there were jagged rocks at the edge of Owen and George's property.

"Yep. It's so weird. Every morning, it feels like he's taller and broader. It's just..." Owen blinked away the tears. "I can see it. George is glowing, having his brother back. It's like it keeps hitting him all over again. Alec's not missing. He's home. He's sitting across the table, eating dinner or playing with my nieces. He's sitting on the patio, full in the sun, watching the waves.

"I've never seen George so happy. Sometimes, if he's home, he goes swimming with Alec. They run to the end of the dock and dive straight out, past the rocks. They gave me a heart attack the first time they pulled that one. And then they're just swimming, cutting through the waves. Their strokes in sync." He shook his head.

"It's crazy. We have a telescope on the deck outside our bedroom. I go up there to keep an eye on them. The first couple of times, they didn't get too far before they turned back. Alec is getting stronger, though. He swims out on his own every day while George is at work. I think he's trying to get strong enough to beat George."

"Sibling rivalry is alive and well, I see."

"Yeah." Owen grinned. "It's amazing, the progress he's made in such a short time."

"Dragon genes," I said, pulling books off the cart. "Is the shifting getting easier for him?"

He nodded. "They've gone as a family out to Drake's Bay twice on moonless nights. Fyr too. Both of them shifted and flew. George says they're doing great, making progress."

"Good."

"You got that right." He picked up the chair and our empty cups before heading back to the bar, giving Fangorn the widest berth he could, given the size of the doorway, which the soldier seemed to find amusing.

Fergus came in to check on me, having just come back from a walk. He sniffed around, got a cuddle, and then trotted off to inspect his territory. It was a nice quiet afternoon of inventorying books. Owen would visit occasionally to shelve some and then go back to the bar when he was needed.

By the time Fyr arrived for his late shift, I had two full carts of books ready to be shelved. Owen took one cart, and I took the other. Unlike George and Alec, we weren't in a race. Both of us shelved slowly, stopping to read book covers, sometimes reading opening pages. We needed to know the books in order to answer questions or make recommendations.

I should have known then that the lovely, book-filled respite would be followed by all manner of ugliness.

When Clive awoke, he found me behind the bar. Owen was finishing up his cart in the bookstore while Fyr and I served the early evening rush. I slid a Manhattan across the bar and then turned to Clive, tucking my head into his neck. His scent always soothed. He was home.

"Good evening. How was your day? Were you able to work on the book order?"

I squeezed him and gave him a quick kiss. "I love that you pay attention to the stuff I tell you, even the not so exciting or life-threatening stuff. And yes, I did! I inventoried almost three carts of books and Owen and I got them shelved." I gestured to the bookstore. "He's just finishing up the last of them. The shelves aren't full, but they're better."

Clive watched Fangorn sitting on the steps, playing tug with Fergus. "Given how relaxed your guards are, I assume that means it's been a quiet day."

"Blissfully so. Just me, books, Owen, and Fergus." I took out my cutting board and returned to slicing lemons.

Fangorn stood abruptly and glared up the stairs. A charged silence hung in the air a moment and then he was up the stairs in a flash. When Fergus tried to follow, we all shouted no. Fangorn returned a few minutes later, wiping blood off his sword, another tucked under his arm. Sheathing his own, he handed me an elven sword and then went back to sit on the stairs and resume his game of tug the pup.

"I mean, aside from *that*, it's been quiet. Anyone we knew?" I asked Fangorn.

"Pawn."

Chess set for the win again. Turning back to Clive, I said, "I'm accruing quite the fae arsenal. Anyway, did you call the nocturne? Is everybody okay over there?"

"I did, right before I came out. Russell answered his phone himself, which told me everything I needed to know. He said he feels a calm and a unity in the nocturne that hasn't been there in quite a while, so it worked."

I put the sword down on the counter behind the bar. "Does that bother you?"

"Not a whit. You forget, we were a powerful, unified nocturne for hundreds of years before Aldith and Leticia began working on my people. Before our relationship riled up the bigots. It makes me very pleased. Russell should have been a Master long before now. I'm glad he chose to accept the mantle. It suits him well."

There was something on his neck. When I reached for the collar of his shirt, he caught my hand and kissed it.

*It's nothing, darling.*

I stared at the red slash in horror. All day I'd been puttering around, life feeling mostly normal and he'd been getting slashed. Dave's dad lied! Why was that shocking to me? Clive had been carved up while I'd been shelving books. My eyes filled with tears.

He pulled me back into his arms. *I'm fine. I don't feel as tired as I've been. Dave Sr. may not have stopped it, but the severity seems to have lessened. Truly, I'm perfectly fine.*

*The wound hasn't faded. You're not fine.* I pulled him into the empty kitchen. *Go ahead.* I pointed at my own neck. *Fresh blood will help, and I've got supercharged blood.*

*Sam.*

*Are you a vampire or not? Come and get it.* I grabbed the front of his shirt and yanked him toward me.

Shaking his head, he grinned. "If you insist."

Pulling me in close, he dropped featherlight kisses up and down the side of my neck. The man could make me forget my own name without even trying. And then I was sitting on the island, his hand down my unzipped jeans, my legs wrapped around him, while his fangs sunk in. A few blissful minutes later, he was done feeding and I was ready for a nap.

After helping me get myself put back together, he grabbed a glass and went into the fridge for juice. "Drink up, darling." He watched me a moment, the red line no longer on his neck. "Do you want to see the progress on the Seal Rock house? You asked about it last night."

I hopped off the island, grabbed his hand, and walked back into the bar. "I would, but first we need to visit a strip club."

Fyr's head turned at that but he didn't comment.

Clive sighed unnecessarily. "I assumed as much. Perhaps I could take you out to dinner before we visit demons."

"Sounds perfect." I glanced over at Fyr. "Are you okay holding down the fort on your own?"

"Sure. Weekday nights aren't too crowded. If you're not back before I close, should I take Fergus home with me? He hasn't been able to bug Alice in a while."

We'd never left the little guy home alone before. "Yeah, could you? I'd appreciate it."

Fangorn bellowed, "I guard!" which made a few of the wicches sitting near him jump, but I was mostly used to it at this point.

Once the rush died down, I ran in back to get cleaned up and changed. I'd figured out how to adjust the straps on the fae axe sheath. It didn't work as well for a quick draw, but it allowed me to go out in public without scaring people. The axe now sat at my lower back, so the handle wouldn't stick up over my head. Awkward but doable. The sword and sheath at my side were less obvious after I put on a long coat. I was ready for dinner and a demon bar.

Before we left, we engaged in our latest pastime: checking the chess set. On the king's side, there were two pieces with new faces. One appeared to be an elf. The other, I couldn't make out. His features were oddly pinched. "Any guess?"

Clive shook his head. "He looks a bit like a seal. Perhaps a selkie?"

Nodding, I said, "So we'll be extra careful around land and sea. Check."

Shaking his head, Clive took my hand and pulled me out on our date.

He was right. Our lives shouldn't only be about survival. The Slaughtered Lamb was covered. He no longer had a million responsibilities hanging over his head, so we went to an elegant

French restaurant in the Marina District. In his gangster glamour, Fangorn stood in the shadows beside the restaurant. We'd shown him pics of the new faces added to our watch list but he hadn't recognized either of them.

Clive had reserved a private dining room for us. It was perfect, filled with fragrant flowers and shimmering crystal. We had our moves down, though we didn't really need them in a private room. We did our act for the servers, appearing to be sharing our food, à la *Lady & the Tramp*. I had a seafood bisque and some beef tartare, lobster, scallops, lemon pepper duck, and quail stuffed with mushrooms, topping it off with a soufflé drizzled with blood orange sauce and a warm Louisiana butter cake with roasted peaches, huckleberries, and vanilla ice cream. In my defense, we're not talking huge portions here and I'm a freaking werewolf.

It was lovely and no one tried to kill us, which was the nicest kind of date.

When we went to collect Fangorn, we found him picking his teeth. Oh, no. "Please tell me you didn't eat someone's cat."

His brow furrowed, thinking. Making a V with two fingers, he motioned to his eye in a clear mask move.

"Racoon?"

He shrugged and belched.

"Was it wearing a collar like Fergus'?" *Please say no. Please say no.*

He shook his head.

Keeping him from eating pets was probably the best we were going to do.

"Okay, guys. Let's go visit the clothing challenged."

# 25

# No Stealing Candy!

Clive opened the back door for me and gave me a kiss. "Anyone around we should be aware of?" Always thinking, this guy.

I slid into the SUV and closed my eyes, accessing that part of my mind that could locate the dead, the mostly dead, and some immortals. "You guys. Most of the vamps are at the nocturne. A couple are…at Fisherman's Wharf? They must be nibbling on tourists. Lots of ghosties, but no one in particular."

"No Charlotte?"

I shook my head. "I'm pretty sure she passed over. The usual fae in Golden Gate Park and the bay. Dragons are all accounted for." I opened my eyes. "I don't think the elf and the selkie—if that's what he is—have crossed over into this realm yet."

"Good. We're as informed as we can be." Clive got into the driver's seat, Fangorn having already wedged himself in. It was a short drive to the Demon's Lair, but Clive didn't have the same luck with parking that I'd had. He ended up finding a spot a couple of blocks away, which was fine, as I really needed to get in the right frame of mind before I went back in that place.

As we got closer, possibly because I'd just been scanning for other supernaturals and was therefore open, I felt a ghost at the side door to the strip club. Clive had my hand, so I had to tug free before I lost her. She was standing in six-inch platform heels, a flimsy floral shortie robe tied loosely at the waist showing off an astounding rack. Her long blonde hair was in a high ponytail and she was smoking a cigarette.

"Hello?" I called.

She glanced over, expression blank, and then her whole face lit up. "You can see me?" She wobbled on the uneven pavement of the narrow alley. "I mean for real, you can see me?" She straightened her robe.

"I can."

She burst into tears and threw herself at me, sobbing on my shoulder. Even in towering heels, she was tiny. After a minute, she tried to pull it together. "I'm sorry. It's just been so lonely, out here all by myself."

"If you want to pass on, I can help you with that." Poor thing. Charlotte had said that when they weren't needed, they just sort of existed out of time in a gray space. Was this poor woman aware and just standing in this alley ever since she'd died?

"Pass on where?" she asked, eyes a soft brown. She exuded an innocence at odds with the outfit and profession. I'd thought the green would have disappeared pretty quickly when patrons were constantly pawing at you.

"To—" I glanced over at Clive and Fangorn, one patiently waiting, the other confused, before returning my attention to her. "To the other side, heaven, whatever you believe."

"What?" Her eyes went wide, her expression a combination of horror and fear. "I'm D. E. A. D?" she whisper-spelled. No idea why.

"I'm sorry. I thought you knew."

She lifted her hand to wipe away tears and flinched at the sight of the cigarette. If it were possible, I'd say she blushed. Ghosts were in the gray to white color spectrum, so there was no blushing, but I felt it.

"I know these are really bad for you," she said, dropping it to the cement and grounding it out with one platformed foot. "I just get nervous and—" She gasped. "Is that how I D.I.E.D?"

"I doubt it."

"I only smoked one a day and only three puffs. My great-aunt Sarah was a smoker and she died of the C.A.N.C.E.R. It was horrible."

Why she said *died* that time but spelled *cancer* was beyond me.

"And my Uncle Lou and my cousin Jeremy." Sighing, she stared down at the smashed butt.

"Lots of smokers in your family, huh?" This was the weirdest conversation ever.

"Yeah, I guess. But most everyone I know smokes. My Uncle Ben has one of those voice boxes in his throat." She leaned forward and whispered, "It kind of scares me. I didn't want to ever end up with one of those, so I promised myself I'd quit." She shrugged one shoulder. "I guess maybe moving to the big city made me backslide some."

Something about this felt off. "Can I ask your name?"

"Oh, sure." She shook her head. "Where are my manners? I'm Candy."

Nodding, I waited a moment. "I meant your real name."

"That is—oh, you mean the whole thing? I'm Candace Marie Miller." She was so eager to answer my questions, to have someone to talk to, it broke my heart.

*Can you look up Candace Marie Miller? I'm not sure how long she's been standing in this alley but given the number of smokers in her family and her phrasing, I'm pretty sure she's been standing here for a while.*

"That's a pretty name." She flushed at the compliment. "I'm Sam Quinn. How long have you been dancing at the Demon's Lair?"

"The…what?" Her eyes bulged as she skittered to the other side of the narrow alley. "Is that what they are?"

"I'm afraid so."

She shivered and then whispered, "Some of them are really scary."

I stepped closer to the dumpster she was hiding beside. "I know. There's one whose whole body is covered in open sores."

Slapping her hand over her mouth, she leaned in again. "And one is really tall and so skinny, you'd swear he'd never eaten anything his whole life long."

"Yep. I've seen that one too, but you don't need to worry about anyone overhearing you. I'm the only one who can hear you."

She shook her head, eyeing the back door. "There's one that's really handsome—he's scarier than the other ones—he looked right at me one time. I was like a rabbit in the high beams. I stared, too scared to move. I think he smirked at me, but it could have been the woman with him." She twisted her fingers in front of her. "I don't want to wish any misfortune on another of God's creatures, but I really hope he wasn't looking at me."

"I understand completely."

*Candace Marie Miller was shot and killed in this alley in 1956. She's from the Central Valley. Her family were farmers. She left home for Hollywood but had trouble breaking into the business. In order to make ends meet, she began dancing. Her family said they didn't know she was in San Francisco. Authorities believe she came out on a smoke break, interrupting a mob hit.*

*Poor thing.*

"Is that man with you?" she asked, staring at Clive.

"Yes. He can't see or hear you, but he knows I can communicate with the dead, so he understands what's happening. Candy, this is Clive. Clive," I said, running my hand down his arm, "this is Candy."

Smiling, he inclined his head a fraction. "It's lovely to meet you, Candy."

"Oh my," she breathed and then slapped a hand over her mouth again and gave me a guilty look.

"It's okay. I know he's gorgeous."

Clive laughed at that.

"Come to that, he knows too. Anyway, the very tall gentleman right there"—I pointed at our soldier—"is Fangorn. He's my guard."

Fangorn grunted. As he didn't seem shocked by my talking to air, Clive must have already clued him in to what was going on.

"Are you somebody important?"

I shook my head. "Nope. I've got a creep who keeps sending people to attack me, so I travel with backup these days. We need to go in this place because a friend of mine is in trouble. You don't have to come with us, but I also don't want to leave you here on your own."

"Please don't go." Her eyes went glassy again.

"If you don't want to come in, you can wait in front and we'll pick you up on the way out."

She glanced around the alley, her home for over sixty years, and appeared terrified of being stuck here for another sixty.

"I can help you cross," I offered again. "I bet your family really misses you."

"Oh," she said, pulling her robe more tightly closed. "No. I don't want to be a bother."

"Candy," I said, trying to get her to look me in the eye, "it's not a bother. At all. You'd be doing me a favor. This weird thing I can do doesn't feel so weird if I can help people like you."

She nodded reluctantly, in acknowledgement, not agreement.

"Do you want to come in with us or wait out front?" I was afraid if we left her, she'd fade before we got back and I wouldn't be able to find her again. I didn't want her to spend eternity in this seedy alley all because she was imagining her family's disapproval. Shame could destroy you, bit by bit, from the inside. Candy might have wanted to hide how she was making a living, but survival was nothing to be ashamed of.

She hesitated, wrapping the end of her long ponytail around her finger. "I'll…I'll go with you."

"Great." I turned back to my guys. "Candy's going to come with us. Go ahead, Fangorn, lead the way."

Grunting—that one was impatient. I was starting to get the

variation in sound down—he opened the door and glowered at the bouncer. Like last time, Lurch came out of the shadows and waved us in. Candy was clinging to my side as I pointed Clive toward the back. Fangorn scanned the room, which was far more crowded than the last time. Candy made a strange sound and I looked over to see her gaping at the stage.

"They're N.A.K.E.D.," she hissed.

I nodded. "That's true."

"But." She looked around frantically. "Won't they get in trouble for that? Oh! They have one of those poles! Stu—he was the manager of the Mermaid Lounge—he was okay. Sometimes they're not, you know."

"Yeah, I know."

"Anyway, he said we were going to get a pole next month. I was going to ask him if I could—" She yelped and I knew she'd seen the creepy bartender's eyes turn red too.

"Candy, it would be best if you tried to be quiet now. I need to concentrate. Okay?" Fangorn led the way into the back hall again.

"Oh, sure, sure. I'll be quiet as a mouse. You won't even know I'm here. Not a peep out of me. No, siree…"

She kept going but was thankfully whispering, which was a little easier to ignore. I got it. She was scared to death and metaphorically whistling in the dark. I'd done the same the last time I was here.

When we stopped at the back wall, I reached for the invisible doorknob, but Fangorn pushed me behind him, grunting at Clive to do it.

"In case there's something scary on the other side, he wants you to open the door." I unsheathed my demon sword, just in case.

Clive moved to the front and reached out his hand. A doorknob appeared and he turned it, opening the door onto the dark alley. A couple of bare bulbs over doorways glowed with a dirty yellow light.

"Charming." He reached for my hand. "No heartbeats, aside from a few rodents."

Candy's fingers dug into my arm. "Did he say rodents?" She was spinning this way and that, searching the ground for rats.

"Unless they're ghost rats, you'll be fine."

"Oh." She shook her head. "I swear, I'm so stupid. I—"

"Nope. I've only known you for a few minutes and I already know you're not stupid. You're not allowed to insult my new friend."

Candy didn't say anything, but her grip relaxed. Fangorn was back in the lead. I was sure Clive was right. It was pointless to search the darkened windows for eyes staring back, but I couldn't stop myself.

At the end of the alley was the ancient door again. It had been closed since our last visit. Clive pulled it open on screeching hinges. When he started to walk in the alcove with the elevator, I pulled him back.

"That wasn't here before," I said, staring into the gloom.

Both Fangorn and Clive studied the small cement room. "What wasn't?" Clive asked.

"That," said, pointing at the roiling black cloud hovering between the door and the elevator. It was sentient. I could feel the menace, the hunger.

Candy's hand's tore at my sleeve, trying to hold on as she was pulled toward the shadowy need. Souleater. That's what that thing was, and it wanted Candy.

## 26

## Why Do Demons Have to Be Such Assholes?

"Sam!" Candy's thin arms were wrapped around mine as she was yanked forward. Like someone in a category 5 hurricane clinging to a tree, her body was soon airborne, her screams echoing in my head.

I knew Clive was saying something, but I couldn't hear him over the wailing, both in the black cloud and beside me. When Fangorn took a step forward, I grabbed his arm and shouted, "No!"

Candy was desperately clutching my sword arm. I switched the sword from my right to left hand. It may not have been my dominant one, but it was terrified ghost free, which made it the better choice. Hopefully, Dave's dad did in fact imbue it with something that'd help keep Candy from being consumed by evil.

*Shit.* Was I a necromancer or what? Drawing on my power, I pulled Candy back and put her outside the door. Leading with my sword, I tried to slice through the shadowy presence and was sucked into the room, the door slamming behind me, trapping me with it.

Darkness enveloped me, cutting off all sound. I switched hands again and then slashed the sword through the air, trying to hit what was hiding. Twisting in the pitch black, my arm arcing in every direction, I attempted to find and skewer the entity fucking with me, but he was having too much fun.

I felt a jab in my side and then another one in my back. Always a second too late, I sliced through the air, hitting nothing. Blood trickled down my skin. I drew the pain into the wicche glass around my neck and tried to concentrate.

Searching my mind, I looked for the flat black-on-black blip that meant demon. The void was too big. There were too many dead. I had almost tipped into the darkness and lost myself when I stopped flailing and tried to find clarity in stillness. Holding the sword in front of myself, my forehead to the flat of the blade, I pulled my focus in. I didn't want Hell. I didn't want the biergarten or strip club. I just wanted the demon with me right now.

There it was, hiding in the corner. I stepped toward it and the room filled with glass-shattering wails and deep guttural grunts. My head went light and my stomach seized. The jabs turned into claw slices. I knew the sounds, the wounds. I'd been having this nightmare for seven years. He was playing the soundtrack of my torture and rape.

A low, raspy chuckle filled the silence between the screams. No. I wasn't being taken down by this. I'd survived it once. The memory wasn't going to take me out. I focused on the laugh. Clutching my stomach, I stumbled forward, making a retching sound. When I was close to the corner, I sprang forward and stabbed.

He slid out of the path and now knew I could find him, damn it! Randy, my rapist, now stood in front of me, hunting knife in his hand, eyes going yellow, his wolf coming to the fore. It took everything I had, but I closed my eyes on him. He was a distraction. That fucking demon was trying to throw me off his scent.

Randy's voice was everywhere, coming from every direction, as he narrated the soundtrack of my torture. Nope. Fuck you. I already killed you. It was the demon I needed now. I searched my mind again and finally found him, hovering directly above me.

Pleading tearfully with Randy to leave me alone, I focused all my energy on holding the demon in place. The sword in my hand had to be upping my power because I knew I held no sway over demons. When I felt Randy's hot breath in my ear, I cringed away and stabbed straight up.

A blinding light filled the room, the screams of many swirling around me, and then it all disappeared, the room finally silent. The door was yanked off its hinges and thrown down the alley. Clive grabbed me and didn't put me down until we were halfway down the alley.

"I smell blood," he said, lifting my clothing, trying to find the wounds.

Candy was suddenly beside me. "You saved me."

"It's okay."

"It's not," Clive ground out, licking any cut he found to staunch the flow and help me heal.

"I was talking to Candy. Keep doing what you're doing." I pointed to my lower back. "Over here."

"What—what was that thing?" She was so scared, she was becoming transparent.

"That was a demon, but it's gone now."

Candy had her hands clasped between her breasts, terrified, her gaze cutting back to the elevator room. "You're bleeding. That thing cut—why is he doing that?" she asked, referring to Clive. Oh, well. She was going to have to know at some point.

"My husband is a vampire." Ignoring her *eep* and murmured prayers, I continued, "He's licking the wounds to help heal them quickly. Vampires can do that. And while we're on the subject, I'm a werewolf and a wicche, a necromancer to be specific, which is how I can see and talk with you. I get that you're scared. You don't have to stick with us. I'm always available to help you cross over to see your family. In the meantime, though, we're going to a demon bar to find my friend. I think he needs help."

She winked out of sight. While not unexpected, still a bummer. I really did want her to cross over. She'd being paying for her perceived sins for far too long. "And we lost Candy."

Clive paused, looking up at me. "Did the demon get her?"

"No. Fear did. This life is not for the fainthearted."

Grinning, he stood and gave me a smacking kiss. "The soul of a warrior, this one."

I don't know why, it was silly, but his words made me tear up. Too many years, I supposed, of hiding from the memories—the scars—of what Randy had done to me, of hiding from my aunt, of berating myself for being weak.

"No, love. That was your origin story. Those years were what taught you compassion. A warrior without empathy soon becomes a tyrant. Your strength comes from pain and recognizes that pain in others. Now, did I miss any wounds?"

I tapped my lips and he swooped in with a kiss that made my knees go weak.

An annoyed grunt broke the spell. Right. We had a mission.

"Sorry. We're ready now." Grabbing Clive's hand, we walked back to the elevator room, now demon-free. Fangorn hit the call button and we waited.

When the door finally opened, Fangorn went in first, sword at the ready. Clive ushered me in and then brought up the rear, hitting the BD button.

"Do we know what the A stands for?" Clive asked, gesturing to the bottom button.

"We do not. Probably something hideous like Agony."

"Antichrist?" Clive responded.

"Argh, Avast Ye Land Lubbers!"

"You think demons have their own pirate ride?" he inquired.

I shrugged. "Stands to reason. If you can do anything, why not have your own pirate ride? Oh, maybe we could have the dragon builders make us one of those," I said.

"Apocalypse," Clive guessed.

"Alligator," Fangorn chimed in, surprising the heck out of me.

"To fight or eat?" I asked.

He shrugged. "Both."

While Fangorn dreamed of battling gators, Clive took my hand

and squeezed. He knew I was scared and was playing along to help settle my nerves. When the door eventually opened, I took a deep breath and stepped out.

The time of day in Almost-Hell-landia was later than last time. It was full dark now, with fireflies bobbing around the flowering bushes. Lanterns, swinging above in the light breeze, lit the path to the Biergarten of the Damned.

Fangorn led the way. The voices were louder than last time. When we rounded the wisteria, I saw why. All the tables were filled. Red-skinned demons with horns and hooves; black humanoid entities, eyes sewn shut, mouths filled with razor-sharp teeth; pale, bloated carcasses that looked to have been dead in the water for weeks, eyes a filmy white; gorgeous men and women interspersed throughout, chatting with the horrors.

A few of them I recognized from true crime documentaries, some from history, like the man in the plaid suit and dark glasses who promised eternal life and a pipeline to Heaven, only to bilk his followers of all their money and encourage them to drink poison—after they'd given it to their children, of course.

Instead of the terror I'd expected, I realized I was overwhelmed with disgust and anger. That damn demon above had reminded me that what had been done to me had been enabled by one of them. What had been done to my mother was thanks to one of them. I unsheathed my sword, because fuck them. They lived in the shadows and traded in pride, greed, lust, envy, gluttony, wrath, and sloth. I wasn't going to give them the fear they fed on.

As one, they all turned to us, their eyes on me and the sword. Yes, I broke out into a cold sweat, but that could be ignored. I stared down as many as I could and then turned on my heel and headed to the blackened structure still serving as their bar, Clive and Fangorn flanking me.

When a fur-covered demon in a dark cloak, ram's horns, and red eyes with vertical slits stood to intercept me, I let my wolf's teeth lengthen and held up my sword, a deep, feral growl rolling through the now silent space.

I felt him pushing, trying to take over my mind. Maybe it was the spelled sword in my hand, maybe he was just low-level enough for it to work, but I found his blip easily in my head. Staring into his arrogant eyes, I crushed it, pictured that flat black blip in my hand as I squeezed with all my strength, channeling the resultant headache into the wicche glass. I'd need to deal with the imbalance soon, but it wouldn't be while I was surrounded by demons.

His goat eyes rolled into the back of his head and he hit the ground. It hurt. Clive was siphoning off the pain the wicche glass couldn't handle. It didn't matter. I had to make a show of strength or they'd attack. Being the selfish demons they were, no one else chose to risk pain for something that didn't involve them. I was aided by their disregard for one another.

Ted Bundy was back behind the bar. He looked me up and down, his sudden smile not reaching his eyes. Taking in the demon still on the ground and my two bodyguards, he didn't bother to say anything, instead heading for the scorched doorway.

"You have visitors," he sing-songed.

There was a crash in the back, some rather angry and creative swearing, and then Dave was barreling through the doorway.

I held up my hands, one still holding my sword, and said, "I just want to talk with you."

His shark-black eyes took in all the tables of demons watching and listening, and then the demon still crumpled on the floor, before returning to me. "What do I have to do to get you to fuck off? What? You're like some damn baby duckling that imprinted on the wrong person."

I could feel Clive's anger boiling over. He wanted to tear Dave's head off.

*Please don't. There's a reason he's trying so hard to push me away.*

*I love you, darling, and I'll try, but there's only so much abuse I can let him heap on you.*

"Can we go somewhere and talk? And then I'll leave you

alone." Out of the corner of my eye, I saw someone moving toward me. Damn it, it was Olivier again.

He leaned on the bar and took in the scene. "Oh, go ahead. Chat her up. She seems like the trusting sort."

"This has got nothing to do with you," Dave growled before turning back to me. "Get out!" he roared and then turned his back on us.

"You'll have to forgive him," Olivier said. "He's always been an emotional one, crying to Daddy if things didn't go his way." He shrugged and gave me a wicked grin. "Would you like to hear a story?"

He sat on a barstool and leaned back, his elbows on the bar behind him. "Let's see. It was a few years ago." He looked up into the night sky, pretending to consider, as though he wasn't positively gleeful telling tales on Dave. "It was seven, almost eight years ago."

Dave was suddenly filling the doorway. "Get out. I mean it, Sam. Now. I'll stop by tomorrow if I get the time, but I'm not talking with you here, not now."

"Relax. It's a fun story. Come on, you can help me tell it," Olivier said.

Dave burst into flames.

## 27

# Sam Isn't Available Right Now. Please Leave a Message

Olivier rolled his eyes at the fiery display and then waved me over, patting the barstool beside him. When I didn't move, he shrugged good naturedly.

"So, there was a lovely and very good little wicche who was on the run, hiding with her daughter from her mean ol' sorceress sister." He cupped his hand around the side of his mouth, as though imparting a secret. "Batshit crazy, that one, with a hard-on for killing her sister." He dropped his hand. "Sister and niece, that is."

My heart was in my throat. Was this the bastard who'd possessed the homeless man and made him carve up my mother?

"Sam, go!" Dave shouted, but I didn't flinch. All my attention was on Olivier and his story.

"The poor little wicche had constant headaches from the sister trying to bore in and discover their whereabouts, but the good wicche tried to make life as normal and happy as she could for her daughter. She was worried, though. She had to find a way to protect her child from her sister. So, the dogged little wicche worked all day and all night, pouring all her magic into an amulet to protect her child. And it worked, but in exhausting herself so much, the sorceress sister was able to break through the good wicche's defenses and discover their whereabouts.

"After that, it was easy to track and torment them. The amulet kept the child safe, but the mother was in constant pain and fear, keeping her daughter on the run. Now, the child grew up and grew resentful of the constant movement, of changing schools, of no friends. The mother was quite literally giving her daughter everything, but it wasn't enough for the little brat."

"Sam," Dave said, the fire having gone out, but I ignored him.

"It was her senior year in high school. She wanted to graduate, wanted to walk in a cap and gown. The mother felt the sister getting closer and told her daughter she couldn't attend the ceremony. They needed to go to be safe. The daughter cried, used her tears to manipulate her mother, the poor little wicche who'd already given everything she could.

"The loving mother relented, of course. There was nothing she'd deny her beloved girl. So, they stayed long past when they should have, and the sister found them. Found them and carved up the mother with a big, sharp knife while the daughter hid in a closet, watching.

"No graduation, no cap and gown, just a funeral for the sweet little wicche who gave everything she could for the whiney, ungrateful daughter. Personally, I thought it was poetic justice when a short time later, the daughter got carved up as well."

Clive wrapped his arm around me. *We're going.*

"Wait," Olivier said. "I haven't gotten to the best part yet. The poor, whiney orphan started to make a life for herself, still safely hidden by her mother's amulet. She opened a bookstore and bar. And who should show up on her doorstep, looking for a job? The demon who'd carved up her mother." Olivier beamed and then laughed and laughed, holding his side as the rest of the demons in the biergarten joined in.

In that moment, the world tipped and the floor dropped out from beneath me. I was free-falling without moving a muscle. My gaze cut to Dave and the truth of it was written all over his face. My brain stuttered to a stop.

The sword was suddenly in my hand. Olivier's laugh wound down as he looked on avidly. I took a step toward Dave, his expression resigned. Hand shaking on the sword, I looked into his eyes and knew he welcomed the blade.

Without a word, I turned and walked back past the laughing demons. I didn't care. None of it mattered. An explosion ripped through the biergarten, tables shooting up and then showering down, as though land mines sat beneath each one. Hell rained down on the demons.

I felt a moment of blinding light and blistering heat before Clive picked me up and flew to the elevator. Looking over Clive's shoulder, I watched demons hit the ground, scrambling away from the other bodies falling, the wooden timbers crashing around them.

The void inside me seemed to get bigger and bigger, sucking in my thoughts and emotions. The elevator opened and Clive stepped in with me, Fangorn bringing up the rear. Clive put me down. I knew he was saying something, but I couldn't hear him over the roaring in my head.

What seemed like a moment later, the elevator opened and we were back in the alley. Strange. I'd found the alley so scary before. I'd been hyper aware of the scratch of every rat's claw. Now? It was like the lights had been turned on in a haunted house. I'd seen the wires and pulleys.

I yanked open the back door of the Demon's Lair and strode through. Fuck all their deep shadows and red burning eyes. Lurch moved into my path to stop me. I shoved him right back out of it. I didn't have the time or interest to deal with lackeys.

Pushing open the front door, I turned for the car. Fangorn took point. I knew Clive was beside me, concerned, but I couldn't. I didn't have it in me to discuss anything that had just happened. The screaming void was keeping me nicely insulated from the world and I was fine with that.

Clive opened the back door for me and I slid in. Instead of closing the door, he framed my face with his hands. The tears came at once. I blinked and shook my head, looking away from him. Kissing my forehead, he let me be.

The drive home was over in a blink. I got out and streaked down the steps into my safe space. I stood a moment at the bottom of the stairs. It was late, but there were still a few customers. Fyr sat behind the bar, reading a mystery. Fergus sat in front of me, being a good boy, trying to get my attention. Scratching him behind the ears, I kept going. I didn't want to be around people.

I intended to hide in our apartment, but when I looked at the bed, I knew it wasn't far enough away, not from myself. Letting my coat fall to the ground, I detoured down the new hall, ducking around the heavy plastic sheeting into our folly.

I'd taken pictures last week from right here, not wanting to disturb the workmen. This time, I didn't stop, walking out into the Shire. I brushed my hands over the tops of tall grasses beside the pond. Fergus had followed me in, racing this way and that, trying to sniff everything at once. I couldn't see him, but I could track his progress by the grass waving and bending.

When I hit the cart path, I started jogging, Fergus right beside me. We passed the cart and the horse that looked amazingly real. Fergus stopped to check out the horse, but I continued on, past large, shady trees and another pond at the base of the tall green hill containing the hobbit holes.

I ran up the footpath, Fergus at my heels again, past blue and yellow doors, up a steep incline directly to the large perfectly round green door with a brass knob in the center. It sat below the massive tree growing at the top of the hill, its branches overshadowing the doorways. Hoping the door was unlocked, I pushed and found myself in the entry. They weren't done, but it was perfect, exactly as Tolkien had described Bag End.

As with any hobbit hole, comfort was key. There was a long hall, paneled in a rich, warm wood that ran straight through the hill. Rounded doorways opened to rooms on either side, bedrooms, bathrooms, cellar, pantry, kitchen, dining room. Each room was filled with squashy armchairs and sofas, the tile floors covered in thick rugs, the walls adorned with art and maps.

The rooms to the left of the hall were the best, as they had windows looking out over the gardens, meadow, and ponds. When I reached the end of the hall, I found a library on the left. Some of the shelves had large, leather-covered tomes, but most were still empty. There was a beautiful desk in front of the window and soft, floral armchairs by the fireplace.

I stepped in and sat, curling my legs up on the seat, tipping my head against the cushioned wingback. A moment later, Fergus hopped into my lap and settled himself, offering comfort or a napping buddy. Whichever I needed.

Dry-eyed, I stared out the window at the Shire, willing myself to think of anything but Olivier's story. Fergus whined and licked my chin. I didn't need to see the pup's ears lift to know Clive was coming. I'd felt it.

He walked in, laying his hand atop my head a moment before crouching in front of the fireplace. "If they're decorating, surely this must be working." He tinkered a bit. "Or perhaps not. Everything is made to look real, but it's a folly, so…" He pushed down on a decorative brick on the hearth and a fire shot up. "Much better. You may not be feeling it right now, but it's quite chilly in here."

Clive slid his arms under me, picking up both Fergus and myself, before taking the seat and holding us in his lap. Fergus slid off and curled up on the rug at our feet in front of the fire. After helping me extricate myself from the axe on my back, Clive wrapped his arms around me and waited. He was good at that.

The tears came almost immediately. I could have held them back, but kindness and sympathy had broken the dam. He took a handkerchief from his pocket, dabbing at my face, but it was no use.

*You know, the only one responsible for your mother's death is Abigail.*

Of course, he knew which part of the story had decimated me.

*It was true, though. She told me we needed to go. We'd been moving for as long as I could remember, and we'd never been caught. I thought she was being overly cautious. It was only a few more weeks. What was the harm?*

*You didn't know.*

*She said she was sorry, but we needed to pack. He was right. I teared up and then went to my room to collect everything on my bed again. My mom came in a few minutes later and said we'd stay until graduation.*

*You didn't know.*

*She did that because of me. She risked her own life because I was a whiny baby who wanted to graduate. With a class I barely knew. We'd only been there a month.*

*You didn't know.*

*But I should have! Just like I should have known she was in constant pain.* I rubbed my forehead, remembering how she'd often done the same. *We sometimes stayed places three or four months. When we had to get out quickly, it was because she'd seen something in the scrying mirror that said Abigail was closing in. I knew that! And because she'd kept us safe my whole life, I'd assumed the threat wasn't that great. What was two and a half more weeks? My mother's torture and death. That was the cost of two more weeks.*

*Love, you couldn't possibly have known. Did she say, 'My sister knows where we are. We have to run now?'*

*No. But the pattern had been set when I was too young to understand the threat. She wanted to protect me as much as she could. She tried to make a game of it, until I became a teenager and started asking more questions. It upset her, I knew it did, but I wanted to know why we had to move so much. Other kids didn't. That became clear every time I started a new school.*

*Everyone else seemed to have friends, have enemies, have kids they'd known since kindergarten. I felt sorry for myself, always being the new kid, always separate from the others.*

He kissed my forehead.

*It was stupid adolescent crap that I'm sure most people go through.*

*I'd been seventeen that last time. An adult in your world, and I'd manipulated her into doing what I wanted.*

*There was no manipulation. You cried because you were upset. That's called being human. You'd gone to pack because you were following your mother's request, even though it meant forgoing yet another rite of passage in your life.*

I shook my head, tucked into his neck. *Demon or not, he was right about me.*

*No, darling, he wasn't. Don't allow his words to color your memories of your mother. She loved you more than anything in this world—a feeling I'm quite familiar with—and she'd never want you to take on this guilt. She was killed by her sister, a sorceress with a lifelong grudge against her, who would have done the same to you if she'd known you were there.*

*And the only reason she didn't is because my mom used her energy to hide me right before she'd needed it for a fight.*

*And that was her choice, wasn't it? She chose as her final act to protect her daughter. Honor her memory, darling. Don't allow a demon's words to stain your relationship.*

He sat with me until I finally wound down, until the tears eventually dried up. Throat tight, heart aching, I felt as though I'd been set adrift with only one line anchoring me to the shore. Clive.

*You know, I've been thinking. What if we put a plaque for your mother under the tree on top of the hill?*

"A bench," I eventually said, sitting up and wiping my face. "We'll add a bench with a plaque for her. Then it'll almost be like she's sitting with us, overlooking the Shire. She used to read *The Hobbit* to me when I was little before eventually giving me all her copies of Tolkien." Looking out the window through tear-filled eyes, I added, "She'd like that."

## 28

# I'm Pretty Sure a Backpack of Snacks Was in the Marriage Vows

Clive studied the room. "I never anticipated living in a Hobbit hole, but I must say, it's quite cozy."

I smiled into his neck. "Hobbits are all about peace and comfort. And multiple meals. I think that was why my mom started telling me Tolkien's stories. She had a bag of snacks at the ready because I was always hungry growing up. I knew we didn't have much money, so I tried to pretend I wasn't, but my stomach would rumble, and she'd ask if I wanted second breakfast or elevensies."

"I'm going to have to start carrying a backpack of snacks for you, aren't I?"

"You did promise in sickness and health, in hunger with snacks."

"Hmm, I don't believe I recall that."

"Strange. I thought for sure Owen put that in there. *Anyway,*" I said, snuggling in, "I don't know if Mom knew I took after my dad or not. I mean, Quinns produced born wolves but only male until me."

"My unique little one."

"Right?" My phone buzzed in my pocket. I checked the screen. "Fyr's closing down now. What was I—oh, so when my mom made the amulet dampening my powers and hiding me, she probably focused on my wicchey side, as the wolfy bits were still in question."

"One would assume the near constant hunger tipped her off." Grinning, he adjusted my sword and settled me more comfortably in his lap.

My phone buzzed again and I looked down. "Fyr's leaving. He's reminding me to lock up."

"Come on," Clive said, standing us up. "Let's head back before the dragons find us." He picked up my axe by the leather sheath—fae metal burned vampires—while the pup hopped up and danced around, excited by the possibilities.

Holding hands, we walked slowly down the hall, looking into the rooms that were approaching done. "Yes," Clive said, pulling my hand to his lips for a kiss. "I think we'll enjoy living here very much."

We paused at the front door a moment while Clive listened. "No heartbeats nearby. The coast is clear."

When he opened the door, Fergus ran out to race up and down the paths along the terraced hill. I hadn't taken a moment to appreciate it before, but the door garden was perfectly lovely. Bag End was built into the top of the hill. In between windows and the door was every shade of green, from the grass-covered hill, the ivy and moss, the wildflowers growing between the slate steps down. Thick, glossy bushes with rich blossoms, a peony here, a dahlia there, bleeding hearts, clematis, everywhere I looked was abundant Middle-earth.

"Hey." I bumped Clive's shoulder with my own. "Speaking of no heartbeats, what did you think of the horse?"

He shook his head as we descended the steps, making our way back to the path that rounded the large pond. "I must admit, though I am quite fond of horses, one without a heartbeat or breath is disturbing. The skill is extraordinary. They have created an incredibly lifelike horse."

"Which you find disturbing."

"I really do. It does make me want my own stables, though." He swung our hands like I often did as we stepped back on the cart path, toward the horse in question.

"I thought real horses didn't like vampires?"

"They're very intelligent animals, so they don't. I was considering, though, if I started with a foal or two, and I raised them to not fear me. Later, I'd presumably have more who didn't fear me." He looked out over the Shire in the magical late afternoon sun. "I miss riding."

"Maybe you could be a vampy horse breeder, training horses for other supernaturals who miss riding. I mean, this folly is going to cost a fortune. I can't support us forever, you know. You're going to have to get a job soon."

Two dragon workmen came through a door in the horizon I hadn't seen.

I waved my free hand over my head. "It's absolutely perfect! You're doing an amazing job! Thank you so much!" I smiled hugely, hoping they wouldn't yell or slow down the build after I'd just praised their work. We were talking about dragons, though, so you never knew. They were a churlish bunch.

They looked at each other, looked back at us, and waited, presumably for us to get the hell out.

"Perhaps we should consider the lack of fire their response and continue on." Clive pulled me forward. Fergus barked twice at the dragons and then led the way back to our apartment.

"Yeah. Probably for the best." There were water lilies floating in the small pond near the apartment entrance. "How do horses feel about wolficches?"

"I suppose we'll find out," he said, wrapping an arm around me while pushing open the heavy plastic sheeting. Fergus ran in first and shot right through the apartment and into the kitchen, barking wildly.

Clive and I spared one glance and then both shot forward. Something was in the bar. Clive got through the door first and I plowed into him. Being Clive, he didn't move, but when I bounced off him, he shot out a hand to hold me upright.

"This must be your husband."

Dave's dad was back. He sat at a table by the window, a short glass of whiskey at his wrist. Fergus crouched out of reach, hackles raised, watching the demon.

"Clive Fitzwilliam. And you are?" Clive held me behind him, which seemed overkill as I had already had a long conversation with the man, but he was a demon, so, yeah, I got it.

"A pleasure to meet you. I'm Dave's father."

"Your name?" Clive inquired.

"Is not something I'll be sharing this evening. I came to speak with your lovely wife, if I may. Ms. Quinn?" Perfect in a dark suit, his white dress shirt lay open at his throat, stark against the near luminous brown of his skin.

I looked around Clive's shoulder. "Yes?"

"I was wondering if you might sit with me. I have something I'd like to discuss with you. Your husband is, of course, welcome to remain."

"How good of you," Clive remarked, causing Dave's dad to grin unrepentantly.

Clive and I sat across from the demon, the axe sheath still hanging from Clive's hand. Fergus hopped into my lap, his paws on the table, staying between the demon and me. Brave boy.

"As I'm sure you're aware, your visit to the biergarten this evening caused quite a stir." Dave's dad took a sip of whiskey. He then held the cut crystal up to the light. "This is my own reserve, by the way. I didn't help myself to your liquor."

"Oh, that's"—I felt Clive's hand on my leg. Right. No need to let him off the hook when he showed up uninvited—"good to know."

Dave Sr. winked at me. "Nice save."

"If you heard what happened," Clive began, "then you know that wasn't Sam's fault. Your son whipped up the inferno."

The corner of Dave Sr.'s mouth twitched. "He did." He took

another sip. "It's an effective reminder to the rest of them who he is and what he's capable of. I'm told you were quite distraught when you left, as was my son apparently. Can you tell me what was discussed?"

I didn't want to carry tales I wasn't supposed to. Then again, fuck Dave! Then again again, thinking of Dave as my enemy felt all wrong. "Why don't you ask that Olivier guy? He was the shit disturber causing all the trouble."

He sighed deeply. "I would but I'm having some trouble finding him at the moment. I'm afraid my son was quite angry with him."

"Yeah, well, I'm not too happy with your son at the moment."

Clive ran his hand up and down my leg in comfort. We hadn't discussed that revelation yet. It was too much. I wasn't ready to confront the betrayal. I held Fergus with one hand and laid my other over Clive's, squeezing.

Dave Sr. cocked his head, studying us. "Hmm, that wasn't the reaction I was expecting. Since Olivier is currently indisposed, would you be so kind as to explain the nature of your conversation with my son?"

"Olivier was doing all the talking," I said.

"Yes, he does have a tendency to do that, doesn't he? I'm not sure why my son puts up with it."

"I believe that stopped today," Clive responded.

Nodding slowly, Dave Sr. said, "It did, didn't it? As Sam and I discussed earlier, my son didn't have an easy time growing up. My home isn't the most conducive to healthy child-rearing."

When I snorted a laugh, Dave Sr. said, "Just so. They were quite cruel to him, as I understand. My son is not without his own, rather formidable, defenses, though, so I never understood why he put up with it."

"Sometimes fighting fire with fire makes you feel like a pyromaniac," I volunteered.

Dave Sr. didn't appear to hear, lost in thought. After a pause, though, he turned to me again. "How do you mean?"

"I'm talking about myself, I suppose. I hid my wolf side for many years. I shifted when I had to and then pretended that side didn't exist. The one who attacked me, tortured me, he was a wolf. I didn't want anything to do with him. If I could have erased it all, for the longest time, I would have. Shifting, as he had, feeling that drive to hunt, as he had, it made me too much like him. I hated him, so I hated and denied that part of myself that was like him."

"I see," he said. "Because my son hates the demons who tormented him, he refused to use his demon gifts to fight them."

I shrugged. "I wasn't there. It's just a theory."

"It'll be interesting to see how things change once he's embraced his true nature."

Glancing at Clive, I said, "I don't think Dave has hidden his nature while he's been living here. I mean…" My mind started down a path I wasn't ready for. "I guess he was hiding other things."

Dave Sr. finished his drink and the glass disappeared. "I really am pressed for time tonight. What was the conversation about that put such sadness in your eyes and made my son blow things up?"

I was feeling decidedly less protective of Dave right now. "My mother." The tightness in my throat stopped me from saying anything else.

After a lengthy pause, he said, "I see." Standing, he buttoned his suit jacket. "This is going to take too long." He held out a hand. "Would you come with me, please?"

I was suddenly across the bar, standing behind Clive, who was holding a squirming Fergus under one arm and my axe by its straps from the other.

Dave Sr. studied us, eyebrows raised, appearing rather impressed. "You've misunderstood my intent. I can offer you safe passage to and from my home."

"No," Clive said.

"I've been fooled by that one before," I said around Clive's shoulder. "The fae king interpreted the safe passage promised by the queen to mean that they could do anything they wanted to me right up until my journey home, which they promised would be pain-free."

"The fae can be rather tricky with their language, can't they?"

I peeked around Clive's other shoulder. "Much like demons." I was sticking behind Clive because I could feel how churned up this whole situation was making him. We'd just walked through our new home, imagined our lives, horses, Fergus racing around, and now here we were again with someone threatening to steal me away to somewhere he couldn't follow.

It had taken living through hours of Sitri attacking him, being unable to do anything to help him, to fully appreciate how crazy it had made Clive when the fae had stolen me from Canterbury. I'd been gone for over a week and he had no idea who had me, where I was, or what was happening to me. So, yeah, I stayed behind him.

"You've had a decidedly interesting life for one so young."

Peeking around again, I said, "It's mostly been the last six months or so that have been off the rails. We're just looking for a nice, quiet life together."

He nodded and then disappeared. Well, that was easier than I thought it was going to be. I felt a hand on my shoulder and my heart stopped.

"That won't start tonight."

Clive spun, eyes vamp black, fangs descended, leaping for me, but we were already gone.

29

# Oh, Hell

My stomach flipped as I dropped straight down into pitch black. All I could think about was the last time I'd visited Hell and splatted on the rocky floor of the visitor's center.

"You've been to Hell before?" Oh, I guess Dave's dad was hanging with me for the trip. His disembodied voice was in my ear.

"Not really, no. I was trapped in a vision by my aunt, who was a sorcerer. I described it to Dave, though, and he said what I'd experienced was all correct. I dropped into the way station, broke every bone in my body, but was still alive-ish. Irdu was my orientation guide. He only stuck with me for a few minutes, though. I wandered off on my own until I was able to pull myself—with an assist—out of the vision."

"Interesting."

The speed with which we were falling in total darkness was making my heart rabbit. Maybe Hell had a stronger gravitational force than Earth. It felt more like pulling than falling. I really didn't want to splat again. It was horrendously painful.

"You'll be fine," he said absently.

"I don't trust you."

"Whyever not?"

"You lied to me. You said you'd stop Sitri from attacking Clive while he slept and you didn't." Asshole.

"I did and don't be vulgar." His voice turned angry and disapproving.

"I believe we discussed the whole mind reading thing and no you didn't."

Oppressive silence filled the void before he finally said, "Your thoughts are quite loud."

"Why are you doing this? We were cooperating with you."

"Not quickly enough. I'll keep you safe, but you need to understand that you're not my priority. My son is my priority. You weren't telling me what I needed to know. I think this will be more effective anyway. Quiet now. I'm thinking."

If he wasn't a super powerful demon, I'd kick him. Right in the 'nads. I tried to see through the dark to the bottom, but the force of the wind had me tearing up. Light-headed, stomach in my throat, and eyes watering, I officially hated this abduction. Stupid, imperious demon. I felt a nudge and then I started to spin. Oh, God. I was going to hurl.

"See? It can always get worse. Stop complaining."

Screwing my eyes shut, I threw my arms out, trying to slow myself down. It took quite a lot of arm and leg movements to try to find the right combination to stop spinning, but I finally got there. Judging by the silent laughter I was sensing nearby, I probably looked like a complete loon, and he had just decided to finally put me out of my misery. Whatever. At least I wasn't spinning anymore.

Godfrey popped into my head. If there was anyone who would enjoy hearing this story, it would be him. I just had to live long enough to get home and tell him.

After a while, it felt like I was sensing color below. It could have been the back of my eyelids. Were my eyes open? I blinked. Yes. Yes, they were. Red. I was seeing a pulsating speck of red—maybe some yellow too—below us. I swore, if he was dropping us into Mordor and the fires of Mount Doom, we were going to have words.

And then it was like we'd jumped to warp speed. Flipped over, I was now plummeting headfirst into a raging inferno that got bigger by the second. *Clive! I love you!* I screwed my eyes shut again and braced for impact.

I could feel the smug bastard rolling his eyes at me, and then we were standing on the edge of a lake of fire, in a huge rocky cavern. The heat was so oppressive, sweat was already running down my back and my lungs felt like they were burning from the inside. My eyes stung and my knees gave out as a hand shot out and grabbed me, holding me upright.

Like a door slamming shut, the heat disappeared. I was standing in the same spot, but Dave Sr.'s hand was on my elbow and I was no longer being burned alive. In fact, the sweat drying on my skin made it a bit chilly.

"I forgot how this would affect you." He gave me a look, though, that said it was payback for the bastard thought.

"When you visited me in the library, you said you guys couldn't hurt people like me."

Silence.

"You told me there were rules and our auras or souls or whatever were obvious, that people like me were off limits."

"Ah, but you forgot the more important detail," he said, scanning the recesses of the gargantuan cavern. Turning to me, his gaze felt heavy and cold. "I can do whatever I want." He looked down at his hand on my elbow and then let go, touching the pommel of my sword.

The door opened and I was consumed by fire again. When my eyes started to roll back in my head, he guided my hand to my sword. As soon as I touched it, the door closed and I was protected from the heat. I could think and breathe again.

Damn him. "Where are we, anyway?" If he wanted me chastened, I suppose he got it. I really did not want to be burned alive.

"Hell," he replied simply. His eyes were trained across the vast expanse of molten, liquid fire.

"Yeah, I got that. I meant does this place have a name?" Did the answer matter? Not particularly. Mostly, I was just recovering from almost dying while trying not to think about the fact that if my hand was knocked off this sword, I'd be burning up again.

"This is the Abyss."

Holy shi—

"Wait here." And he disappeared.

Oh, no, no, no, no, no. He did not just take me to Hell and then ditch me! Keeping a death grip on my sword, I spun, making sure no one was sneaking up in me. *Shitshitshit.* This wasn't a vision. There was no getting pulled out this time.

Screaming. I was hearing screaming. It just registered over the sound of the fire echoing off the walls of the cavern. Louder and louder; my head pounded. When it felt like my skull was going to explode, I almost took my hand off the sword to cover my ears. I covered my left ear with my hand and then unsheathed my sword and blocked my right ear as best I could with my shoulder.

It didn't work. The screaming was inside me and I now hated Dave's dad more than just a little. Movement in the periphery of my vision had me looking up. Oh, God. People, a huge jumble of people, tumbling over one another, were sliding down a steep rocky slope, headed directly for the Abyss.

I raced forward, closer to the edge, as they dropped into the molten, liquid fire from the other side of the flaming lake. They just kept coming, toppling over one another, limbs at odd angles as they rolled, bounced, flew, and then dropped into the hissing flames.

Face burning, too close to the edge, I moved back, my stomach heaving. I stumbled to a rocky outcrop and vomited, tears streaming down my face. It was too much. The unending wails, the explosions of fire as another dropped in, soul-crushing despair. I was a necromancer surrounded by the evil dead. I had every defense in my arsenal engaged and it was like a toothpick trying to stop a tsunami.

"Mr. Dove!" I called, looking for the angel that had saved me last time. "I need you!" He was probably still hanging around Meg's church.

"How did you make it across the Abyss?" A demon—Olivier—walked out of the shadows toward me. "Oh, it's you. Did you hit the wrong button on the elevator?"

Did I—Oh. A for Abyss. "So I guess you didn't get hurt in that explosion." I was gripping my sword like my life depended on it, because, of course, it did. Did I already mention Dave's dad was a jackass!

"We're demons. We're made of fire. It'd be like you getting caught in the rain. So," he said, moving closer, "why are you here?" His gaze traveled over me. "And why are you gripping that sword so tightly?"

An arm wrapped around my waist. Jolting, I looked up into the face of one of those goat-headed demons and nearly wet myself.

"Fresh meat," he growled, rubbing his junk against my hip. "I love it when they give us new toys to play with."

I panicked. I'll admit it. When he grabbed me, I was back in that shack seven years ago and I froze. Light-headed-dry-mouthed-heart-stopped-stomach-dropped frozen. For two seconds.

And then I flipped the fuck out, slamming my razor-sharp claws up through the bottom of his jaw, hooking them around the bone and swinging him over my shoulder before slamming him to the ground. Stomping a foot on his chest, I pulled my clawed hand back and drove the sword in my other hand through his forehead before yanking it out and slashing it through his neck. He popped out of existence, the floor of the cavern rumbling in his wake.

"Now I definitely want to see that sword." Olivier pushed, trying to influence me, trying to get inside and possess me. He'd tried to do this at the biergarten and had failed. He must have thought he'd have more success on his home turf.

Thankfully, it was easier to keep him out with my hand on the sword. "You can go now," I said, flicking my fingers. "I'm waiting for someone."

"I don't think so. As I'd prefer not to be speared with those claws of yours, though," he said, circling in front of me, "I'll let my friends handle it."

Those destined for the Abyss tumbled down from up above, wailing mournfully in the dark before being consumed in the lake of fire. As the bodies sunk, little black spirits rose and raced over the bubbling surface, right toward me. Olivier took in my expression and began to laugh.

"Just because you're a demon, it doesn't mean you have to be an asshole!" More and more popped out of the lake of fire and zoomed toward me.

"Sure it does." He stepped back, out of the baby demons' path.

They swarmed me, each taking little bites, most concentrating on the hand holding the sword. Blocking as best I could, I thought back on that spell I'd used before, accidentally dragging Dave down to Hell. Yes, we were already here, but maybe it'd drag Olivier to another part of Hell and give me some peace.

Focusing, funneling the bites into the wicche glass, I worked on the spell a moment until I had the wording correct in my mind. I didn't want to screw this up. As I began chanting, the bites lessened until there were none. With one last push, I opened my eyes and watched Olivier get surrounded—not just by the baby demons, but bigger, nastier ones as well—and dragged off.

I looked down at myself. I was covered in blood, my clothes ripped and torn. I'd feel the pain in a minute. Fear and adrenaline were holding it back right now.

I fixated on a swath of my belly that was exposed, the section Gloriana had healed when I'd almost died in a kelpie attack. Gloriana had smoothed my skin—returned it to factory settings—when she'd healed me. I'd had scars from neck to foot for seven years and then little by little the last few months, I'd begun to lose small patches of them, to fight my way out from under the roadmap of pain weighing me down.

And now they were back. My skin was once again filled with bite marks and slashes. I held back a sob. I knew my trauma didn't define me. I knew that, but here I was again, covered in blood and pain because someone felt they had the right to do as they pleased and I had to live with the consequences, because—let's be honest—I didn't matter. I wanted to scream at the injustice.

Blowing out a breath, shaking my head, I tried to clear my thoughts. This wasn't the time or place. Survival was key. I moved farther from the edge of the Abyss. I'd deal with the scars later.

"Real nice safe passage, you bastard!" My shout echoed off the cavern walls and then was drowned out by the next group headed for the Abyss. A demon walked by, and I almost jumped. He looked me up and down, stared at the sword a moment, and then moved on.

"What happened to you?" Dave Sr. was back. He studied me a moment and then stared out past the Abyss.

"Your idea of keeping me safe?" Yes, he scared the hell out of me, but he had promised to protect me, said there were rules against targeting the non-evil.

"And as I've told you a few times, those rules don't apply to me. If you'd like, I can take you to meet Lucifer. You can plead your case, see if you get anywhere with him."

"No thanks," I mumbled.

"Thought not." His gaze never wavered from whatever was on the far side of the lake of fire. A demon walked by us and bowed to Dave Sr. before continuing on. "By the way, handy little spell you used on Olivier. It didn't do much other than annoy him, but I found it amusing.

"Here we are," he murmured. "Be a dear and yell, would you please?"

When I just stared at him, confused, he stole my sword away. As the fire consumed me once more, I added my wails to those already echoing off the dark cavern walls. My knees buckled and then the sword was back in my hand. "Son of a—"

# 30

# Dave Has Entered the Chat

"No!" Even over the thunderous fire and never-ending screams, I heard Dave's roar of anger.

I could barely see anything through the heat waves over the fiery pit. I turned to Dave Sr., looking for answers. I'd definitely heard Dave—I'd know that roar anywhere—but I wasn't sure if the red I'd seen was his face or a flash from the lake. His dad had disappeared, though, leaving me alone again. *Ass*hole!

Dave popped in where his dad had been standing a moment before. "The fuck! How did you even get here?" He grabbed my arm and started dragging me away from the Abyss.

His dad returned, blocking Dave's path.

"Was this you? We don't hurt innocents, remember?" Dave's grip on my arm was really fricking painful, but I didn't want to get between a father and son.

"I suggest you let her go before you break her arm or burn her again." Dave's dad, who hadn't seemed gigantic a moment ago, loomed over his muscular, six-three son.

Dave's hand dropped. "Let me take her home."

Considering, his dad finally said, "No. I don't think I will."

"Why? Trust me; You don't want her around. She's nothing but trouble." Dave crossed his arms over his impressive chest.

*Nothing* seemed a bit harsh. While they bickered, I kept seeing dark shadows swoop in the periphery of my vision. When I turned, they were gone. Then I'd see a flash of something hazy and white, followed by another dark swoop. What the hell *was* that?

"Use my study," Dave Sr. said.

Swoop, swoop.

"We have nothing to discuss."

Jeez, these two. I was never getting out of here. Dark eyes shone from the shadows, watching.

"Son."

Dave dropped his arms and set off in the opposite direction. Mr. BigFuckingDemon, forevermore known as BFD, pointed imperiously at his son's back, so I followed Dave. Swoop, swoop.

I kept the sword in my hand as I crossed the stone cavern floor. The orangey light from the lake of flames made shadows dance and jump. Combined with abject terror and swooping shadows, my steps were a might unsteady.

Dave reached a wall between two jagged boulders and extended his hand. A doorknob appeared. Glancing over his shoulder, he flung open the door and waited.

Not trusting anyone around here, I stopped at the doorway and looked in. Oh, this was nice. I felt a shove and then the door slammed shut. I had a moment of panic before Dave brushed past me and sat down in a leather reading chair.

The room was beautiful, with the old-world style Clive was partial to. With dark colors, polished woods, and leather furniture, it felt like a combination study and smoking room. I would have loved to check out all of BFD's knickknacks, but I had a ragey asshole to deal with instead. Since he took the chair, I sat in the corner of the sofa, as far from him as I could get.

"Why are you here?" His dark eyes bore into me, acting like all of this was somehow my fault.

"Your stupid dad abducted me. Clive and I wer—"

"What!" he bellowed.

His outbursts had stopped making me jump years ago.

"My father brought you down here?" He sat forward, anger and disbelief coloring his expression.

"He showed up at The Slaughtered Lamb and wanted to know what we were talking about at the biergarten before you blew it up."

"And what did you tell him?" There seemed to be more than just curiosity in his tone.

"Nothing. For some unknown reason, I kept your secrets." Shaking my head, I focused on an antique map framed on the wall opposite. "Such an idiot. You kill my mom and I still try to protect you from your dad."

Dave fell back, collapsing in the chair. All the distrust and rage drained out of him. "Why did you?" he finally asked

My throat tightened and my eyes flooded. No, damn it! I wasn't crying in front of him. Turning my head, I tried to blink away the tears. There was no room for grief in my heart. I hated him. He'd tortured my kind, gentle mother who'd never harmed anyone, who'd sacrificed any semblance of a normal life in order to protect me. I had to remember he wasn't my cranky, foul-mouthed friend. He was a fucking demon.

Looking anywhere but at him, we sat in silence for an uncomfortable length of time before grief and betrayal got the better of me. "How could you have done that to her? And why befriend me afterward? That's some next-level evil, right there."

He closed his eyes and dropped his head back. "Your mother was an accident."

"You tripped and cut her to ribbons?" I laid the sword across my lap with trembling hands.

"I'm not going to hurt you, Sam. You don't need to white-knuckle the sword." His voice was deep and growly and had me longing for the days when that voice made me feel safe. This was what he'd done to me. He'd destroyed my life and then made me love him. My first impulse was to protect the man who'd torn up my mother, sending me down the path to my own torture and rape. None of that would have happened if it weren't for him.

Even knowing that, instead of giving him up to his dad, I'd still tried to protect him, making me a gullible moron and the most horribly disloyal of daughters.

His eyes remained closed.

"I should use it to cut the head off the man who tortured my mother. I should hate myself for still harboring even the smallest amount of concern for you." I took a deep, calming breath. "This sword is the only thing keeping me alive right now. Your dad spelled it. I have to hold onto it to keep from dying a fiery death."

He tipped his head forward and opened one eye. "He did? Interesting." Dropping his head back, he lapsed into silence again.

My skin was crawling. I couldn't sit here with him like everything was fine, like he hadn't done what he'd done. I was ready to take my chances out there, to go in search of the elevator so I could go home. I had stood to do just that when he finally spoke.

"My mother Mathilde was a sorcerer, like your aunt."

Dropping back onto the couch, I said, "I know. Your dad told me." I hated myself for hoping that under it all, he had a reason for what he'd done, but if he didn't, then what? He had just been toying with me for the last seven years to make this moment hurt more? It didn't make sense.

He lifted his head again, brow furrowed. "He did? We never discuss her."

"He popped in on me at the nocturne after my first visit to the biergarten." At Dave's look of disbelief, I continued, "He really does seem concerned about you. He said the other demons were dicks to you and he didn't know why you put up with it."

"Dicks? Really?" Eyebrows raised, he stared me down.

I shrugged. "Paraphrasing. Anyway, why did you? Put up with it?" My fingertips moved back and forth over the word engraved in my sword, *Fior*. True.

He sighed. "I've never told anyone this, but I need you to understand." He blew out a deep breath. "I remember everything from my birth on. My father rarely showed up. He was more of a dark, looming presence that came and went." He paused. "And she was a complicated woman. Picturing her now, I can see she was little more than a child herself, but at the time—" He shook his head. "She was just Mother.

"When we were alone and she was working in the garden or brewing potions, she was...content, I guess. I don't recall her ever being happy, but she seemed content, puttering away, humming. When people visited, even women looking to buy her remedies, she'd tense. She didn't like anyone invading her territory, especially men.

"Even with my father, she seemed more excited to be near his power. Whenever he left, she'd talk for days about him teaching her ways to keep us both safe. Her face glowed with a fanaticism that was scary. After a while, though, it would fade and we'd be back to wandering through the woods, her pointing out plants, explaining their uses."

He stared ahead in silence for a time. "If she'd been left to grow up, not brutalized by her father and husband, her life would have been so different." He shook his head in disgust. "I wouldn't exist, but whatever, because she wouldn't have been broken and twisted. She could've been a content little wicche, her village's wise woman. Shit, she could've had forest animals following her wherever she went. Instead, she was stiff and jumpy, constantly looking over her shoulders, carrying weapons in her pockets."

He got up and poured himself a glass of amber liquid. "I remember the world covered in snow four times, so I guess I was about that old when I heard my mother yell. I was in the woods, playing with a squirrel. I ran as fast as I could and found a man pinning her to the frame of the open door of our broken-down cabin.

"She was fighting him, one hand twitching with a spell, when he punched her, knocking her out. She fell partly in the cabin and he dropped to his knees, pushing up her skirts. I came up behind him and when he turned, I put my hand on his face and burned him. He screamed, trying to push me off, but I didn't let go. It felt good.

"Mother woke and pushed me aside. He was dead, his head scorched, but still recognizable. She raced around the cabin, grabbing her most important possessions and was hitching the horse to our small cart when the villagers appeared. They'd heard the important man's yell and discovered him dead. Assuming my mother had cast some spell on him, they declared her a witch and dragged her to the center of the village to deal with.

"When one of the women grabbed me to drag along, I intended to burn her too, but my mother shouted, 'No!' They probably assumed she was talking to them, but I knew she was telling me not to hurt anyone else." He downed his drink.

"It didn't take long. Mom and I were tied up and held behind a cabin. A farmer with a scythe guarded us, though he refused to look at us, not even when she begged him to keep me safe.

"She couldn't hear them, but I listened to all the petty complaints, the accusations of wicchery from the same people who'd come to her for potions. It's always the same." He shook his head. "They were justifying to themselves and their neighbors why they were taking the life of a young mother. While they whined and wrung their hands, men were building a post and collecting kindling for a good, old-fashioned wicche burning.

"I felt it when she drew on my father's power. Four men were tying us to the post, shoving me back every time she tried to give me to one of them. One copped a feel while pushing me back. He was the first to die. The other men were setting the wood on fire and didn't notice right away. All she wanted was someone to care for me. When they ignored her, she showed them exactly what she was capable of. The one with the scythe stepped over the dead men and tried to cut her in two, but she pushed him back, had him slice himself open.

"The fire grew quickly, consuming us. My father finally showed up. Too late. She was past saving. I dropped and he snatched me out of the flames, looked around at all the people on their knees, screaming, trying to ward off evil, and decided Hell was the better option for me."

Closing his eyes a moment, he said, "I don't think I've talked this much my entire life. It's exhausting. Anyway, it's not like Hell is known for having stellar daycare. Nannies who killed their charges? Sure. Tons of those. People you'd trust to care for a child? No. You may have noticed there aren't a lot of kids down here. Lots of pedophiles, though, so that was fun."

At my horrified expression, he explained, "They only try it once. Having your cock burned off still hurts like fuck when you're a demon.

"For years, I wished I'd had the quick exit my mom'd had. Instead, I had an eternity here, preyed on, looked down on. I was a mutt, a demon-wicche crossbreed, a target for any demon looking to cut his teeth on a new victim.

"With the lesser demons, it was pure hatred. I was a mongrel and yet I sat at my father's knee, had his ear, inherited some of his gifts." He ran his hands over his bald head. "I inherited magic from my mother as well. She was gifted with an affinity for plants and animals. The Hellhounds followed me around as a small child, protecting me when they could."

"Aw—" When I remembered who I was talking to and what he'd done, I snapped my mouth shut. I had trouble breathing as the guilt swamped me. It was so hard. For years, he was the one person I could count on. I may have annoyed the crap out of him, but he was the angry, fire-breathing rock I relied on. He was the scary guy, swearing in the kitchen, who would battle back any comers in my defense before insulting me and going back to the kitchen. He gave me away at my wedding. I couldn't make my brain bend the right way for this to make sense.

"I was stuck in Hell," he said. "Not because of anything I'd done, but because of who my parents were. It was miserable and… lonely, I guess. Being a symbiote for a sorcerer is a shit job. Usually only the lower-level demons do it. You get summoned day and night. You deal with a lot of sociopaths. You have to loan them your power to fuel some pretty fucked-up magic.

"I started doing it as a kid, maybe five or six years old." He got up and refilled his glass. "The first sorcerer I worked with was batshit, but"—he took a big gulp—"he was someone to talk to. I didn't like helping him with his magic, but he could be funny sometimes."

Shaking his head, he finished the drink. "I think the others around here assumed I was low-level in terms of power because I continued to be a symbiote. And I didn't fight back when they attacked."

"Why didn't you?" And why did I still care?

Staring at the empty glass, he finally said, "Penance, I suppose. If I hadn't burned that man, my mother would've lived. After everything she'd survived, she died badly because of me.

"Later, I did some truly evil shit for the sorcerers just so I could have someone to talk to." He shrugged one beefy shoulder. "Seemed only right I got my ass handed to me."

"Weren't there any—I guess not." It was stupid to ask if there weren't a couple of nice demons he could befriend. They were stinking demons.

"What?" He sounded tired.

"I don't know. I just wondered if there were any decent ones like you."

"The fact you can call me decent," he muttered. "I thought I'd found one. You met him. The one who talked to you in the biergarten. Olivier. He's Nephilim too, son of one of the Fallen. He played it so well, I bought it down the line."

"What did he do?" I really hated that guy.

"He was older, one of the group that often targeted me, but he started to hang behind, act like he was checking to make sure I hadn't been hurt too badly." Dave turned his head, met my eyes. "Years. He took years to set me up, to go from one of my tormentors to one of the bored who just watched. Eventually, he sought me out to talk. It was masterfully done. I'll give him that."

He scratched his cheek. "I thought I'd finally connected with someone. All along, I'd been working as a symbiote with different sorcerers. After some pretty ugly situations as a kid, I'd come up with ground rules. I wouldn't harm the innocent. You want me to gouge out someone's eyes and relocate their intestines? Sure. It just needs to be someone already slated for Hell. The morally compromised are our bread and butter.

"Other demons may not have had those lines, but they also didn't have my power. You want me, you follow my rules."

He kicked out his legs and crossed them at the ankles. "So I had a friend, and I had a few sorcerers I worked with. I still hated it here, but I'd created a livable existence. Olivier came to me one day, asked for a favor. He had a sorcerer he worked with." He glanced at me again. "All part of the setup. When you have nothing but time, there's something really satisfying about a long con.

"He came asking for a favor. His dad needed him. He was proud to be called on, but he had a sorcerer who needed him as well. Could I cover for him this one time? I'd already been working with one of mine over—I don't know—a day and a half maybe. I was tired, but this was my friend asking for a favor so, of course, I did it.

"He gave me the background. Sorceress trying to hide from family who were hunting her. Only got into sorcery to protect herself, blah, blah. He took enough elements from my own mother's story that I'd be sympathetic and act without investigating."

Meeting my eyes for a moment, he turned back to the glass. "I believed him. He was my friend, after all. I believed her when she told me, tears streaming down her face, that her sister had finally found her and she needed to get rid of the threat once and for all."

I didn't see his arm move but I jumped when the glass he'd been staring at smashed into the door. Glass flew everywhere but at me. It was like he'd put an invisible wall in front of me.

"Fuck. I knew better than to trust anyone. I knew!" He thumped his fists on the arm of his chair. "So I did what Olivier told you I did. It wasn't until I heard the extra heartbeat and realized there was someone else in the apartment that I stopped to study the players.

"The woman being killed was pure light. The child in the closet, the same. The sorcerer I was aiding had a soul as dark as demons themselves. I'd broken my cardinal rule because I was weak and pathetic, and so fucking desperate for someone to like me." His sigh felt like surrender.

"There was nothing I could do. The wicche was dead. I pushed your aunt out before you realized your mom's spell of paralysis died with her. I figured you were a second from busting out and I wanted your aunt gone."

This didn't add up. "But then you knew. The whole time I was being hunted and trapped in visions, you knew who was after me, but you never told me, never stopped her. You lied."

31

# Fiery Death: Do Not Recommend

"I didn't lie. I just never told you who I thought it was." At my scoff, he continued, "When I left Hell, I was stripped of most of my abilities. My dad was pissed that I'd taken off. Did I assume it was your aunt? Yes. Could I have caught her? No, and I *did* try. Olivier was hiding her. I'd felt it that day I shared her mind. She wanted you dead too. After…what happened, Olivier and the others thought it was hilarious that I was rolling around in the muck with them, that I'd tortured an innocent wicche, one with the same last name as my mother."

"Same name? Your mother was a Corey?"

He rubbed his forehead. "Yeah. How 'bout that?" He gave his head a little shake. "I couldn't stay here. I was consumed with guilt, self-loathing, hatred for everyone around here. I knew your aunt would never stop hunting you, so I decided to protect you, if I could, to try to make up for what I'd done."

"Too bad you weren't there to help me in the woods." In the shack. I hated thinking about it, but if Dave was telling the truth, his timing sucked. If he'd moved to the human realm a few months earlier, he could have prevented Randy from raping and torturing me.

He drummed his fingers on the arm of the chair and then finally said, "I was."

Stomach dropping, I stood abruptly and moved to the door. He killed my mother and then stood by while I was brutalized? "Fucking demon," I hissed, pulling at the doorknob. It wouldn't open. I spun, keeping my back to the door, my sword pointing at him. "Let me out. And point me toward the elevator. I'm done with you."

"Don't blame you, but I didn't lock it. He did. Neither of us are getting out until he says so." He crossed his arms over his chest again. "And I didn't just sit back and watch you get attacked. Abigail was screwing with your head, upping the pain and terror, literally trying to scare you to death. It was a race as to whether Randy or Abigail would kill you first."

I didn't want to talk about this. I needed Clive. The sword trembled in my grip, but I didn't let go as I yanked on the door again.

"I pushed her out of your head, flicked the switch your mother's pendant was hiding."

I turned slowly at his words.

"You needed your wolf to fight him off, to break out of those bonds. Your mother's magic hid the wicche and the wolf. I pushed your wolf to the fore so you'd have a fighting chance."

Leaning back against the door, I listened, unsure of what to believe anymore.

"You got yourself free and then attacked him. He ran and you tore off in pursuit, but then she and Olivier pushed in again and stole the memories, stole your triumph, leaving you with nothing but fear.

"I've been alone and drifting most of my life." He stood and moved farther away from me, leaning against the wet bar counter. "Watching over you gave my life a focus. I didn't know or care about you, other than I felt like I owed your mother. I thought, well, I'll just keep an eye on her while I figure out what I want to do next.

"At that point, I was sure I'd end up going home. And then, things started to change. You were scared of your fucking shadow, but you were trying so hard to act like you had it all together. I thought, hell, if she can toughen up, create a new life for herself completely alone, I can too."

"So you weren't really working for someone else?"

He gave me a blank look.

"You said you were watching me for someone else."

He nodded as though remembering and then shook his head. "Demons lie, Sam. You know that."

"You mean like now?"

"Except for now. Anyway, I watched videos and taught myself to cook, taught myself how to bank and shop in the human world. What I thought was a temporary obligation became a life, one that made me happy. I can't tell you how foreign that feeling was. I didn't recognize it for the longest time. And when that bitch found you, I knew it. I knew it was all going to come out. That I'd lose the child I was trying to protect. That this new life was over."

It made sense. I hated to admit, but it made sense. I understood why he'd done it, but I didn't know if I had it in me to forgive him.

The door I was leaning on moved. I jumped out of the way, not wanting BFD to fling me into the wall. It wasn't Dave's dad who walked in, though. It was Olivier.

"There you are," he said to me, his smile razor sharp. Glancing at Dave, he added, "Your father told me where to find you. I don't think he appreciated you using his study." With a smirk that said he was giddy that Dave was in trouble, he turned back to me. "Payback's a bitch, sweetie."

He reached for me, and I held up my sword. I was done with this asshole too, but Dave was suddenly standing between us. Olivier flicked his fingers at Dave and started to move in, but Dave hadn't budged. Whatever Olivier thought he'd done, it hadn't worked.

Dave grabbed Olivier by the neck and lifted him off the ground before crushing his throat and slamming him against the door so hard, it strained the hinges. Flames jumped from Dave and engulfed Olivier. When Dave let go, the fire went out and Olivier crumpled to the floor in a heap.

Looking shocked and more than a little embarrassed, Olivier climbed to his feet and said, "Well, that was new. Look who's all grown up." Laughing, he opened the door an inch, allowing a legion of dark shadows to swoop around the door and swarm Dave. Punctures appeared in Dave's skin almost immediately.

He didn't flail or fight. He stood, staring at Olivier while the shadows tried to devour him. His lips split in a ferocious grin that would have had me wetting my pants. The humor on Olivier's face faltered and he reached for the doorknob.

A powerful pulse shook the room. I lost my balance and fell back on the couch. The shadows sprang from Dave and hung in the air around him. Dave's stare never left Olivier, who was grasping futilely at a door that wouldn't open.

With a nod of Dave's head, all the shadows raced across the room to Olivier, biting and slashing. He spun, trying to fling them off, but they stuck. He must have tried something like what Dave had done, but instead of the frenzied swirling shadows being thrown off and sailing across the room, they snapped back, biting and clawing Olivier again.

As much as I hated that demon, watching him being ripped apart was making me sick. Unfortunately, when he flung his arms out, he sent a passel of the shadowy demons straight at me.

Sword up, I swung. A few disappeared in a bright light and a wail, while the others moved in to bite the shit out of me. The swooping shadows reminded me of ghosts. So, as I couldn't slice the a-holes on me without stabbing myself, I instead closed my eyes, trying to block out the mayhem around me, to access my necromancer side.

The demons, I could do nothing about. I could see the black-on-black beings, but I couldn't seem to grab them, as much as I tried. What I noticed, though, was that the white haze I'd noticed earlier was confused ghosts who'd been tricked and held. That, I could do something about.

I was stronger than the demons in this respect. The ghosts were the dead. They fell under my purview. I pulled, separating them from the demons who held and fed off them, and then I offered myself as a conduit to the other side. I wasn't sure how many of them would accept, but a cool rush ran through me as they all crossed over.

The demons were like angry bees, crawling all over me, desperate to make me pay for taking their prisoners. I heard a loud crash and my eyes flew open. Dave had thrown Olivier across the room, where he'd slammed into the wet bar, decanters and glasses shattering.

When Dave moved in to help me, Olivier jumped him. Dave swatted him off, his focus on me, but Olivier pulled a knife, his face a mask of rage. There was something about the knife. It felt off. Evil. I had a split second to decide what to do. I knew my survival depended on my holding the sword, but I was also positive that knife was about to kill Dave.

No time to weigh options, I let the sword fly. It sailed over Dave's shoulder and pinned Olivier to the wall. Screaming and white light filled the room as I fell back on the couch, my lungs seizing, my body starting to burn. There were crashes and shouts; I didn't care. I was dying a fiery death.

And then the sword was shoved back into my hand. The shadowy demons were gone and BFD was filling the doorway. His very angry son held the black dagger Olivier had been wielding.

"Why didn't you tell me what was happening?" BFD stepped in and closed the door behind himself.

"My problem. I needed to deal with it." Dave weighed the dagger in his hand. "How did he get one of these?"

BFD held out his hand for it. "Ah, that's how he did it." He paused, considering the knife. "My guess is Sitri, but I'll be asking Olivier's father exactly that. This and his son's actions should explain why he was unmade." He took the knife from Dave, and it disappeared. "I'll take her home. Will you remain so we can talk?"

Dave looked like he was about to say no and then paused. "If you want."

"I do." BFD was a powerful demon and all, but in this moment, he was a father trying to connect with his son.

Every part of my body hurt, my breathing was labored, my eyes stung, but I kept silent. This felt like a real chance for Dave to regain his family—or maybe to have one for the first time.

Dave stuffed his hands in his pockets. "Yeah, okay."

"Good. Have a seat. I'll be right back." BFD grabbed my arm and then we were flying through the void again.

The cool breeze felt wonderful on my roasted body. Part of me wanted to give him shit about lying to me, saying he'd make sure I wasn't hurt, that he'd stop Clive's torture, but the other part wanted to make sure he knew how lucky he was to have a second chance with Dave. I kept quiet, though, as I'm not an idiot and I really wanted to get home.

"Thank you." The deep voice was in my ear.

"For?" I was really hoping he didn't get pissed off and send me spinning again. Considering how horrible I felt, I might just hurl up a lung.

"My son."

"Oh, well. I was mostly just nearby when crazy crap happened." As much I was conflicted about Dave and whether or not I wanted him in my life, his father shouldn't be. "Your son's a good man. You should definitely get to know him better." My breathing was leveling out. Hopefully, that meant my lungs weren't scorched.

"You can say that in spite of his role in your mother's death?" His voice seemed to come from every direction in the dark.

I wasn't sure I knew how to explain what I was feeling. "My mother's death will always be horrific for me. I'm not sure if I can ever think about Dave the way I used to, but the blame for my mother should be laid at the feet of the person responsible, her sister, my aunt. Dave was merely the weapon."

"Interesting."

"Can I ask you a question?"

"You may."

"From the story you told me about Dave and his mother, Dave should be about fifteen hundred years old, but my mother was only killed eight years ago. His reactions to the other demons and his supposed age don't make sense to me."

"May I tell my son you believe he was behaving like an angsty teen?" I could feel BFD's humor filling the void.

"Kind of wish you wouldn't."

"Suffice to say that time runs differently in Hell."

"Gotcha." I'd figured it was like Faerie and that time was weird, but I'd wanted to check. Age made a difference. For instance, when I'd first read *Hamlet* and he couldn't decide what to do—had his father been murdered? Was the ghost telling him the truth? Should he kill his uncle? All of that made sense because Hamlet was a teenager.

Later, I watched a couple of films that had actors in their forties playing Hamlet, and it completely changed the story. It was no longer a young man, unsure of his course. It was now a cowardly adult who made excuses not to act. One, I could sympathize with. The other, was a lot harder.

"One other question?" I wanted to know what was so special about that black dagger.

"It's the *Daemonium Ferrum*, the demon blade. There are only a couple in existence, and they are to be secured at all times."

"What does it do?"

After a long pause, he said, "I won't divulge all its properties, but it is able to cut between planes of existence to, perhaps, cut a vampire as he sleeps."

"What?" That little asshole!

"Ready?"

"For what?"

32

# Quoth the Crow, "CAW"

And then I was standing in The Slaughtered Lamb again, Clive—eyes black, fangs locked and loaded—diving over me to attack Dave Sr. My husband caught himself before he knocked me down just as BFD disappeared.

Clutching me to him, he raced up the stairs to the parking lot. "We have to get you out of here." After he'd stuffed me in the front seat of his SUV and plopped Fergus in my lap and the axe at my feet, he slid in and fired up the engine.

"Stop." I ran my hand down his arm as he gunned it, heading for the exit. "Clive, stop. It's all over."

He paused before pulling out onto the road. Eyes still vamp black, he turned to me. "Over?"

"He already took me to Hell. Unlike Faerie, when you return, it's at the exact moment you left." I squeezed his hand on the stick shift. "I'm okay."

Clive pushed out an unnecessary breath. "You're okay? You're —" He stared at me in horror. "You're covered in blood." He put the car in reverse. "I'll call Dr. Underfoot. See if he can—"

"Clive. It's okay. I'm fine." I looked down at myself. I was a horrible mess. My clothes were scorched and ripped. My hands and arms were covered in bites and slashes that were already starting to heal. Awesome. More scars. To take my mind off that, I said, "You haven't shown me the Seal Rock house yet. We have time now."

Searching my face for signs of worry or injury, he wrapped his hands around either side of my head and pulled me in for a long, soft kiss. When he finally pulled back, his eyes were once again stormy gray. "You're sure you're all right?"

"Mostly, which is enough for now."

"Okay." Even though he was still worried, he went along with my suggestion and pulled out onto the road, driving half a block before turning on a side street and directly into a driveway. "We could have walked here faster." It was the middle of the night and quiet, though the sound of the nearby surf was a constant roar.

Clive got out and met me on my side of the car. I didn't have Fergus' leash, but I knew he'd stick with us, unless a cat distracted him. I was about to leave the axe in the car and then thought better of it. Hopefully, the demons would leave us alone now. The fae, though, were an ever-present danger. Strapping on the axe, I plopped Fergus down.

While the pooch raced around sniffing, Clive took my hand and led me up the steps. The exterior was complete, with dark brown brick, white stucco, thick, dark wooden beams. It was absolutely gorgeous. The original building was boxy and forgettable. They'd changed the lines, gave it beauty and character. They'd made it a work of art.

"It was two stories and now it's three, which allows for the peaked rooves."

"It looks like rooms were added, walls pushed out, to get the Tudor architecture." It was stunning and I was giddy to see it all. "And chimneys! We have fireplaces."

"We do. They changed exactly as much as could be changed and considered a remodel. I'm very happy with the work so far. See what you think." Clive took keys out of his pocket and opened the front door. Scooping me up, he carried me across the threshold.

"I guard!"

Startled, I looked over Clive's shoulder and saw my soldier jogging up behind us. "Sorry. We didn't see you when we left. This is our new home. It's still under construction. Would you like to come in and see it?"

Fangorn pushed us aside. "I search." He stood in the entry, polished dark wood floors under his battered boots. Unsheathing his sword, he tilted his head, listening. A moment later, he was racing up the stairs.

Clive put me down and then leaped straight up and over the third-floor banister. I grabbed Fergus before he hit the second step in pursuit. Holding him up so we were nose to nose, I let my eyes lighten to wolf gold and said, "Stay," before putting him down at my feet. I pulled both my axe and sword, backing across the dark first floor.

Clive was right. The house was stunning, the walls light and warm, with exposed beam ceilings and a huge stone fireplace in what appeared to be a great room. Large French windows overlooked the park and ocean. I almost laughed when I moved past what had to be the dining room and saw the crystal chandelier.

"Stop. Please stop." Candy was back in her towering platforms and tiny dressing gown. "There's something scary in there."

"How'd you get here?" I whispered.

Again, I could have sworn there was a ghostly blush. "I followed you before."

While I wasn't happy about spectral stalkers, I had more important things to deal with right now. Fergus moved silently with me. It was odd that I'd heard nothing from upstairs. The longer it was silent up there, the more I was positive Candy was right and the problem was down here. *Clive? Are you okay?*

No response. A soft susurration of sound dropped a chill down my spine. A piercing *caw* rent the air and made my blood run cold. Sitri was supposed to be gone. Who was fucking with us now? *Dave!* I knew it wouldn't work, but I figured it was worth a try. Unfortunately, I also knew Dave was chatting with his Dad in Hell right now.

Candy shoved my shoulder. “Go! Why aren’t you going?”

Scanning the dark corners of the empty rooms, I finally saw two shiny black eyes watching me from a perch at the top of a bookcase. I didn’t know who was behind the eyes, but I knew I was in deep shit.

Candy squeaked and then went running for the front door. “Come on, doggie! Your mommy’s crazy.”

A loud, cacophonous flapping sounded behind me, making me jump as dozens of crows tumbled out of the fireplace at my back. Claws outstretched, they swooped in a coordinated attack. I swung my axe and sword. When I hit them with the sword, a burst of light filled the room as a dead crow hit the floor. The axe killed them as well, but there was no white light. The demon sword was needed to get rid of them for good.

Fergus trembled between my calves. The crows kept trying to snatch him away from me, but the pup growled and snapped at any that got too close. The dead crows were piling up around me, but more kept coming through the fireplace.

I heard a snort of breath and realized it wasn’t only the crows. Red eyes glowed in the dark. A shaggy, muscular canine slinked down the stairs toward us. A Hellhound. Sure, why not?

The blades were barely a blur as I moved in a circle, hitting anything coming for me. Their claws tore at me and blood dripped everywhere. I heard a strange ringing tone under the piercing *caws*. I had no idea what it was, but I also had more than enough to be getting on with.

A crow clawed my forehead and I had to brush away the blood with my wrist to keep it from running into my eyes. When the sword moved closer to my face, the tone grew louder. It was coming from the demon sword. The timing wasn’t right for it to be connected to the crows. It might have been my own blood causing the sword to ring.

The blade felt different in my hand. Charged. Deciding it was worth a try, I held the sword, spattered with my own blood, in front of my mouth while I swung the axe. “Dave! I need you now!”

The Hellhound leaped, knocking me over and driving me to the ground. Fergus yelped and I prayed he got out of the way, that he wasn't crushed beneath the bulk of the demon dog. Red eyes trying to mesmerize me, it opened its maw. Long, razor-sharp teeth glistened as drool dripped onto my face, burning my skin.

One of his paws pinned the arm wielding the sword to the floor, but my other arm was free, so I hacked at his neck with the axe, though it didn't seem to bother him much. Candy popped back in and tried to punch the Hellhound. While I appreciated the assist, it had no effect on the demon.

When he reared back to bite my head off, I was able to rip my arm out from under his claws. Arm now shredded, I righted the sword so when he lunged forward, the blade punched through the roof of his mouth, into his brain. His fangs pierced my skin as white light filled the room. A percussive pulse shook the floorboards, and it was gone.

Candy jumped up and down, clapping. "You did it!"

Light-headed, I sat up and looked for Fergus. He was sitting by my side, growling at a second Hellhound stalking toward us as crows tore at my scalp and back. Climbing to my feet, I was shoved back down.

Candy yelped and then ducked into the dining room to escape.

BFD and Dave stood on either side of me. BFD flicked his hand and all the crows were gone. Dave moved forward, arm outstretched, before placing his hand on the Hellhound's head. Its butt plopped down as it waited for Dave's command. Dave put his hands on either side of the Hellhound's massive head, leaned down, and whispered for it to go home. It disappeared.

When Dave turned, he looked horrified, so I assumed I wasn't looking my best. "Father?"

BFD turned, took in my state, and sighed. With a nod of his head, the pain disappeared. Getting slowly to my feet, I braced for twinges, but there were none.

"Thank you." I turned to Dave. "Clive and Fangorn ran upstairs when we got here, but I haven't heard anything since."

"Who's Fangorn?" he asked.

"The fae soldier I brought with me to the Biergarten of the Damned. He's my self-appointed bodyguard." I sheathed my weapons and then picked up Fergus, who whined and flinched at the pain. I held up my gangly pup to BFD, who rolled his eyes but nodded at Fergus, who stopped shaking once the pain went away.

My beautiful great room was filled with crow corpses and blood spatter. "I don't suppose…"

BFD shook his head in annoyance and waved a hand, getting rid of all the crows and blood.

"Thank you. It's our new house."

He was watching the stairs for his son's return, but now looked around. "Nice."

When his gaze traveled to the dining room, Candy gasped and disappeared. I doubted she'd be back anytime soon.

Finally, I heard movement upstairs. *Clive! Are you all right?*

*Coming, darling. Your soldier and I were trapped in some kind of Hellish portal by Sitri. Dave just freed us.* And a moment later, he was standing in front of me, pulling me into his arms.

Dave and Fangorn pounded down the stairs. The soldier was looking a little shaken. I doubt he'd considered being trapped in a Hellscape a possibility when he volunteered to guard me.

Still holding on to Clive, I turned my body toward Dave Sr. "I thought you took care of Sitri for us?"

"I did," he said as he walked toward his son.

Dave shook his head at his father. "This was Sitri's work."

Dave Sr. stopped mid-stride, cocking his head to the side. "I see. A few things are making more sense now." He pointed to a spot on the floor and a person popped into existence. I'd recognize that asshole anywhere. Chiseled features, dark hair hanging almost to his shoulders, magnetic eyes.

Sitri bowed to Dave Sr. "Why have you summoned me, my lord?"

"You're still targeting these two after I told you they were friends of my son's." BFD radiated such intense power, he was difficult to look at.

Bowing again, Sitri said, "That is the problem, my lord. I discovered it was Daeva who betrayed me."

"Fath—" Dave began, before BFD flicked a finger and Dave had what looked very much like a scold's bridle attached to his face. I'd only ever seen drawings in a book, but they were ancient metal torture devices attaching to the heads of women who men deemed to have a wicked or overactive tongue. A metal bit sat painfully in the woman's mouth, compressing her tongue, making it impossible for her to speak.

BFD nodded to Sitri. "Continue."

## 33

# Who's the Scold Now?

"Thank you, my lord. This vampire"—he gestured to Clive—"attacked me, tearing off my head, ripping apart my human body. I later found out Daeva knew what he was planning; in fact told him where to find me. I have been wronged, my lord, and am only seeking revenge."

"I see. But you weren't only trying to hurt the vampire, you were trying to possess him. Trying and failing."

There was a flash of annoyance and then Sitri smoothed his features. "I only needed to weaken him a bit more and he'd have been mine. My lord, a Master vampire at my disposal? Vengeance and a tool for chaos and destruction? I believe lord Lucifer would approve."

Judging by BFD's expression, he understood Sitri's threat and dismissed it. "What was Olivier's part in this?" He didn't even glance at Dave, whose real name seemed to be Daeva.

"A loyal protégé who has had dealings with Daeva since he was a child. He knows him to be weak and cowardly, currying the favor of whoever he believes will protect him."

This seemed like a weird defense to me. Was he really slamming BFD's kid as a way to get out of trouble? Or maybe this was how shitty parent-child relationships were in Hell.

"Understood. So, you recruited Olivier to enact your revenge on Daeva, while you focused on these two. Is that correct?" BFD flicked his finger and a leather wingback chair appeared. He sat and waited.

"Yes, my lord, exactly. I only sought my due." Sitri bowed again, his shoulders relaxing.

"And the *Daemonium Ferrum*? How did Olivier obtain that?" BFD asked, opening his hand, the black dagger appearing.

Sitri paused, looking like a deer in headlights. "I…can't be sure."

"Come now. Surely, it isn't too difficult to remember stealing this from Belial's storeroom. He was quite surprised when I returned his blade and explained that Olivier had tried to use it to kill *my son*."

Sitri froze before falling to his knees, his forehead to the floor. "My lord, please forgive my ignorance. I had no idea that Olivier would go that far. Daeva's life is too great a price to pay for his betrayal. I merely wanted his lies discovered and his relationships ruined."

"Yes, I see," BFD said, the black blade disappearing once again. Turning his head toward Dave, he flicked his fingers and the metal mask vanished. "Have you anything to add?"

Sitri sat up. Expression relaxing, he seemed to assume Dave would back him up. I knew I was a novice when it came to demon backstabbings, but this was deeply fucked. Did he really expect Dave to offer himself up for punishment to save Sitri? Did he not understand who Dave was at all?

Dave bowed his head. "You know the story, Father, and what part I played in it."

"I do." BFD snapped his fingers and the scold's bridle was now on Sitri's face, with a chain from the bit to BFD's hand. The floor opened up between Sitri and BFD; glowing flames and horrendous heat filled the room. I grabbed Clive's hand and we both held the handle of my sword while moving far away from the opening. Fangorn, holding Fergus, went out the front door.

Sitri screamed behind the metal mask as BFD tugged the chain, pulling the demon closer and closer to the Abyss. Sitri fought, arms and legs scrabbling on the wooden floors, trying to save himself, but he was no match for BFD.

Dave Sr. turned to his son. "Would you like the honor?"

Dave shook his head.

"Just as well." BFD stood and addressed Sitri. "You think to come before me and confess your plans to kill my son as your due?" He yanked the chain, dragging Sitri closer to the drop-off. "I'll make allowances for petty revenge schemes and hurt pride, but arrogant stupidity combined with a lack of respect *for me*? No." He sighed, staring into the eyes pleading with him through the mask. "You have been judged." Wrapping the chain around his hand, he smiled and then yanked. Sitri flew forward and tumbled down into the Abyss.

Sitting back in his chair, BFD waved his hand again and the floor returned, the light and heat disappearing. Furniture appeared where the Abyss had been a moment before. "Sit."

Clive and I moved cautiously to the couch. I really hoped that little portal to Hell was gone forever. Dave strode to the other wingback chair and sat. I saw movement in the window and panicked, thinking the crows had begun reforming for an offensive, but then I recognized the huge blocky head of Fangorn.

"It's all clear. You can come back in," I called.

The shadow shook its head. "Stay here!"

"Can't really blame him," Clive murmured, and I nodded.

"I can't promise that Sitri and Olivier haven't recruited others to harass you, but I can tell you that my personally carrying out, or approving of, their destruction will give all but the most powerful pause." Leaning forward, he placed a finger on the wood floor and said something under his breath. "I'll do the same for your bookstore."

"Um. Okay?" What had he done?

"He just warded your home against demons," Dave volunteered.

"Oh! Thank you," I said, feeling some of the tension weighing me down start to ease.

"Good. Your home and work will be protected, even from the use of emissaries, like the crows." He studied me a moment and then cricked his finger, beckoning me forward.

"No, thank you."

He dropped his head, staring at me under his brow. "Come here."

"I'd prefer not to, but thank you for the invitation." I folded my hands in my lap and hoped BFD would let it go.

"Do stop calling me that." He turned to his son. "You trust these two?"

"Yes, Father. She means no disrespect. I've been telling her for years to never go willingly to a demon, and the last time she was near you, you abducted her. The wariness is well earned."

"I suppose. If you have need of me in the future," he said to me, "I don't recommend trying to contact me. If you must, though, talk with my son. Now," he said, cricking his finger again. "Do you want me to get rid of all those wounds and scars or don't you? You seemed quite annoyed with me earlier for not keeping you safe."

I was covered in blood, old and new, from the demons, the crows, the Hellhound. I glanced at Clive and then stood, crossing the room to BF—he held up his finger in warning.

"You said you'd stop reading my mind and what the heck am I supposed to call you? I don't know your name."

He held out his hand. Clive was suddenly at my back, his arms around me. If this was another abduction, Clive was going too. Taking a deep breath, I held out my hand and placed it in Dave Sr.'s outstretched one.

*Hold on to that sword. You may have use of it in the future. And my name is Abaddon.* He winked and was gone.

Clive moved his arm, laying a hand over my racing heart. "It's over now," he whispered.

I turned to Dave. "Is he really…?"

Dave eyebrows shot up. "Did he give you his name?"

Nodding, I tried to swallow, but my mouth had gone dry.

"He must have taken a liking to you. He doesn't do that." Dave shook his head, brows furrowed. "My guess is the fact that you continued to risk your own safety in order to help me has—well, *endear* is too strong a word—has given him a certain partiality for you."

"Good," Clive said, pulling me back to the couch. "She can use all the help she can get."

I studied Dave. He'd come when I called, just as he always had. I didn't know what to do. "So, we're both Corey wicches, huh?"

He nodded.

"I guess you actually *are* my grumpy, foul-mouthed uncle." Did that make it better or worse?

Leaning forward in his chair, he rested his elbows on his knees. "Sam, just tell me what you want. You want me to disappear, I will. Say the word." His perpetual scowl was gone. He was asking if I was banning him from this new life, the one that had brought him happiness.

Was I? "Sometimes," I began slowly, still deciding what I could live with, "we do incredibly shitty things. When it's done out of cruelty and malice, that's one thing. When it's done out of ignorance or weakness or misunderstanding, that's another. One, I can forgive. The other, I can't. You made a mistake, a horrible, heartbreaking one, but you've worked hard ever since to make up for it."

He was braced, waiting for my judgment.

"I don't think my mother would be very proud of me if I punished you for the lies others told."

His eyes went glassy a moment, but then he blinked, and they were dry.

"We could really use a cook at The Slaughtered Lamb. Our customers are wasting away."

Nodding, he sat back in the chair. "I could do that."

"Good. So," I said, gesturing around the room. "It's nice, right?"

Chuffing a laugh, he bowed his head, gave it a little shake, and then stood, glancing around the first floor. "It is." He glanced at Clive. "How much longer do they say?"

"Perhaps a week until we move in. The folly, though, is far more elaborate. They'll be finishing that in stages. The Shire, which is closest to the bar, should be completed quite soon."

"If the dragon crew will allow me, I can lay wards against demons throughout the tunneling from this house to The Slaughtered Lamb. Sam refused to have me ward the bar before because I'd told her I could only do it through blood sacrifice. That was how the sorcerers I worked with had done it. My father taught me how to do it as he does. He also returned the powers he'd stripped from me when I'd left without talking to him years ago."

"When did he do that? He winked at me and disappeared."

"You weren't included in that conversation, so your timeline skipped over it." Dave ran his hand along the staircase banister. "The wicche crew you have here does beautiful work. I might hire them myself," he added absently.

"Are you and Maggie getting a house together?" My, my, lots of changes were happening.

Scoffing, he sat on the stairs. "I have to get her back first."

I moved to the staircase and sat beside him. "What happened?"

"Things got ugly while you were in England. I knew what Sitri and Olivier were capable of, so I sent Maggie back to Ireland. When I called to check on her, her family said she wasn't there. Hadn't arrived. No one knew where she was. Or at least they weren't telling me."

Patting his arm, I said, "Maybe she's hiding in Faerie."

He looked suddenly stricken. "I hope not. She's had nightmares ever since that little trip you took into Faerie. If she had to go into Faerie, Olivier must have found her in Ireland before she'd reached her family." Standing abruptly, he growled, "Fuck!"

"What have you remembered?" Clive asked.

"Olivier. When I was working in the biergarten, he asked me for a Guinness, said he'd recently developed a taste for them. Then a fight broke out and it was mayhem. Even the demons can't stand Albert Fish. I forgot. Damn it."

"Maybe Fangorn can help. We can ask if he's willing to go to Faerie to look for her." I wasn't sure if that was asking too much.

"As he and Fergus are outside, let's lock up and go ask them. We're approaching dawn." Clive wrapped an arm around me and walked us to the door. "Next time, you can see the upstairs."

"You really think we'll be able to move in next week?" I couldn't wait to get out of the cramped apartment.

Clive nodded. "I believe so."

"Is the backyard fenced for Fergus?" I wanted him to have his own yard. Right now, he had to rely on people taking him for walks. Granted, I knew he loved his walks, but just being able to go out and roll around on the grass sounded pretty awesome.

"It is. When we brought him home from Britain with us, I discussed our fencing needs with the contractor. The landscapers will be working on the front of the house tomorrow." Clive closed the front door and locked it.

When I turned around, Dave was leaning against the side of Clive's SUV. Oh yeah; he had popped in with his dad. No car. I walked around the side of the house, looking for Fangorn. Fergus tore across the lawn and spun, standing in front of me, growling back into the dark shadows by the far window.

Clive had gone to talk with Dave. I heard him offering Dave his ride so Dave could get home. After all, we were half a block from The Slaughtered Lamb. I only had part of my mind on their conversation, though. Fergus was growling and I hadn't seen Fangorn yet.

A shadow moved and then the silhouette of the soldier moved toward us through the gloom. Fergus moved back to stand between my calves. Something was off. Was there another demon out here? My gaze lifted to the nearby trees. More crows?

34

# Sam and Clive Begin Their Nice, Quiet Life Togeth—Oh, Come On!

"Good," I called to the soldier. "We're headed back now. Are you ready?"

"Yes. Let's go."

Fergus trembled against my legs. I heard it too. That wasn't our soldier. I picked up Fergus and held him under my left arm, not looking at whoever was wearing my soldier as a glamour. *Clive, I need you now. Act as though nothing is wrong.*

"Here," he said and there was the sound of keys hitting a palm. "Take her." His voice was getting closer. "We can walk home. Is my family ready to go?"

"You bet." I half turned toward Clive. My focus, though, was still on Not-Fangorn. "The house is beautiful! I can't wait to move in." I glanced back at the fae assassin not two steps from me. "We have a room for you, Fangorn."

"Good," he said.

Moving as fast as I could, I tossed the pup over my shoulder with my left arm, while my right seized the axe strapped to my back, and swung. He was fae, so he should have had excellent reflexes, but he hadn't realized I'd made him so he hadn't seen it coming. His eyes had just begun to widen when his head rolled from his body. As the remains disappeared, the face changed. It was barely a half second, but I'd seen the elf's true face.

"Beautifully done, darling. That face. He was one of the chess pieces, wasn't he?"

"Yes. Meanwhile," I said, looking around, "what did he do with the real Fangorn?

Clive gave me a quick kiss and then moved silently around the far side of the house.

"What chess set?" Dave asked, holding the pup and scratching him under his chin.

"I thought I tossed Fergus to Clive?"

"You did," he said, "but I caught him. I figured Clive would want his hands free for a fight."

"Good point."

"I guard!" His voice was more snarly that usual, but it was good to hear.

Clive walked Fangorn back around the corner. "It seems the assassin used a magic rope on our soldier, similar to the one they used on you in Faerie." He moved to my side again, his arm wrapping around me.

"Are you okay now?" I asked Fangorn.

He gave a grunt of assent. "King escaped."

"The fae king escaped the queen's prison?" *Shitshitshit.*

Fangorn grunted in agreement. "Elf said." The concern was clear on his big, blocky face.

"If you'd like to return to Faerie to check on the queen, I understand." I felt Clive tense, but Fangorn's first loyalty was to his queen. "And if you decide to go, my friend here"—I pointed to Dave—"his girlfriend Maggie is a banshee. No one has seen her in quite some time. We're worried she's trapped in Faerie."

Brows furrowed, he blew a quick breath out of his nose, thinking. After a lengthy pause, he pounded on his chest and growled, "I guard queen!"

"I know you do. And she'll need your strength with the king out."

He grunted, this one filled with agitation.

"Go. It's all right." I'd miss the big guy, but I knew he'd only volunteered to guard me because he thought his queen was safe.

Nodding, he moved to Dave and patted Fergus goodbye. He smiled when the pup licked his hand. "Maggie?" he asked Dave. When Dave nodded, Fangorn grunted his understanding. He glanced back at Clive and me and then took off at a run.

"Darling, I wish you'd spoken with me before releasing your bodyguard." Clive watched the soldier run off into the night.

"Nope. He needs to be with his queen. Plus, look what happened tonight. Fae can glamour themselves to look however they want. Taking on Fangorn's form gets an assassin closer to me."

Dave put Fergus down on the grass and said, "She's got a point."

"Yes, I know. I just don't like her being without another line of defense, especially as there's nothing I can do during the day." Clive took my hand and we started to walk back to The Slaughtered Lamb.

"I won't be in tomorrow," Dave said. "I'll come back, but right now I have to find Maggie. I can't search in Faerie. I tried," he said. "I went to The Wicche Glass and broke in. I tried to go through the mirror you used, but it was just a mirror for me. I have ways to search for her in this realm, though, gifts my father returned to me. I'll use those while I wait for Fangorn." He turned to Clive. "Still okay to borrow your car?"

Clive nodded. "Fine."

"Wait," I said, and Dave stopped, glancing back. "What about all that money you put in my account? Take it back to buy a house."

He shook his head and kept walking. "I'm loaded. Consider it your twenty-fifth birthday present." He hit the key fob on Clive's SUV, got in, and drove off.

Ocean roaring in the distance, my little family crossed over the grassy field. I saw Candy winking in and out at the end of the parking lot. *Candy's back.*

Clive ran his hand down my back. *I hope she's all right, as you need sleep.*

"Are you okay?" I called. She looked quite upset. Of course, she did just witness a demon battle.

"I—I changed my mind." Her hazy form kept popping in and out.

"About what?"

"My folks? I'm so scared, but that was H.E. double L., wasn't it?" She hugged herself, waiting.

"Yes. When the floor opened, that was the Abyss, where the damned go after death."

Nodding slowly, shifting her weight from one foot to the other, she whispered, "I don't deserve that for taking off my clothes, do I?"

"Not even a little bit."

"I was worried before. If I passed on, maybe I'd go there. I'd never see my family and I'd be in H.E.L.L. I didn't move on because I was so scared."

"How about now?" I really hoped she'd found the courage to do the thing that terrified her.

She took a tentative step toward me and I opened my arms. Like ripping off a bandage, she ran into me. I held her tight and gave her the little push she needed to get across. A cool, contented breeze and empty arms told me all I needed to know.

"Was that Candy passing on?" Clive asked.

"Yes." I took his hand again, the wind from the ocean whipping stray hairs across my face.

"I almost felt it through you. Fascinating."

My little family and I headed down the stairs. Passing through the ward, I felt something new and smelled a whiff of smoke. It looked like Abaddon had kept his word.

The phone in Clive's pocket buzzed and he pulled it out. "Good evening."

I recognized Russell's voice on the phone, but I wasn't listening. My poor little guy's water bowl was empty. Once I filled it, he drank, and then trotted into the apartment and flopped down in his bed.

"I'm with you, buddy. I'm exhausted." Before bed, though, I had to get cleaned up. A quick, not-too-hot shower later, I toweled off. It took my overtired brain too long to realize what I was seeing. I wiped the mirror and stared at myself a moment before bursting into tears.

Clive raced in and found me sobbing. I wrapped my arms around him and he held on, holding me every bit as tightly as I needed.

*What happened?*

*Look at me.*

He studied my face. *What?*

"Look!" I backed up so he could see all of me.

Reaching out, he ran his hand down my body, neck to waist. "I rather miss them."

I swiped at my streaming eyes, laughing. My scars had been my identity for too many years. It was only recently that I'd relegated them to their proper importance. Scars were a symbol of survival. Now, though, when they were finally all gone, I was strangely nostalgic for them too. "I feel naked without them."

"You are naked, darling." He slid his hand around my waist and pulled me back in. "I get to learn your body all over again." When he kissed me, my racing thoughts slowed to only one: Clive.

True to his word, he picked me up and carried me to bed, where he showed me just how much he loved me and how happy he was to have me back in his arms. Lips and fingertips glided over my skin again and again until I was ready to explode.

When he finally settled between my legs, I wrapped myself around him, scars and demons forgotten. There was only the feel of our bodies moving against one another. There was only us.

Later, when I was starting to drift off, Clive said, "I got a call from Russell."

Oh, yeah. "I heard."

His hand brushed up and down my back. "I'm afraid that nice, quiet life we're looking forward to may need to be postponed a little longer."

I pushed myself up on my elbow so I could see him. "What's happened?"

"Apparently, one of Garyn's people called this evening, asking Russell for permission to visit San Francisco. He has no grounds to refuse her. She's threatened no one."

Garyn was Clive's maker. After she'd shared the dark kiss with him, she tried to keep him with her forever. Clive had learned the basics and taken off; he'd had his sister's murder to avenge.

Garyn didn't take well to being abandoned. She'd actually been Aldith's maker as well. The two had plotted together to make Clive pay. Aldith had made good on her threats. Garyn, though, had done nothing that we knew of, so Russell had no grounds to bar her.

I took a deep breath. "I felt her when we were in England. I think she might be a little crazy and more than a little fixated on you."

"Well, she can't have me. I'm taken." His hands settled on my bottom.

"Why do you think she's coming? You haven't seen her in a thousand years. Why now?" I snuggled in, afraid I was in for another fight for him soon.

"Maybe nothing, maybe revenge for Aldith. We'll find out soon enough and we'll deal with it."

"Demons, fae, your crazy maker; we'll handle it together."

Nodding, he wrapped his arms around me. "We will. Oh, I forgot." He reached up and pulled a thin gift-wrapped package from behind his pillow. "Happy birthday."

I shook my head. "I told you I didn't need a gift."

"Hush." To bypass the fuss, he lifted the top off the shirt-sized box.

Tissue paper. Rolling my eyes, I flipped open the tissue paper and saw—tears filled my eyes. I sat up and wiped at them, trying to stop the flow down my face. He'd found my parents' wedding photo and had it framed for me. "How? I've never even *seen* this. I thought all my mother's belongings were destroyed. I don't understand how you found it."

"I hired an investigator." He ran his hand up and down my back as I held the sheet to my eyes.

"But there's been no time. I just told you."

He pulled me back down into his arms. "I told you, darling. I'm very fast." When I hiccupped a laugh, he kissed the top of my head. "All things are possible. Sometimes even the impossible."

# Excerpt from BEWICCHED: THE SEA WICCHE CHRONICLES

Keep reading for a sneak peek of BEWICCHED: THE SEA WICCHE CHRONICLES, first book in Seana Kelly's new series. Don't worry, Sam & Clive will return in the fall of 2023.

## They Weren't Kidding When They Called Me, Well, a Wicche

Ursula, a villain who did not deserve the label, was my favorite. She was a working woman, offering a service, and was vilified for it. The payment was obvious. The whiners knew the consequences. They just thought they were special, that they could get magic without paying for it. That's not how magic works. You always have to pay. Plus, octopuses were amazing, so I refused to support fairytales disparaging them.

*Little Mermaid* aside, I was calling my Monterey seaside art gallery and tea bar The Sea Wicche because I, Arwyn Cassandra Corey, was a sea wicche, or at least I really wanted to be. The wicche part was true enough.

It was a perfect day, with clear blue skies and a cold salty wind on the California coast. I went out the back door of my studio to the deck that ran along the ocean side of a small, abandoned cannery I was having renovated. The deck gave a little with each step. Strangely enough, weathered, rotting wood was a bit of a safety hazard. I loved this place, though, even with the standing water and the rusted machinery.

I used to break in and run around here when I was little. Mom worried I'd hurt myself, but Gran said she'd seen in a dream it would be mine and to leave the poor child alone. In wicche families, the older you are, the more powerful. No one messes with the crones. I was, therefore, looking forward to getting old. The crones do not give a fuck. They've seen and done it all and have lost the ability to be polite about it. They'll tell you what they think to your face, because what are you going to do about it? That's right. Nothing.

I couldn't wait. Anyway, Grandmother said the cannery was mine, so it was mine. Even at seven, it was all mine. It sat on tall pylons that were mostly submerged at high tide. Now, though, at low tide, the barnacles, oysters, coral, and algae were visible. There were even a couple of gorgeous orange starfish that had made my pylons their home.

I sat on the edge and leaned over, holding on to the weather-warped wood with my ever-present gloves. The two starfish were still there. One was clinging to a portion of the support pole that was covered in a carpet of purple and green algae. I needed photos. Tourists snapped them up, especially this close to the Monterey Bay Aquarium.

Tipping back, I rolled over onto my stomach and took my phone out of my back pocket. Dangling over the deck edge, I framed the shot and took it. Perfect. Yes, my DSLR camera would be better, but the light was magical now. The colors were so vibrant, they'd pop out of the frame. If I ran back in for my camera, the light could change, and I'd lose the shot. I'd made that mistake too many times. I had a phone with the best digital camera on the market and I could tweak the image once I got it on my laptop.

I wear special gloves all the time, not just when touching

rotting wood. They are a thin, soft bamboo fabric with connective threads on the fingers so I can still use my smartphone. Touch is a problem for me; clairvoyance is not for the faint of heart. I see too much, hear too much. You try shaking someone's hand and hearing that he thinks you're a money-grubbing fake taking advantage of his mother, that you're bilking her out of her last dime, and he wished you'd drop dead. All of that the moment his hand touched yours.

Or, even better, how about finally getting a kiss senior year from the guy you've had a crush on since sixth grade, only to learn that he really wished your boobs were bigger and he hoped Rachel heard about his kissing you because he was trying to make her jealous. Oh, and he actually thought you were a weirdo, but a boob was a boob, so…

Yeah, dating sucked ass when touch meant picking up every stray thought and emotion. For a while, I self-medicated with booze. If it weren't for alcohol, I'd still be a virgin. That wasn't a sustainable plan, though. I hated drunk Arwyn and hated even more the predators who moved on me when they saw I was wasted enough to dull the voices. So, new sober me wears gloves and has sworn off dating and sex. It's a modern world. There are electronic alternatives that don't close their eyes and think about someone else.

I took a few more shots as long as I was hanging here, none as perfect as that first one, though. A text popped up on my screen and I flicked it away. It was my mom again, reminding me that Gran expected me at dinner tonight. They'd been trying to get me to join the Council since I was in my teens—maiden, mother, and crone.

The Council oversaw all disputes, heard pleas for help, granted magical aid, usually for a fee. Now that I was back from England—and my chess set was finally in the hands of the werewolf book nerd it was intended for—they were pushing hard for me to join. It wasn't that I wouldn't help when they needed me. I didn't want to be tied to the regularity. I had my work and really did not care about the day-to-day petty bullshit. If they needed me to power a spell, fine. The rest of it, not so much. Mom and Gran knew the toll it took on me, knew I lived through the worst horrors the people petitioning us carried with them, but they didn't experience it, so it was easy to forget the price I paid for my magic. I hadn't had a full night's rest in ever. The nightmares haunted me as though they were my memories.

So, gloves, isolation, and my ocean buddies. There was movement in the water below. A tentacle almost broke the surface. Yes, my octopus friend was still hanging out below the cannery. "Hello, Cecil! I hope you have a lovely, watery day!" The way he moved was mesmerizing to watch. So much so, it took me too long to realize what was happening. Damn it! I was going to end up in the ocean.

Throwing the phone over my shoulder, I gave it a magical push to get it to the deck and then hoped for the best. Lights went off in my head and my vision went dark. *Snarling. I heard that first. Often the sounds and scents came to me before the images. Growling and the scent of the forest. Two yellow eyes, huge, staring into me, before the scene formed.*

*A forest at night. Huge, dark paws pounding the underbrush. Howling in the distance. The muffled thud of many paws chasing. Or retreating. Am I predator or prey? Anger and grief fill me. Long sharp claws tear through the packed earth. A clearing ahead. Room to gain speed. No, ambush. A pack of wolves growling in a semi-circle. More behind. Snarls and yips as those chasing complete the circle.*

*A man stands in the distance, hidden from the moon by towering trees. His scent enrages me, but the pack is moving in for the kill. I want to leap over all the others and get to him, rip his throat out, let his blood drip from my jaws as I move to his torso and feast. Instead, the wolves attack and the man slips away unnoticed.*

My body tipped forward as I watched the wolves tear each other apart. Damn it. I was about to drown, watching wolves kill each other.

I wasn't in the water, wasn't wet. What I was, though, was

hanging in the air. A very tall, very strong man was holding me a foot off the deck, a hand gripped my hair around the back of my neck. I stared into warm brown eyes and shouted, "What the fuck? Put me down!"

He dropped me like I was on fire. Thankfully, my balance was pretty good and I kept my feet under me.

He cleared his throat and pointed toward the water. "You were sliding in." He handed me my phone.

"Thanks," I said, "for picking up my phone and grabbing me before I went in. I'm an epileptic." Not really. I just needed a cover for my habit of hitting the ground. "This is private property, though. You shouldn't be here." I shaded my eyes. Oh, my. He had to be six and a half feet tall, a perfect muscular specimen, with dark hair starting to curl around his ears and a full dark beard. A thin scar trailed down his cheek and into the beard. He wore faded jeans, sturdy work boots, and a t-shirt topped with a flannel. I might not be able to touch, but I could look.

"I'm on the construction crew. Stan asked me to stop by to take measurements on the deck." He stared at me as though he was pretty sure I was insane but was too polite to say it.

Ha, joke was on him. People had been calling me nuts my whole life. It didn't even register anymore.

"So you're okay?" He had a deep growly voice. "You threw your phone at me and then just flopped over the edge, like dead weight dropping into the ocean."

"Seizure," I said, checking out my phone. "I'm fine now." No scratches on the screen. Score! "Go ahead," I said, gesturing to the rotting deck. "Do your thing." I started back into my studio and stopped. "Wait. Why are you working today? It's Sunday, right?" I checked my phone for the date.

"I wasn't doing anything, so I figured I might as well get started." He shrugged one beefy shoulder. "Plus, I'm trying to make a good impression. I need the work." He pulled a measuring tape off his belt. "Do you want the deck any different, or am I replacing this one exactly?" He took a receipt and a pencil from his shirt pocket, starting to take notes.

"You can do it without dropping planks into the ocean or pounding on the pylons so hard you disturb the ecosystem, right?"

"Ecosystem?" He walked to the edge and leaned over, peering down. "Is that what you were looking at?"

"My starfish Charlie got a new friend." I peered over the edge and saw the guy's arm move, like he was ready to grab me if it looked like I was about to go in. "The friend kind of looks like a... Herbert." I slid the phone back in my pocket, brushing the dirt from my gloves. I owned many pairs, all washable.

"Herbert and Charlie, huh? Which one is which?" His balance was amazing. He'd been leaning out past the edge of the deck for a while and not a bobble or tremor in sight.

"Herbert is closest to you." Wicches can see auras. We can tap a part of our brains that allows us to see a person's aura, essentially to see what kind of person we're dealing with. The brighter and shinier the aura, the more trustworthy the person. The smokier the aura, the more we needed to watch our backs. Yes, I was a strong wicche who could take care of myself, but six and a half feet of muscle on a psycho was probably something I should prepare for.

Letting my vision relax, I sized up this guy who wanted to work here while I was alone in my studio. No aura, just a snarl of fur and claws. Ah, the reason for the vision. Which one was he, though? One of the pack? The man in the shadows? He couldn't have been my conduit to the vision—the wolf being chased. There was no way that poor bastard took on twenty wolves and lived. Fingers twitching at my side, I readied a spell, just in case. "Werewolf?"

Poor guy looked like he'd been smacked in the face with a shovel.

"It's okay." I pointed at myself. "Wicche."

"I know, but how did you?"

"*You* knew?" I'd never laid eyes on this guy before. How did he know?

He tapped his nose. "You have a scent."

I felt my face flame. I'd showered this morning, hadn't I? *Shit.* When I got involved in a project, I lost track of time and personal hygiene.

Chuckling, he clarified, "Wicches as a group, not you in particular. You smell like plaster and paint. And the ocean."

"Oh." Well, that was okay then. Not all werewolves were psycho killers. In fact, very few of them were. Still, I let the spell dance between my fingers.

He wrote something on the paper in his hand. "What kind of railing do you want?"

"None."

He raised one eyebrow. "You'll need some pretty good insurance to cover all the lawsuits from people falling off this thing."

"The plaster and paint you're smelling are from the tentacles I'm building. They'll be thirty feet tall and come up from below the water, curving this way and that to keep people from falling in. It'll look like a sea monster is pulling us into the ocean."

His eyes flicked from the ocean to the edge of the deck. "Nice." After pausing a moment, he asked, "What about kids? The curves will leave holes, the perfect size for little heads."

I stopped the automatic denial and thought about the design I had in mind. I waved him in the back door of my studio so we could look over the plans. My art studio took up about a third of the cannery building and was the first section remodeled. I needed a place to work. The gallery could wait.

I stopped him before he stepped over the threshold, though, my hand on his chest. "Wait. What's your name?"

He stared down at my hand until I moved it. "Declan."

"Declan what?" I'd be texting all the cousins first chance I got to see if anyone knew anything about this guy. I hadn't had that vision about bloodthirsty werewolves for no reason. And that man in the shadows... Even now, the memory sent a chill down my spine.

"What's it to you?"

"Maybe you're a serial killer." Or a man who kept to the shadows, watching the carnage he'd set in motion.

He stared at me, his intense brown eyes making me lose my breath. "You're the wicche," he said, leaning in. "Am I a serial killer?"

Instead of answering, I put up a hand, stopping him from following me. "Why don't you wait out there? Do your measurements. I'll go grab the plans." Being a werewolf, I couldn't read him easily, not without touching him. Erring on the side of caution, I started to close the door, a spell ready if he gave me trouble.

"You know, I'd like to know your last name too?" A second man's voice made me jump.

Who the hell was that? I swung open the door and ducked my head through to find another muscular guy on my doorstep. Luckily, I knew this one. Logan, Alpha of the local pack. Six-four, tawny hair, tanned skin, blue eyes, he was the golden child of Monterey. Women flocked to him, and he'd never met one he hadn't liked.

"Arwyn." His gaze traveled from my out-of-control curls down to my paint-spattered sneakers. "Good to see you again, although I can't say much for the company you're keeping."

My cousin Selena had dated Logan in high school when he was the star athlete on every team. She was head over heels, but he was working his way through the female student body, so it didn't last long. She said he wasn't a jerk about it. He was just a guy who loved women and couldn't rest until he'd pleasured all in his path. Everyone needed a hobby, I supposed.

When he turned to Declan, the physical change was extraordinary. Relaxed and flirtatious morphed into clenched jaw, puffed chest, hands fisted. "You know the rules. You can't come into my territory without meeting with me and getting my approval. I'm Alpha." Logan crossed his arms over his chest and glared at Declan, his eyes going wolf gold.

Declan didn't flinch. "I'm not in *your* territory. Pack grounds are in Big Sur. I live and work in Monterey. Eve is the Master of Monterey."

Logan growled, "Bloodsuckers don't rule us. You want to stay here, you meet with me."

Ah, shit. Not again. *Large wolves circling one another, one jet black, the other gray and tan. The gray lunges. The black meets him, clashing tooth and claw. Blood flies as they shake off the pain, circle, and charge. It's vicious and violent. I don't want to watch, don't want new nightmares. The gray one, bloody and limping, cringes away when the black one howls, but then the black wolf is set upon by another who drives him into the dirt…*

Blinking, I stare up into cool blue eyes.

"Hey, now, are you all right?" Logan, with his warm, muscled arms around me, put me back on my feet. "I forgot. You're epileptic or something, right?"

I nodded, frustrated and annoyed. Twice in one day. It had been almost two weeks since my last vision. "Gentlemen," I said, trying to defuse the hostility, "I have reason to believe this won't end well. What do you say you just shake hands and walk away? In fact," I added, glancing back in my studio, "I can offer you both a freshly baked fudge brownie with a layer of caramel in the middle. Can you smell them?" Being werewolves, they'd never back down from a fight, but it was worth a try.

Declan studied me a moment, his expression dark, before lifting his head to scent the air. "I'm in." He stuck out his hand and waited.

I did *not* expect that.

Logan smacked Declan's hand away.

That, I expected.

Declan blew out a breath, streaks of gold now visible in his brown eyes. Leaning against the doorframe, he growled, "Where and when?"

"Pack grounds. Full moon. And since I had to track you down, you'll join our hunt instead of meeting me in my office. You think you can handle that?" Logan sneered.

Declan shook off the anger. "Sure."

"Arwyn," Logan said while glaring at Declan, "if you lose one of your workmen, I'll make sure to send Stan a replacement. We take care of our own around here." When Logan grinned, for just a moment, his teeth seemed too long, too sharp, but it could have been a trick of the light.

And then his eyes were back on me, the affability returned. "You Corey girls sure do have the biggest, prettiest blue eyes."

"Green," I corrected.

"Right. So, I've been meaning to ask you, there's a new Mexican restaurant in town I'd like to take you to. What do you say?"

"Well, I'll have to think about that, won't I?"

"You do just that." He winked. "And I'll see you again real soon." With a warm grin, he sauntered off.

I stuffed my hands in my overall pockets. Logan had been doing his damnedest to seduce me since I was fifteen. When I turned back to Declan to discuss railings, though, he wasn't watching the threatening Alpha leaving. He was watching me.

BEWICCHED: THE SEA WICCHE CHRONICLES
out May 2, 2023

# Acknowledgments

Thank you to my husband and daughters for putting up with me as I raced to finish this book. Thank you also to the fine makers of chips and chocolate, helping to get me through long writing sessions.

Thank you to my kind, funny, and supportive critique partner C.R. Grissom. The poor woman has read everything I've ever written. For that alone, she needs a medal and a case of good whiskey. Get you a friend like C.R. If I called her in the middle of the night, needing help with a dead body, she'd show up wearing all black, with a shovel in her trunk, and no questions on her lips.

Thank you to Peter Senftleben, my extraordinary editor. You have the enviable knack of getting to the heart of the story and then helping me to see my own work through a different lens. Thank you to Susan Helene Gottfried, my exceptional proofreader who always knows exactly where the commas go (unlike myself).

Thank you to the remarkable team at NYLA! You've made every step of publishing a little easier with your wit, compassion, and expertise. Thank you to my incomparable agent Sarah Younger, the fabulous Natanya Wheeler, and the incredible Cheryl Pientka for working together to make my dream of writing and publishing a reality.

# Dear Reader

Thank you for reading ***Biergarten of the Damned***. If you enjoyed Sam and Clive's fifth adventure together, please consider leaving a review or chatting about it with your book-loving friends. Good word of mouth means everything when you're a new writer!

Love,
Seana

## Want more books from Seana?

If you'd like to be the first to learn what's new with Sam and Clive (and Owen and Dave and Stheno…), please sign up for my newsletter ***Tales from the Book Nerd*** here: https://geni.us/BLuT6 It's filled with writing news, deleted scenes, giveaways, book recommendations, first looks at covers, short stories, and my favorite cocktail and book pairings.

**The Slaughtered Lamb Bookstore & Bar**
Sam Quinn, book 1

Welcome to The Slaughtered Lamb Bookstore and Bar. I'm Sam Quinn, the werewolf book nerd in charge. I run my business by one simple rule: Everyone needs a good book and a stiff drink, be they vampire, wicche, demon, or fae. No wolves, though. Ever. I have my reasons.

I serve the supernatural community of San Francisco. We've been having some problems lately. Okay, I'm the one with the problems. The broken body of a female werewolf washed up on my doorstep. What makes sweat pool at the base of my spine, though, is realizing the scars she bears are identical to the ones I conceal. After hiding for years, I've been found.

A protection I've been relying on is gone. While my wolf traits are strengthening steadily, the loss also left my mind vulnerable to attack. Someone is ensnaring me in horrifying visions intended to kill. Clive, the sexy vampire Master of the City, has figured out how to pull me out, designating himself my personal bodyguard. He's grumpy about it, but that kiss is telling a different story. A change is taking place. It has to. The bookish bartender must become the fledgling badass.

I'm a survivor. I'll fight fang and claw to protect myself and the ones I love. And let's face it, they have it coming.

**The Dead Don't Drink at Lafitte's**
Sam Quinn, book 2

I'm Sam Quinn, the werewolf book nerd owner of the Slaughtered Lamb Bookstore and Bar. Things have been busy lately. While the near-constant attempts on my life have ceased, I now have a vampire gentleman caller. I've been living with Clive and the rest of his vampires for a few weeks while the Slaughtered Lamb is being rebuilt. It's going about as well as you'd expect.

My mother was a wicche and long dormant abilities are starting to make themselves known. If I'd had a choice, necromancy wouldn't have been my top pick, but it's coming in handy. A ghost warns me someone is coming to kill Clive. When I rush back to the nocturne, I find vamps from New Orleans readying an attack. One of the benefits of vampires looking down on werewolves is no one expects much of me. They don't expect it right up until I take their heads.

Now, Clive and I are setting out for New Orleans to take the fight back to the source. Vampires are masters of the long game. Revenge plots are often decades, if not centuries, in the making. We came expecting one enemy, but quickly learn we have darker forces scheming against us. Good thing I'm the secret weapon they never see coming.

**The Wicche Glass Tavern**

Sam Quinn, book 3

I'm Sam Quinn, the werewolf book nerd owner of the Slaughtered Lamb Bookstore and Bar. Clive, my vampire gentleman caller, has asked me to marry him. His nocturne is less than celebratory. Unfortunately, for them and the sexy vamp doing her best to seduce him, his cold, dead heart beats only for me.

As much as my love life feels like a minefield, it has to take a backseat to a far more pressing problem. The time has come. I need to deal with my aunt, the woman who's been trying to kill me for as long as I can remember. She's learned a new trick. She's figured out how to weaponize my friends against me. To have any hope of surviving, I have to learn to use my necromantic gifts. I need a teacher. We find one hiding among the fae, which is a completely different problem. I need to determine what I'm capable of in a hurry because my aunt doesn't care how many are hurt or killed as long as she gets what she wants. Sadly for me, what she wants is my name on a headstone.

I'm gathering my friends-werewolves, vampires, wicches, gorgons, a Fury, a half-demon, an elf, and a couple of dragon-shifters-into a kind of Fellowship of the Sam. It's going to be one hell of a battle. Hopefully, San Francisco will still be standing when the dust clears.

**The Hob & Hound Pub**

Sam Quinn, book 4

I'm Sam Quinn, the newly married werewolf book nerd owner of the Slaughtered Lamb Bookstore and Bar. Clive and I are on our honeymoon. Paris is lovely, though the mummy in the Louvre inching toward me is a bit off-putting. Although Clive doesn't sense anything, I can't shake the feeling I'm being watched.

Even after we cross the English Channel to begin our search for Aldith—the woman who's been plotting against Clive since the beginning—the prickling unease persists. Clive and I are separated, rather forcefully, and I'm left to find my way alone in a foreign country, evading not only Aldith's large web of henchvamps, but vicious fae creatures disloyal to their queen. Gloriana says there's a poison in the human realm that's seeping into Faerie, and I may have found the source.

I knew this was going to be a working vacation, but battling vampires on one front and the fae on another is a lot, especially in a country steeped in magic. As a side note, I need to get word to Benvair. I think I've found the dragon she's looking for.

Gloriana is threatening to set her warriors against the human realm, but I may have a way to placate her. Aldith is a different story. There's no reasoning with rabid vengeance. She'll need to be put out of our misery permanently if Clive and I have any hope of a long, happy life together. Heck, I'd settle for a few quiet weeks.

**Bewicched**

The Sea Wicche Chronicles, book 1

*We here at The Sea Wicche cater to your art collecting, muffin eating, tea drinking and potion peddling needs. Palmistry and Tarot sessions are available upon request and by appointment. Our store hours vary and rely completely on Arwyn—the owner—getting her butt out of bed.*

Hi, I'm Arwyn, the sea wicche, or the wicche who lives by the sea. It requires a lot more work than I'd anticipated to remodel an abandoned cannery and turn it into an art gallery & tea bar. It's coming along, though, especially with help from a new werewolf who's joined the construction crew. He does beautiful work. His sexy, growly, bearded presence is very hard to ignore, but I'm trying. I'm not sure how such a laid-back guy got the local Alpha and his pack threatening to hunt him down and tear him apart, but we all have our secrets. And because I don't want to know his, or yours for that matter, I wear these gloves. Clairvoyance makes the simplest things the absolute worst. Trust me. Or don't. Totally up to you.

Did I mention my mother and grandmother are pressuring me to assume my rightful place on the Corey Council? That's a kind of governing triad for our ancient magical family, one that has more than its fair share of black magic practitioners. And yes, before you ask, people have killed to be on the council—one psychotic sorceress aunt stands out—but I have no interest in the power or politics that come with the position. I'd rather stick to my art and, in the words of my favorite sea wicche, help poor unfortunate souls. (Good luck trying to get that song out of your head now)

***And for something completely different…***

**Welcome Home, Katie Gallagher**

*This romantic comedy was my first book published. Remember, don't judge a book by its (truly hideous) cover.*

Nobody said a fresh start would be easy

A clean slate is exactly what Katie Gallagher needs, and Bar Harbor, Maine, is the best place to get it. Except the cottage her grandmother left her is overrun with woodland creatures, and the police chief, Aiden Cavanaugh, seems determined to arrest her! Katie had no idea she'd broken his heart fifteen years ago…

# About Seana Kelly

Seana Kelly lives in the San Francisco Bay Area with her husband, two daughters, two dogs, and one fish. When not dodging her family, hiding in the garage to write, she's working as a high school teacher-librarian. She's an avid reader and re-reader who misses her favorite characters when it's been too long between visits.

She's a *USA Today* bestseller and is represented by the delightful and effervescent Sarah E. Younger of the Nancy Yost Literary Agency

You can follow Seana on Twitter for tweets about books and dogs or on Instagram for beautiful pictures of books and dogs (kidding). She also loves collecting photos of characters and settings for the books she writes. As she's a huge reader of young adult and adult books, expect lots of recommendations as well.

Website: www.seanakelly.com

Newsletter: https://geni.us/t0Y5cBA

twitter.com/SeanaKellyRW

instagram.com/seanakellyrw

facebook.com/Seana-Kelly-1553527948245885

bookbub.com/authors/seana-kelly

pinterest.com/seanakelly326

Printed in the USA
CPSIA information can be obtained
at www.ICGtesting.com
LVHW011436290924
792443LV00043B/823